SOMEBODY TO LOVE

Ryker Falls Series

LANI BLAKE

RYKER FALLS

Somebody To Love is a work of fiction. Names, places, and incidents either are products of the author's imagination or are used fictitiously.

Somebody To Love is published by Lani Blake

Lani's Books

The Lake Howling Series

A Promise Of Home
The Texan Meets His Match
How Sweet It Is
It Only Took You
Don't Look Back
A Long Way Home
Then Came You
Faith And The Rockstar

Ryker Falls Series

Somebody To Love
From This Moment
Love Me Tender
Only Just Begun
Hold Me Close

This one is for all the people who have walked through my life.
Too numerous to name, but so special they deserve a mention.

"Some people come into our lives and quickly go. Some people move our souls to dance. They awaken us to a new understanding with the passing whisper of their wisdom. Some people make the sky more beautiful to gaze upon. They stay in our lives for awhile, leave footprints on our hearts, and we are never, ever the same."
-Flavia Weedn

Chapter 1

THERE WEREN'T TOO many things in life Joe Trainer couldn't stomach. He could put on a load of wash without it upsetting his day, even clean up the mess some idiot made in his bar after drinking more than he could stomach. But grocery shopping, that was right up there with brussels sprouts to his mind. This issue usually reared its ugly head when he opened the fridge and found a wedge of moldy cheese, stale milk, and something suspicious growing on a plate that had been shoved to the rear, but little else. There'd also been the issue of washing his hair with soap because he'd run out of shampoo. Not too much of an issue as far as Joe was concerned, but his aunt would have plenty to say if she noticed. Although why she felt it necessary to check out his shower supplies when she dropped by, he had no clue.

"I just want guy shampoo," he muttered, looking at the shelves before him. Three down, four wide. The bottles ranged in color and shape, like pretty wrapped candy. *Nothing pretty here, however*, he thought picking one up.

"What the hell is paraben and why don't I want it in my shampoo?" Putting it back, he reached for another.

"You doing okay there, Joe?"

"God's truth, Bit. I just want guy shampoo. Honest-to-goodness stuff that I put in my hair. It foams up, then I wash it out, usually getting it in my eyes at the same time." Reading the label, he added, "Why would I want to put ylang-ylang on my head? Better still, what the hell is it?"

"Honestly, Joe, get more aware. The cananga tree has flowers called ylang-ylang, which is where the essential oils in that bottle you're holding come from."

Joe studied the tiny woman standing at his side. He'd only ever known her as Bit, even though she was actually Mrs. Rosemary Yardly. Her nickname came because she was a tiny bit of woman with a huge personality.

"How come you know this stuff?"

"This is my store. I need to know what I'm selling when morons like you come in clueless. It makes me feel smart."

"Harsh but true." Joe nodded.

She had white hair cut short, a round body, and wore a red apron with a can of beans on the front.

"Nice apron."

"Thanks, you want one? I have a spare."

"All good, you leave it for the staff, I'd hate to deprive them."

"You're a good man, Joe Trainer."

"Everyone's saying it," Joe muttered, picking up another bottle of shampoo and reading the label.

"Buzz's dog biscuits are on special if you want to pick him up some more."

"I'll do that thanks."

A loud crash rang through the store.

"What the hell was that?" Joe said.

"The sound of my profits. What idiot has dropped something now?"

Bit left at a run, leaving him no closer to his shampoo choice. Joe closed his eyes and reached out, selecting the first bottle he touched. He then placed it in the cart and continued down the aisle, making random selections. Joe wasn't a list shopper... in fact any shopper. He bought what appealed, end of story.

Turning, he was hit with the tang of pickles. Deciding that he didn't need anything from that aisle right at that moment, he took the next, and stopped several feet down it. A woman was standing on the toes of her peach-colored sneakers, trying to reach something on the top shelf. On the slim side, she had long legs in fitted, worn jeans boasting a label that told him they'd been worth some serious money when they were new. His eyes travelled to the outline of two ribs he could see between the small band of smooth skin and the waistband of her white long-sleeved T-shirt.

"Need some help?"

"No, I got it, thanks."

He watched as she reached for something, but failed.

"Just a few more inches and you may just do it," Joe encouraged.

Her blonde hair was on top of her head in a messy knot that women seemed to favor, and he had to admit to liking it.

Checking the label on the box she was inches from reaching, Joe felt the small sting of pain he always felt seeing Bailey's favorite candy. *It's been fifteen years, bud, time to let her go.* Joe wondered, as he often did, how Bailey Jones had made such an impression in his life the two years she was in it.

"Right here whenever you're ready to concede defeat."

She let out a huff of breath, then stepped back a few feet to look at him. He saw a face that needed a few pounds and some sleep, but for all that she was pretty, actually more than, Joe thought. Sweet. Satin-smooth skin. Color rode high on her pronounced cheekbones. His eyes fell to a full lower lip that had dropped open as she looked at him.

"Is something...." Joe's words fell away as he noted the shocked, smoky-gray eyes. "Bailey?"

"Joe?" She whispered his name. While he grappled with who stood before him, she cleared her throat and spoke again, this time louder. "Hello, Joe."

Gone was the little girl he'd held sobbing in his arms all those years ago; the vision was now changed for life by the twenty-eight-year-old Bailey Jones who stood before him. *"You have to follow me, Joe. Come for me and bring me home. Promise me."* He still remembered the last words she'd spoken to him.

"Bailey," he said again, because he had nothing else. Emotion thickened his throat, blocking words, and his head was suddenly filled with visions of a past he'd left behind long ago.

"C-could you pass me that box, please."

"What?" He shook his head, trying to clear the images of what he and Bailey Jones had once shared.

"Th-the box of Apple Sours." She turned her face away and looked to the top shelf. "Could you pass it to me, please?"

Joe made himself walk by her, and reach up. He didn't know what else to do. Bailey was home. "Just the one?" His voice sounded normal, as if the last time he'd seen this woman was yesterday, not fifteen years ago.

"Three, thank you."

He handed the boxes to her. "My pleasure," he said, as

if the woman before him hadn't once been the best friend he'd ever had. At thirteen, Bailey had understood him better than anyone else. She'd been the one person who believed in him.

She put the boxes in the basket over her arm, and gave him a small, tight smile that didn't reach her eyes. Eyes that had dark smudges underneath. Tired eyes.

"You here for a vacation?" He made himself talk, act natural, and not give in to the shock that was ricocheting through his body.

"Yes," she said. "I'm n-not sure how long yet."

He stood silently while she fiddled with her groceries. They were strangers now, he realized. Of all the scenarios he'd thought up about this day, if it ever came, it hadn't played out like this. He'd thought they'd laugh, discuss the past like old friends. Instead they were uncomfortable with each other, the distance between them a chasm.

"Well, thanks, Joe. It's good to see you again."

"Ryker Falls is sure a long way from Boston to come for a vacation, Bailey." He made himself talk while he struggled with the fact that she stood before him. No longer a child, but a beautiful woman.

"How do you know I was still in Boston?"

"Maggie."

"Of course." She shot him a look, and he saw she wasn't as composed as she appeared. Her eyes were darker, a sure sign she was emotional. He remembered that, and so much more about her.

"Maggie is very proud of her famous friend."

"Once famous. I don't do that now... haven't for a while."

"Really? Last I heard you were still wowing crowds everywhere."

She shook her head. "Ha, no, not for months now."

"True? Maggs never said. So what's next for you?"

"I-I... ah, I'm t-taking a break."

He frowned as she stuttered over the words. Bailey had never stuttered, she'd spoken in a clear, concise voice. He watched her inhale deeply, twice. Of course, more than he had changed in the years since they'd last seen each other, he knew that, he just hadn't expected.... Hell, he had no idea what he'd expected.

"I decided to come here and see Maggie." The words were spoken slowly.

See Maggie, not him.

"Quite a lot has changed in fifteen years, Bailey."

She nodded, but said nothing more. Another change; the old Bailey Jones had filled every gap with words.

She started moving. Reaching his side, she stopped briefly, and looked up at him. Joe noticed a small crescent-shaped scar high on her cheekbone that hadn't been there when she was thirteen.

"Thank you for reaching the Apple Sours for me."

He made himself speak. Pushed aside the myriad of feelings choking him, and forced a smile onto his face.

"No worries, I know what your addiction to them was once like. It's good to see that hasn't changed. Nice to see you again, Bailey. I'm sure I'll see you around."

She gave another jerky nod, and something flickered over her face. Sadness, maybe? Whatever, it was soon gone. She managed a shaky smile. He remembered that too. The little girl who had taught herself how to hide away from things that hurt or upset her. She'd often hid her troubled thoughts behind a smile.

"Goodbye, Joe," she added before leaving.

He had the foolish urge to go after her. Take her hand, make contact with her. Instead, he stood where he was, and inhaled. He did it again and again in an attempt to calm himself. Instead, he smelled her. A soft floral scent hung in the air.

"I'm fairly sure this is the confectionary aisle. Yoga is two over."

"Ha" was all Joe could manage. He felt like someone had clamped a vise around his chest. Bailey was home, and she looked…. Christ, how did he explain even to himself how she looked? Beautiful, exhausted, haunted. How had he picked up all that in the few minutes he'd been with her?

"Hell of a scent in the air, and I like pickles," Findlay Hudson said.

"Yeah, clean up in aisle three." Joe ran a hand through his hair. He and Fin had been friends for a while now; both had pasts that were best left buried.

Tall like Joe, Fin had brown hair and blue eyes. He was the head ranger in Ryker Falls. He wore his khaki uniform of shorts and shirt, aviators pushed up on his head.

"You okay, bud? Looking a bit tense around the eyes."

"Had my weekly run-in with Ms. Howard," Joe said, instead of 'I just walked into someone who had once been my savior, and we're now strangers.' "Usually it doesn't bother me, today it did." Joe shrugged. His friend knew him well enough to see something was bugging him, so he gave him a variation of the truth.

"The woman was born to hate, Joe, we both know it. She's not happy unless she's making someone else feel the same. You gotta sympathize with her husband."

"True that," Joe grunted. "I can handle her, but sometimes it just pisses me off more than others."

"You've been back years now, Joe. There's only a few who have long memories and aren't willing to forget. Unfortunately, she's one of them, and vocal about it."

He nodded.

"So you're good? Or is there something else you need to unload on me while I'm playing Dr. Phil?"

"You need to stop dating Mandy, bud. She's making you way too in tune with your emotions." Joe tried to lighten the mood.

"The hell you say!"

"Sissy is what you are. It's damn unsettling to see it happening, too." Joe felt the tightness ease inside his chest as he and Fin went at it like they always did.

Fin slapped his chest. "I'm a goddamned park ranger, Trainer, nothing sissy in that career choice. Unlike you going all soft on me and running a bar."

"Which I happen to own, and if you want that table tonight, you better be nicer."

"True that," Fin sighed. "I'm bringing a date, so chuck on a white cloth and some flowers. A candle wouldn't hurt either."

"I live to serve, you know that," Joe said. "Mandy?"

"Nah."

"Who?"

"New to town," Fin said.

"Tourist?"

"Uh-huh."

"Got a sister?"

"Nope."

"Shame," Joe said, slapping his friend on the shoulder as he passed, because it was expected of him. "Gotta get Buzz some food or he'll start on the furniture again. Then I'm heading back to the bar, and work on rosters. Two down with illness."

"I gave Buzz a biscuit, he should be good for a while."

"What biscuit?"

"The one I had in my pocket."

"You're carrying biscuits around in your pockets now

for my dog? Seriously, I swear this town loves him more than me."

"Well hell, that's a given."

Joe flipped Fin the bird, and continued with his shopping. He left thirty minutes later with four bags of groceries containing a random selection of things that he neither needed nor wanted. Buzz, however, had his favorite biscuits and a large bone that would send him into ecstasy —he'd managed to get his head straight enough to ensure that.

Well, hell. Bailey Jones was back in town, and for some reason Joe had a feeling his life was about to be flipped on its head.

Chapter 2

BAILEY WASN'T sure how she got through the checkout, or managed to acknowledge the lady who served her.

"You here for the parade?"

"Parade?"

"It's the annual end of summer parade."

She remembered the parade, because she'd once been in it on the school float. What she hadn't remembered was that it was usually in the month of September.

"I'm not sure I'll be here."

"We have a street party after. It's worth staying for." The girl had tight blonde curls and a perky smile. *Young and innocent, and still full of self-belief.* Had she ever been like that? Thinking back, she doubted it.

"I'll think about it, thanks."

Parting with some of her precious cash, she then headed out the door, and only when she was back on the street did she breathe easier.

After fifteen years, she'd come back to Ryker Falls, and twenty minutes in, Joe was the first local she'd seen. "What are the chances?" Muttering these words to herself, Bailey tried to regroup. She was no longer a thirteen-year-old girl who thought the sun rose and set because of Joe Trainer.

Friends for life, he'd said to her that final day. Later, when a few years and many miles passed between them, she realized how foolish she'd been to believe that. Life had no certainties. The scars on her arm and hand told her that.

Bailey pushed some hair that had come free off her forehead, and realized her hand was shaking. Making herself move, as she was standing in the main street staring at nothing, she headed to where she'd parked her car. *Get a grip, Bailey. You've had worse shocks, and you knew coming back here meant there was always the possibility of bumping into him.*

She'd seen Joe.

At thirty now, he was a seriously handsome man. Big and broad shouldered, his hair darker, the thick black locks cut short. Piercing green eyes, black lashes and brows, and his face had fewer hard angles than as a teenager, and more chiseled planes and interesting lines now. A strong jaw, high cheekbones, and a nose that started out straight, then veered slightly to the right. His father had done that to him.

Bailey had kept in touch with her childhood friend Maggie by writing a letter each week. Her grandfather had not been able to take that away from her. She'd never asked about Joe though, because no one knew what they had once meant to each other. The urge had been there, but she'd fought it. He was a taboo subject as far as Bailey was concerned. *Which begs the question as to why I came back?*

"Hey, watch out!"

Hands grabbed her, lifting Bailey off her feet. She watched a car pass, and realized she'd been about to walk out in front of it.

"You need to check left and right before stepping off the curb, ma'am."

"I'm sorry, I-I wasn't thinking clearly."

Her rescuer was tall, with dark hair, and had a nice smile that reached his green eyes. She knew those eyes.

"We don't get many people run down on the main street of Ryker, but you were about to be one of them."

He stuck out a hand, and Bailey found herself shaking it. It felt large and warm wrapped around her fingers.

"Luke Trainer."

Joe's baby brother. Bailey's memories of him were of a sad, solemn boy who was always dressed in his big brother's castoffs that hung on his skinny frame. There was no resemblance in the healthy, handsome man before her.

"Hi." Bailey didn't give her name. She was already off-balance, and didn't need another reunion right now. What she needed was to reach her car and regroup. Seeing Joe had unsettled her way more than she'd thought it would.

"You're a firefighter?" Bailey read the words on his navy cap.

"I am."

"I'm glad," Bailey said, because she was. Joe had once worried about the youngest Trainer, confiding in Bailey that he thought Luke had suffered the most at the hands of their father, and that he'd bear the scars for many years, if not always.

"So am I." He gave her a gentle smile, and Bailey guessed that was because she'd sounded crazy telling him, supposedly a perfect stranger, she was happy he was a firefighter.

The sound of a dog baying had them turning.

"Shut it down, Buzz, I'll be there in second," Luke Trainer said.

The dog was huge, like a small black bear with a thick shaggy coat and orange ruff around its neck. He had a white patch of hair on his forehead and each paw.

"He's my brother Joe's dog, but he's pretty much loved by everyone around here."

"I want a big, black shaggy dog when I get a place one day, Bailey." She remembered that conversation clearly, like she did so many of the ones she and Joe had shared.

"Ah, thanks, Luke, for helping me." She dragged her eyes from the dog. "Bye." Lifting a hand, she looked left and right, then ran across the street clutching the small bag of groceries.

Fumbling with her keys when she reached the car, Bailey managed to get the door open and scrambled inside, slamming it behind her. Dumping her things on the passenger seat, she leaned on the steering wheel, closing her eyes.

"You shouldn't have come back." Banging her head twice, Bailey told herself to turn the key in the ignition and drive out of Ryker Falls. She had been a fool coming here, and didn't even know what had possessed her to do so. Curiosity? Longing? Closure? Scrunching her eyes tight, she tried to find focus. Find a direction to head in.

Opening the bag of groceries, she found the Apple Sours, ripped open the box, and poured them straight into her mouth. The sweet, sour hit jolted her senses.

"Better." She inhaled again, then swallowed down a few more.

A year ago Bailey's life had derailed, and she'd been unsettled ever since. Three months ago she'd packed up her things and taken to the road, going from one place to another, but in her heart, she had always been heading here, to the place she was born. What she didn't know was why. Why come back to the memories and pain of the life she'd once led in Ryker Falls?

Turning the key in the ignition, she fired her sedan to life and headed down the main street of Ryker Falls.

The last time she'd walked through this town, things had looked vastly different. The shops had been tired, and the town a small community with little to recommend it to tourists. Her father had loved it here, and her mother had always wanted to leave, which had not made family life harmonious.

Passing the quaint storefronts, some brick, others wood, in varying shapes and sizes, Bailey thought it looked good now. Some had striped canopies, others hanging baskets. Color was everywhere she turned. And the many people on the streets told her Ryker had come a long way in the years since she'd left. Wrought iron lamps had frosted globes that Bailey imagined were pretty at night. Trees had been planted, and offered shade to those who sat on the benches underneath.

Reaching the end of town, Bailey went left and followed the river road that looped back to the beginning of town. She found medical facilities, and the school had been extended. The boardwalk had changed too. No longer just a long stretch of boards, it now had a row of shops adjacent to half of it, looking over the sea. Parking the car, Bailey got out and wandered for a bit, finding a football field and basketball courts further down the road.

"Morning."

"Morning." Bailey acknowledged the elderly women who were walking by. Both were dressed immaculately in floral dresses, their hair snow white and cut in matching bobs. Both wore heels high enough to give Bailey a nosebleed. She knew instantly who they were; if she hadn't, the shoes would have given them away.

"A bit cooler now, but still pleasant."

Bailey looked at the sky. "Certainly looks like it will be a nice day, Miss Marla."

The women came closer, and she noted the lines that

had not been there before. She guessed the Robbins sisters were close to sixty-five now.

"Bailey Jones!"

"Hello, Miss Marla, Miss Sarah." The sisters had been teaching when she'd last been in Ryker Falls. In fact it was Miss Sarah who had first introduced Bailey to the piano.

"Marla, it's Bailey Jones!"

"I have eyes, Sarah, I can see who's standing a foot in front of me."

Bailey remembered that about them too. The arguments.

Miss Sarah hurried forward. "Dear, we are so proud of you."

"Thank you." Bailey leaned into the hug, even though she wasn't big on touching. Her face was then cupped between two soft hands, and she was studied.

"Well now, my dear. I think it's past time you came home. You come on in to the tea shop when you're passing. Right up on the main street, you can't miss it, and the first cup's on us."

"Tea shop?"

"We don't teach anymore, Bailey," Miss Marla said. "We now run Tea Total."

"Here in Ryker?"

"The locals needed a bit of refining, and we were just the girls for the job," Miss Sarah said. "And now we need to get on, Bailey, dear, as we left Mandy in charge."

Mandy was their niece who they'd raised after her father had died suddenly, she remembered that because they'd been in the same classes at school. Watching them walk away, she swallowed the tightness in her throat. Back in town a few hours, and she'd met Joe, Luke, and now the Robbins sisters. Shaking her head, Bailey headed to the shops. The one she wanted was third in the row. She looked in the store windows as she walked, and saw a herbalist, massage place, and a greengrocer... with the emphasis on green. Lots of leafy vegetables and baskets of fruit with "organic" written in large lettering. It would be a place to explore, Bailey thought. But for now the shop she wanted was up ahead.

"Artsy Fartsy?" Bailey read the sign, shaking her head. "Really, Maggie?" Pushing the door open, she walked inside.

The interior was white, the walls covered with a variety of art, and the shelves and floor held sculptures in a variety of different materials.

Bailey would have recognized Maggie Anderson anywhere. At thirteen she'd had that shock of red hair, and the promise of the height she now topped. She had a phone cradled against her shoulder while she did something on the computer with her hands. They'd been inseparable and shared everything from their first meeting, until Bailey had left Ryker Falls. *Well, not everything*, Bailey remembered. She'd told no one about Joe Trainer.

"Can I help you?"

Bailey watched Maggie replace the phone and round the counter to head her way. Her hair was shoulder-length and still curled in every direction. Those hazel eyes had once seemed almost too big, but now sat perfectly proportioned in a pretty face. She had a curvaceous body, clothed in a soft, floaty mint-green dress. On her feet were red ankle boots.

"Maggie." For the second time that day she felt a fierce surge of emotion, but this one was warm and good. "It's me, Bailey."

Her friend's painted red lips opened wide, but no sound came out, except a loud squeak. She then ran at Bailey, arms open, and hugged her hard.

"Bailey!"

Bailey hadn't had a lot of hugs in her lifetime; she came from a family that didn't communicate with physical gestures. In fact, they didn't communicate at all.

"Oh my God, Bailey."

She was held by the shoulders and studied, then hugged again.

"Maggs, it's so good to see you." And it was, Bailey realized, better than good. Closing her eyes, she leaned in to her old friend and held on.

"Oh, and you too!" Her friend squealed, holding her at arm's length again. "You look tired, Bays."

"I am. I've driven for miles to see you."

"How long are you here?"

"I—ah, I'm not sure, actually."

Her friend frowned. "Why haven't you written me in the last year?"

"I've been busy travelling, you know what my schedule is like."

"You always found time to write, Bays. Why did you stop, and don't lie, I'll know."

Bailey found a smile. Seeing Maggs was lifting her spirits already, even if she was asking questions Bailey didn't want to answer.

"Let's leave the in-depth probing into each other's lives for now, Maggs. I want you to show me around your gallery, and then I need to find some accommodation."

"All right, but I will have the in-depth story before you leave, Bailey."

"Sure," Bailey lied. No way was she discussing the train wreck that her life was, or that now it had derailed, she wasn't sure how to get it back on track.

"And you can stay with me while you're here. I have a spare room."

"I can't do that, Maggs. It wouldn't be right, with you having a boyfriend."

Her friend waved her words away. "If we want to have at each other, we can go to his place."

"I can't believe you just said that." Bailey felt color fill her cheeks.

"Don't tell me you're still a prude, Bailey Jones. You've been travelling the world playing piano in exotic places, meeting any number of hot, sexy, rich men. I'm sure you've seen and heard things that would make my hair stand on end."

Bailey made herself laugh, when the truth was she'd been sheltered and protected her entire life. The usual life lessons hadn't come to Bailey until she'd escaped from the viselike grip her grandfather had on her. He'd protected her, he'd said, in case she hurt herself, or worse yet, her hands. And yet no amount of protection had saved them in the end.

Chapter 3

"DO we have to do the blindfold thing, Miss Marla?"

"That's the deal, Joe, because otherwise you'll cheat."

"How?" Joe sat at the table as Miss Marla moved in behind and tied the scarf around his eyes.

"You can see the tea."

"You know that makes no sense, and you're just sore because you can't fool me."

"Don't fight it, Joe."

He snorted at Mandy's words. She was Miss Marla and Miss Sarah's niece, a quiet woman who rarely spoke, and usually stayed out the back of the teashop. Joe had known her for years, but had to say he knew her no better now than he had when first they'd met.

"Bring out those scones when you come back, Mandy."

"Yes, Aunt Sarah."

He listened to the door opening and closing, then the click of one of the Robbins sisters' heels.

"How come you don't have sore feet?"

"Practice. Plus, they do good things to our legs," Miss Marla said.

"Sure, you're both hot, no disputing that, but don't you ever wear flats?"

"When we exercise."

"That makes sense. It'd be hell jogging in those."

"Such a smart mouth for a handsome boy. Luckily I love your dog; he's your redeeming feature."

"Tell me you didn't just open that door and let him inside."

"I didn't."

"You didn't just slip him a biscuit either, right?"

"No."

"So who's crunching then?"

"Sarah."

He laughed, because it was obviously Buzz. "This town is gonna make him fat."

"We wouldn't do that, would we, sweetie?"

"Now put him outside before he gets hair everywhere."

They grumbled, but he heard the doorbell seconds later. He then heard the sisters say hello to customers.

Tea Total Tea Shop was an odd thing to have in a Colorado mountain town, and yet it worked. The sisters had been here for years, immigrating when they were in their twenties, to look after their brother's child after he was killed in a car accident. After teaching the town's children to conjugate verbs—a major fail on his part—they'd started the tea rooms, where people could get homemade scones, crumpets, and any kind of tea they wanted... and in Joe's case, plenty he didn't.

"Oh now, this is a lovely sight."

"What's a lovely sight?" Joe turned his head, but couldn't see what Miss Marla was looking at.

"Here's our Maggie, and she's brought Bailey Jones with her, Joe. Not sure if you remember her. Lived here years ago, and Sarah taught her to play the piano. She went on to be a famous concert pianist." She whispered the words to him, Joe guessed so Bailey couldn't hear.

"We done here then?" He wanted the blindfold off, wanted to look at Bailey. Two days she'd been back, and he hadn't seen her again until now... or not, as the current case may be.

"You just hold on there, Joe. Sarah's bringing your tea, and there is no way you will get this one right." She patted his shoulder.

"Morning, Miss Marla, Miss Sarah. Hey, Joe, you tasting again?" Maggie arrived first, her voice bright and cheery.

"I just came in for a scone, Maggs, and they got me in the chair."

"They're persuasive, but here's the thing, Joe. If you gave in and got some of the tests wrong, they'd ease up on you."

"You know I can't do that, Maggs. I have standards." He listened for another set of footsteps, his other senses on high alert for when Bailey drew near.

"You remember Bailey, Joe?"

"Sure. Hey, Bailey, how you doing?" He reached for the blindfold, but a hand slapped it away.

"Introductions can wait. Here it is, Joe. I bet you can't tell me what it is."

"What's he doing?"

The words came from Bailey, as did the scent that settled around him. Her voice was soft, almost a whisper, and totally different from the one she'd had as a thirteen-year-old.

He took the cup Miss Marla put in his hands and sipped, while behind him Maggs explained what was going on to Bailey.

They'd been doing this for three years now. He always

guessed right, and it infuriated the sisters. So much so that it had become a weekly ritual. He tasted what they put before him, and always guessed right. Okay, maybe he'd missed one or two, but for the most he got it bang on.

"You really didn't try too hard with this one, ladies," Joe said, lowering the cup to its pretty pink saucer. "Marshmallow root, lemon balm, rose hips, with a hint of cinnamon. No, wait." He held up a hand as Miss Marla started cackling. "There's lemon in there too."

She hissed out a breath.

"Boy, you don't even know what ylang-ylang is, how is it you know what's in that tea?"

He wasn't giving that secret away, or the fact that he pored over the internet and ordered teas himself, so he knew what was in theirs.

"It's a gift, what can I say?" He took off the blindfold and looked into the frustrated face of Miss Marla. Behind the counter, Miss Sarah was scowling at him. He then made himself stand and look at her.

"Hi there, Bailey." She wore a lemon-yellow sweater over a denim skirt. On her feet were sandals, her toes unpainted. Her hair once again was up in that messy knot.

"Hello, Joe."

"You eaten all that candy yet?"

One side of her mouth lifted as she nodded. "I saw Joe in the grocer's a few days ago," she explained to Maggs.

"She devours that stuff, just like you, Joe," Maggie added.

"It's good." He shrugged and made himself look away from Bailey. He felt warm in his chest just knowing that she was standing here beside him.

"What's paraben then?" Miss Sarah stepped into the conversation—literally. She now stood before him, hands on hips.

"Now, now, we're not talking about what's in my shampoo, but what's in your tea, ladies." Joe bent to brush a kiss on a soft, paper-thin cheek that smelled of musk. "Have to head off now, have work to do. Come in later, and I'll pour you a glass of that hideous sherry I stocked just for you, and I can bask in my success."

"If I didn't love you so much, Joe Trainer, I'd dislike you intensely."

"Now you don't mean that, Miss Sarah. I'm your favorite, admit it."

"Actually, you may have slipped down to second favorite, as of two days ago."

"My heart's breaking here." He wondered why he was so aware of a woman who was now a stranger to him, but he was. He knew when she walked away, and made himself stay focused on the older woman instead of following Bailey with his eyes.

"Sarah's star pupil is back in town, aren't you, Bailey. So to be fair, she has to take first place, seeing as we've been following her career for years."

Because they were talking about her, he could look at her. She was standing beside the counter, looking at the scones.

"So she's back in town a few days, and my position slides? Hardly seems fair."

She looked up at him and smiled. It was natural, and made her look sweet, which he did not notice.

"What can I say?" She shrugged. "It's a gift." She repeated his words, making everyone laugh.

He had to leave then, because work was piling up. What he actually wanted to do was sit and talk to Bailey, but instead he made himself walk to the door. "I want you two to try harder with the next tasting, because that effort was pathetic."

"How do you know about marshmallow root?" Miss Marla asked.

"I have a plant."

That got them scoffing, because everyone knew Joe was no gardener.

"See you round, Bailey, Maggie."

They waved at him, and Bailey caught his eye, but then looked away. Joe felt that look right to his toes. Closing the door, he made himself walk out into the sunshine under the huge blue-and-purple teacup.

"Let's go, Buzz." His dog fell in beside him as he walked.

"Joseph Trainer, the noise coming from your establishment last night was too loud!"

"You have to be kidding me," Joe said beneath his breath as Mary Howard approached him. "If I say bite, you get to it, boy."

He looked down at his dog, who simply wagged his tail.

"Some kind of protector you are."

"You look at me when I'm speaking to you, boy."

Dressed for exercise in a pair of stretchy black leggings that challenged the laws of gravity, Mary Howard stood bristling before him. Her mouth was set in an angry line, as it always was when she was anywhere near him. He and this woman shared bad blood.

"I'm thirty years old, Mrs. Howard, please don't call me a boy. And I can assure you the sound the band made last night was well within the limits. As a town councilor, it wouldn't be right for me to try and break those limits, now would it."

"Don't you answer me back, boy, I know what I heard."

Her eyes narrowed as she leaned toward him. The

corner of her zip dug into the flesh under her chin, which had to hurt.

"I'm not checking them again, Mrs. Howard, because they haven't changed since last time you complained." Joe usually went for the path of least resistance when he encountered her, but sometimes, like today, when he was feeling edgy, he struck back.

"You'll do what's right because you owe this town, and some of us more than others."

The burn of anger slowly filled his body. He tamped it down.

"I haven't forgotten what I owe *some* of the town, Mrs. Howard." He put emphasis on "some," because this woman was definitely not one of them.

"You and yours are bad blood, and to my mind that doesn't change. Drinking, drugs, and stealing, that's all you're good for."

"With all due respect, Mrs. Howard, I've been back ten years, and not been in one scrap of trouble. Jake's running a successful business at the ranch, and Luke's a firefighter, so I'm not entirely sure what we have to do to prove we've changed. Furthermore, I'm about done trying."

Not that he or his brothers' gave a shit what this woman thought of them, but she was like a burr under his skin sometimes, which was never comfortable, but something he could live with if he had to.

"How's your son doing, by the way?"

She was now the color of a tomato.

"Don't you speak about my boy. He's ten of you."

"If you say so, but then how would anyone know? He left town same time as me, and never returned. You have to wonder why?" He wasn't a mean person by nature, but sometimes it came out, and usually when he was around this woman.

"My boy has important business, and has no time to come back to this small town."

"The small town you live in, Mrs. Howard?"

She spluttered, but rallied. Nothing kept this woman's mouth shut for longer than ten seconds.

"Hello, Mrs. Howard."

Joe hadn't heard the tea shop door open, or Bailey move to his side.

"Who are you?" Mrs. Howard looked Bailey up and down rudely.

"Bailey Jones."

The beady eyes narrowed. "I heard you were playing piano in New York."

"Yes, and other places."

"Well, you just keep away from him and his." She looked Joe's way.

"Pardon?" Bailey's question was cold enough to have ice on it.

"Bailey—"

"He's bad," Mrs. Howard interrupted him. "Always was."

"Well now, I guess that's a matter of perspective then, isn't it," Bailey said.

"And what does that mean?"

"Perspective? Let me see if I remember what the dictionary definition is."

Joe snorted.

"I know what it means!"

Bailey's expression was innocent. "Excuse me, but didn't you just ask me what it meant?"

Joe wondered if the top of Mary Howard's head was about to blow off. He really shouldn't be enjoying her discomfort so much, and especially not as it would put

Bailey into her firing line, but hell, he was only human, and this woman was a bitch with a great big fuck off capital *B*.

"You just watch yourself, girl. I have weight in this town," Mary Howard snarled. Then glaring at both him and Bailey, she turned, looked down at her shoelace, and bent to do it up. Joe wasn't entirely dismissing the fact that it was a deliberate act on her part to do this; Buzz, however, never missed an opportunity, and wandered on up and put his nose where it shouldn't be.

"Argh!" Mary Howard was once again upright. "That dog just violated me."

"Naughty boy," Joe said in the tone he used to order supplies for the bar. Bailey giggled, which earned her a glare. Mrs. Howard then stomped away.

"I'm sorry you had to be part of that, Bailey, but thank you for saying what you did." He turned to face her, now only a foot separated them. Her eyes looked blue more than gray out here in the sun. She was still pale, and to his eyes tired, but for all that, she was beautiful. He found the scar on her cheek again. *What put that there?*

"I don't like mean people, and she's always been one."

"With a long memory."

"We all have those," she said in a quiet voice. "Good-bye, Joe."

Before he could stop her, she moved around him to give Buzz's head a scratch, and tell him he was a good boy, then she'd walked away. Resisting the urge to follow, Joe made himself head in the opposite direction, wondering what Bailey Jones remembered from those two years they'd been in each other's lives.

What did she remember? Like him, was it everything?

Chapter 4

RYKER FALLS WAS at the foot of two huge mountains, and Joe took a few seconds to look at them, to steady himself, before heading back to work.

The twins, the locals called them. The Ryker family who founded the town had two children, twins, Roxanne and Phillip, so the left-hand mountain was called Roxy, and the right Phil. Identical in height and breadth, they could be seen from miles away. They were a year-round tourist town, because when people weren't skiing down them, they were tramping up them to see the falls. A river ran down two sides of the town, and met the sea. This allowed more activity for those keen on water sports, or fishing.

"Afternoon, Joe, Buzz." An elderly man appeared at his side. "That she-devil, Mary Howard, been giving you trouble again?"

"Hey, Mr. Goldhirsh. Nothing I can't handle," Joe said. "When's the race?"

Tall and thin, Frederick Goldhirsh had lived in Ryker for fifty years, and his age was as yet unknown. He never told anyone, no matter how often he was asked. "Age," he said, "is just a number." Of Jewish descent, he started his life in a concentration camp in Nazi Germany, and considering how he had suffered by losing his entire family, the man was the most positive person Joe knew. He ran marathons year-round in every corner of the globe. He was jogging on the spot before Joe now.

"Six weeks on Sunday, and I expect your support, as it's the annual Ryker Falls run."

"I'll be at the end clapping like every other sane person. Aunt Jess will be back too."

The man's eyes crinkled at the corners as he barked out a laugh. He'd been in love with Joe's aunt for at least ten years.

Mr. Goldhirsh was dressed in a tank top that said London Marathon, and a pair of blue shorts. On his head was a red cap. Joe watched as he dug around in the pocket at the back of his shirt and pulled out a biscuit.

"You have to be kidding me."

"He expects it," Mr. Goldhirsh said, handing Buzz the biscuit.

"He's going to be the size of a grizzly soon."

"Wouldn't do you both any harm to do some training with me, Joe."

"God's truth, Mr. Goldhirsh, I'd be dead before we hit the first mile mark."

"And that's the problem with the youth of today," the man said, lifting a hand. He was obviously done with making Joe feel inadequate, and ready to move on and find someone else to hassle.

As he didn't finish that sentence, Joe did it for him as he started walking again. "No resilience."

Ryker had two parts to the town. The "green belt," as Joe called it, was for those who wanted healthy alternatives for their body and soul, like alfalfa sprouts and meditation. You could get a beet and kale smoothie, though why the hell you'd want to was beyond him, and someone to get your chakras back in line and find inner peace.

"Not that I couldn't do with some of that," he muttered. His inner peace had been shattered two days ago when he found Bailey in the grocery store. He hadn't stopped thinking about her since, and now that he'd just seen her, and she'd supported him with Mary Howard, he was even more aware of her.

Then there was his part of town. The place where you could get a meal and pay as little or as much as you wanted. Shops sold everything from hand-painted crockery to high-priced jewelry. Over the years, Ryker had learned to cater for everyone who entered it.

He and Buzz crossed the road and entered his bar. He'd bought the place five years ago, and he'd been making changes ever since. The facade was red brick, the front doors white, like the frames on the two front bay windows. A sign curved over the doorway with the letters *A* and *S* on it, and at night it was lit by twenty bulbs.

Joe loved this place because it was his alone. He shared several investments and properties with his siblings, but not this.

With polished wood floors, and muted lighting, the bar area had plenty of seating or leaning spaces. One wall was bricked, and to one side sat a small stage. Joe looked at the piano and thought of Bailey.

"And that has to stop," he muttered, walking to where his manager was standing, poring over the bookings for the night. He had to get his head around the fact that she was back, and different, and that they no longer meant anything to each other. How could they after fifteen years?

"Hey, Buzz. We're full tonight."

"How come he gets a greeting and I get 'we're full tonight.'"

"He's cuter."

"You pull out a dog biscuit and you're fired."

"What bug crawled up your ass?"

He waved a hand, dismissing the question. "I want to say great, but with the staffing issues, we're gonna be pressed, Em." Emily Paul was short, with a big attitude. She had a cap of straight blonde hair, and several piercings that made his eyes water. She had been the best applicant he'd interviewed by far, even though she was younger by a good five years. Joe believed in gut instinct, so he'd employed her, and never regretted it.

Passing the bar he'd had another friend build with one long slab of local timber, Joe ran his hand along the smooth length before heading to his office. Buzz made a few circles on his bed, then settled down with a heavy sigh.

"Yeah, like your life is so hard."

The dog ignored him and was snoring like the buzz of a chainsaw minutes later. Looking at the clock, Joe noted the time as 4:00 p.m. He'd be lucky to see his bed by 1:00 a.m., and wasn't displeased. If he was busy, he couldn't think about her.

Chapter 5

"A DRINK, a meal, nothing more, Bailey. Seriously, you can't just hide inside for your entire stay. It's not healthy. You're pale, with bags under your eyes, and way too skinny. You're coming out with me tonight."

"Don't hold back, Maggie, and I didn't stay inside today. Day two, I might add. I had tea with you at Miss Marla and Miss Sarah's tea shop, then we walked down to the boardwalk." The tea shop where she'd seen Joe. And then outside where she'd heard that bitch Mary Howard abusing him. The old Joe wouldn't have just stood there and taken that. He'd have yelled back. Like her, lots had changed, it seemed.

"Do you want me to hold back, Bailey?"

"No, I always liked that you told me what you were feeling, Maggs. It's taking me a while to adjust, okay? I haven't been around anyone like you in years."

"I'm not sure that's a compliment."

"I assure you it is," Bailey said. She did want straight talking, because it was the truth she needed in her life now. No more lies or platitudes. No more empty words because people thought they were what she wanted to hear. "I value your honesty, Maggs. But I've been back two days, surely I get some time to just be a sloth?"

Two days of staying in Maggs's wonderful home. It was close to the mountains, in the less-populated part of town. With two bedrooms, the body of the house was not overly large, but what it lacked in size it made up for with the view from the conservatory. Glass walled the room on three sides and the roof, and it offered never-ending views of the twin mountains. The minute she'd walked into that room, Bailey had fallen in love with the little house.

"Good. Because lying is not what we do, Bailey. And yes to being a sloth—if I believed that was what you were doing."

"You don't?"

"No, I don't, but as yet I'm not sure what's going on with you."

"Does there need to be something going on? I mean, can't I just be here to see you and take a holiday?"

"Hmmm." Maggs made a noise that was neither agreeing nor disagreeing.

They were driving down the main street of Ryker, looking for a place to park. Her friend had dragged her out the house with the promise of good food and wine.

"I've talked at you for hours. Shared my entire life story, yet you've told me nothing about yourself, Bailey, other than everything is wonderful... fine, in fact. What I really want to know is why you've stopped performing, and where you've been since?"

Bailey didn't want to talk about that stuff, because it was painful.

"You know what I've been doing, Maggs. I wrote about it in the letters I sent you. I went to Juilliard, then performed around the world. I didn't have time for much else." Her life had been a strict schedule of practice and engagements, which she had enjoyed until they started to suffocate her. Then one day, everything had changed.

"What about people you know or things you've done outside music. Got drunk with friends, the night you lost your virginity. I want to hear those stories."

"Ha ha." Bailey made herself laugh. "That would take hours." In fact, it would take seconds, because other than a few brief rebellions that involved leaving hotel rooms and walking about cities alone, there wasn't anything to tell. Losing her virginity had also been spectacularly unsuccessful, and painful.

Bailey looked out the window at the streetlights; she still found it hard to believe that she was actually back here in Ryker.

"I'll share the virginity story if you will."

She laughed again.

Maggie sighed. "I'm worried about you."

"Don't be. Instead, help me find some work for the time I'm here."

"Why do you need work? Aren't you rich?"

"Hardly that, and I want to work. Maybe there's somewhere I could play at nights?"

"But you're on holiday."

"I get bored easily."

"So what were you doing before you came to Ryker, if you stopped performing?"

"This and that."

"And?"

"And I need a job, Maggs. I promise to fill in the gaps soon, but for tonight can we just have fun?"

She felt Maggie's eyes on her, but kept hers out the window. She had money, she just wasn't able to access it, and wouldn't be able to until she gave in to her grandfather. Yet another stupid mistake on her part. Bailey shuddered at how gullible and easily manipulated she'd allowed herself to be. She was in this predicament because she had no backbone, but that was changing now.

"Okay, fun it is."

Maggs found parking, and they got out and headed up the street. The weather was cooling in Ryker, summer drawing to a close and fall approaching. She followed Maggie into a bar that she'd told Bailey was the place to go in Ryker.

"A.S. is owned and run by Joe Trainer—you met him this morning, Bailey. We'll go find him later, because he may need an entertainer, although I'm not sure someone of your caliber wants to play here."

"Don't be a snob, Maggs," Bailey said as her heart sank to her toes at the thought that she was entering Joe's bar and would see him again soon. "There are some amazing piano players who aren't on the stage."

"I stand corrected."

Joe owned this. Looking around, Bailey was impressed. The space was big, but tastefully decorated, and already full of people. He'd changed a lot since she'd last seen him, and not just in appearance, it seemed.

"As you should. Bad girl," Bailey said, looking for Joe. She had to get this under control if she was to stay in Ryker for a while. She couldn't stiffen up whenever he was near, and her heart had to learn to keep a steady rhythm. Exposure to him should sort that out. She hoped it did, anyway.

"I missed you, Bays."

Maggs's words gave her a sharp stab of pain. Bailey had missed her friend too, but after a while she'd learned how to shut those feelings away.

"Missed you too, and you look amazing by the way." She looked Maggs over.

Dressed in a pair of tight jeans, pink top, and another pair of sky-high heels, her friend exuded confidence and style, unlike Bailey, whose clothes hung on her because she hadn't been able to put on the weight she'd lost after the accident.

"A.S. has great food and entertainment."

"Hey there, Maggie, how you doing?" one of the staff greeted them.

"Good, thanks, Em. This is Bailey, and we're going to find a seat near the piano and order some snacks."

"Sure, no worries, I'll bring you some menus."

Joe had put a great deal of thought into making the people who walked in here feel comfortable, Bailey thought. The lighting was soft, the colors neutral until you reached the one wall that was a vivid jade. Black-and-white prints of actors hung in different sizes and shapes on it.

"Is the boss in, Em?"

"Sure, he's in his office," the woman said, handing them menus.

Relieved that she didn't have to see Joe right off, Bailey relaxed enough to look at the bar menu. The hum of voices told her people were enjoying a drink and conversation. Through a set of doors, she saw more seats.

"That's a restaurant, if you want to have a quiet meal," Maggie said.

They found a high table with several stools. Once they'd ordered, Bailey let her eyes settle on the pianist. He was good, a natural, Bailey thought. There were two types of pianists to her mind. Those who didn't have the raw talent, but practiced hard to become competent, and those who were born with the need to play. She was one of the latter.

"So, Bailey, I see you haven't lost your bad food addiction."

"Loaded fries and a glass of red wine are not bad, Maggie. If I ordered a sundae after, now that would be bad."

"But of course we're having a sundae." Maggie looked shocked Bailey would think otherwise.

With her fries and red wine, and excellent music in the background, Bailey felt comfortable, and was suddenly glad she'd come with Maggie. Her reaction to Joe didn't mean he felt the same way. Sure they'd had an awkward moment today, but it didn't have to happen again.

"Mary Howard is still a bitch, Maggs."

"She is, and not sure why you said that now, but let me tell you, the woman's one to stay clear of."

"I overheard her speaking to someone today. It was ugly."

"Woman's a born bitch, nothing else to say on that matter."

They chatted, but didn't touch on anything personal, and for that Bailey was relieved. Plenty of people stopped to say hi and were introduced to Bailey.

"Hey, Buzz."

Bailey looked down at the large dog that appeared at their table.

"He's kind of like the town's unofficial mascot. Joe's convinced if there was a vote between him and Buzz, Buzz would win any popularity contest," Maggie said. He's usually in Joe's office sleeping, but someone has obviously coaxed him downstairs.

"He's a sweetie," Bailey said, getting off the stool to crouch down and give him a pat. She hadn't had much exposure to dogs, but she liked them, and this one was a big, gentle giant, everyone had told her so.

The pianist stopped playing suddenly, and then ran from the room.

"What the hell's that about?" Maggie frowned.

The woman who had served them moved to the microphone.

"Apologies, we just have a technical hitch to work through."

The hum of voices started as she walked away.

"That'll annoy the customers," Maggie said.

"Why? Can't they just put some music on?"

"Sure, but everyone loves to hear Vinnie play his honky-tonk, and come here especially for that. This place will soon be full of people who have driven from far and wide to hear him."

"That's a shame then."

"Because I'm nosy, I'm going to see what's happened."

Bailey sat again, and ate her fries. Buzz wandered away to greet someone else. Nothing was pressing in on her here. She didn't have her grandfather or agent in contact, demanding she return to New York, and for the first time in months, she could actually breathe. Maybe being in Ryker wasn't so bad. She'd seen Joe twice, and if she saw him again they could be polite, and she wouldn't feel like the rug had been pulled out from under her feet.

"So Vinnie has a stomach upset and he's been sent home. Joe could play, but they're short-staffed so he's working," Maggie said, returning.

"Joe plays?"

"Sure. He's not a natural, but good enough. Em's calling around trying to find a replacement, or they'll just have to run the music through the system. However, I did tell Joe you were here, and he said to beg if I have to."

"I could play." Bailey said the words slowly, testing them to see how she felt about them. *Okay.* For the first time in many months, just like her appetite, Bailey felt her fingers itch. She wanted to play. It was Joe's bar, but what did that matter? She wanted to play, so why not?

"Are you sure?" Maggie looked shocked and a little excited. "Can you play honky-tonk?"

"Please." Bailey gave her friend a pitying look. "I cut my eye teeth on honky-tonk, much to my parents' and grandfather's horror."

Getting to her feet, Bailey didn't look at the faces of the people around her. Nerves had always been a problem, but she'd countered them by not making eye contact. Not that she'd have been able to do that when the audience was in the hundreds, but still, it was Bailey's ritual to go into herself before she played. She did that now.

Seating herself at the piano, Bailey took a couple of deep breaths. Turning her hand over, she looked at the scar running up her palm and wrist. She hadn't played a lot since the accident, but she was ready, she could feel it. The man, Vinnie, had left his music, so she went through it, selected a piece to start with, then placed her hands on the keys and began to play.

Chapter 6

JOE WALKED behind the bar as Bailey started playing. When Maggs had said she'd offered, he hadn't been about to refuse. A. He was in a bind, and B. Well hell, she was Bailey Jones. So he watched and listened as he served. She was playing honky-tonk, as Vinnie had been, but there was little doubting her class. Looking around the room, he realized she had the customers fixated, and she was only on the first song.

"That's the woman who arrived with Maggie. How come she's playing?" Em asked as she lowered empties onto the bar.

"She's a famous pianist, actually. Used to live here, and then went away and made it big."

"Really?" Em looked impressed. "Fancy that."

Joe knew how good Bailey was because he'd followed her career, and once he'd been in the audience, but he'd never expected to see her play in his bar.

"She's good, and when you add hot to that," Mike, his barman, said, "they're eating out of her hands."

Ignoring the need to glare at his staff for calling Bailey

hot, Joe thought about what Maggie had told him. Bailey wanted work. What he wanted to know was why. She had to have money after the performances she'd done, so where was it?

"Hey, Joe."

"Maggie, what can I get you? In fact, it's on the house seeing as you brought your friend with you, and saved my ass."

"And what a fine ass it is."

Maggie was one of those people who were confident in their own skin. She always dressed slightly different and classy. She also liked to embarrass Joe and his brothers at any opportunity that arose.

"We've discussed this, Maggs. You need to get up way earlier to embarrass me. Now Luke, on the other hand, he would be beet red by now."

"Hard-ass." Maggie turned to look at Bailey. "So, you like your new pianist, Joe?"

"She's a bit raw, but I think the crowd are starting to warm to her."

"Ha ha, she's bloody brilliant."

He knew that, and a lot about the woman they discussed, but Maggie didn't know that.

"So you and she stayed friends after she left Ryker?"

Maggie's pink lips lifted. "We started out friends in school, then when she left we exchanged letters. We never moved to emails, just kept writing, although not so much in the last few years on her part."

Joe already knew they were friends.

"When I saw her in the grocery store, I didn't recognize her, but then it's been years, like you said. Still... she looked like a gust of wind would knock her down." Joe didn't feel guilty pumping Maggie for information on Bailey, because he didn't think he had a shot at the woman herself sharing anything with him. "Pale and drawn, was what I thought."

"That's what I think too, but I don't like to talk about her behind her back. She was always sensitive about that kind of thing."

"She may have changed some in the last, what is it? Fifteen or so years."

"Sure, but I think if anything she's more private."

Joe had been a barman for a while now, and he was good at getting people to talk. He knew the art of silence. It didn't take long. Maggie was a nurturer, it was in her DNA. If she was worried about Bailey she'd want to discuss it with someone, and he was showing interest.

"It's just... well, the thing is, Joe, I'm worried about her."

Why had that made his stomach clench? All those years, it seemed, hadn't eradicated his protective streak where Bailey Jones was concerned.

"Not sure why you would be, considering the life she's led and money she must have." He got the glasses out of the washer and started drying them. "Plus, like you said, you've not seen each other in years."

Maggie looked at Bailey again, which meant Joe could. Her hands flew over the keys and her entire body seemed to move with the music. She'd come alive seated at his piano playing honky-tonk.

"Seems happy to me."

"Because she's doing what she loves. She's brilliant, isn't she?" The words weren't loud, but Joe heard them. "You see where Buzz is. That dog is a great judge of character."

His dog was leaning on the seat Bailey sat on, which was kind of odd, because he didn't usually take to people he didn't know well. He was polite, but didn't stray far from Joe.

"Yes, she's brilliant."

"Why are you worried about her, Maggs?"

"I don't know, just a hunch."

Which frustratingly told Joe nothing.

"Well, you go on back to your table, and annoy my brothers who've just arrived, and I'll take Bailey a drink."

"How could I resist that offer?" Maggie laughed, and took the drink he'd just poured her and headed back to her seat.

Joe got down a tall glass, added ice, then poured in soda. He then walked to the piano as Bailey finished another song.

"Thanks for saving my hide and filling in, Bailey." He placed the soda he knew she'd liked as a twelve-year-old on the small table beside her.

She turned her body on the seat to look up at him "A.S., Joe?"

"Apple Sours."

"You named your bar after those sweets?"

"I did, it seemed to fit." He'd also named it Apple Sours because he felt he owed Bailey something for the support she'd given him all those years ago.

"You called your bar Apple Sours." She was smiling now. Not the wide, flash-all-your-teeth kind, but it was another genuine one.

"I think we've just established that."

"I-I just thought to fill in for a few songs, as your man was sick."

"And because you love playing honky-tonk?"

"There is that, too. I guess I should leave now?"

She was beautiful under the soft lighting. Her face still looked tired, and her eyes smudged, but her lips were glossy, and her hair was still in a messy thing on her head. She wore a long-sleeved, loose peach shift-type dress. It hit midthigh, and on her feet were tan wedges. Her scent was subtle and now familiar, and damned if he didn't feel a flare of intense pleasure at knowing she was here in his bar. His Bailey, as he'd once thought of her. His friend, he reminded himself. He eyed the delicate heart-shaped locket around her neck and wondered who'd given it to her.

"Why would you leave?"

"B-because of.... Just because...." Her words fell away.

"I have no idea what that meant."

"Me either." She looked confused. "I heard your pianist was sick, like I said, and found myself seated here the next minute."

She was flustered now, her eyes going to him, then away again.

"Maggs told me, and we were once friends, Bailey, so I'm sure I don't have a problem with a world-famous concert pianist playing in my bar, if you don't have a problem with it."

She didn't smile; in fact, she frowned.

"However, I'm not sure I can afford you," he joked, trying to lighten the mood.

"I don't expect you to p-pay me more than any of your other staff."

"That's a relief, because I don't think I could afford your appearance fee."

"I'm enjoying this more."

The minute she said the words, Joe knew she wished she'd kept them in her head.

"I mean... I-I like playing honky-tonk, b-but don't often get a chance to."

Her words were flat and cold. Once, with him, she'd been full of emotion. Full of fun and sunlight. She'd filled the dark places inside him for a few hours every week for two years.

"Do you want work, Bailey?"

She didn't meet his eye as she nodded. "Sure, I get bored easily, so work would be good."

She was lying, he knew that, just not why.

"Okay, I can slot you in. How about for now you play two nights a week while you're here?"

"I can do that, thank you."

"Bailey, are you in some kind of trouble?"

Her eyes flared briefly with panic. "No, why would you think that? My life is great... wonderful. I'm taking a holiday, and I-I want to practice while I'm h-here."

Joe didn't buy it.

"You said you haven't played a concert for a year; what have you been doing?"

She shrugged. "This and that."

He rested a hand on her shoulder as she prepared to rise. Her skin was warm beneath his fingers.

"I'm pleased you're happy, Bailey. Really," he added. "But if you want anything, you need only ask."

She shook her head and turned back to the piano. "I don't need anything. But thank you for offering."

Unlike him, Bailey had always had impeccable manners.

"You'd be saving me, working here. Vinnie, my regular guy who was playing before you, has a stomach upset, and the other performer we had has a sick family member and left town for a while."

"I'm not sure how long I'll be here, Joe. But while I am I can come in when you need me."

"Give me your phone number, and I'll confirm what days when I speak with Vinnie."

"I don't have a phone."

"Pardon?"

"I don't have a phone."

Joe looked at her to see if she was serious. "You're messing with me?" He could honesty say he didn't know anyone who didn't have a cell phone.

"I don't want one." Her face was now closed completely, no emotion on show.

"But what about when you're driving and get a flat? What about contacting people?"

"I use a pay phone." She said the words slowly.

"I didn't realize they were on every road these days."

She didn't smile.

"Fine, I'll get hold of Maggie." He didn't push it anymore. *Who doesn't have a cell phone?*

"No, I'll come in and see you tomorrow. You can let me know then when you need me."

He couldn't stop his hand lifting, or the finger he ran down her cheek. She pulled back, and looked down at Buzz, who in turn was gazing at her as if she was the last piece of steak in Ryker Falls.

"I-I saw Luke. He's a firefighter, which must please you."

"Yes, he's happy." Joe rolled with the change of subject. "And Jack is doing well also."

"Maggie told me you own some land. I'm so pleased you're all settled here."

This was genuine, Joe thought. She really was happy that he and his siblings hadn't ended up on the wrong side of the law, or worse.

What was clear to him, however, was that Maggie hadn't told her which piece of land he'd purchased, because her reaction would be way different. Joe should tell her, she'd given him the perfect opening, but something held the words in his head. Instead he said, "And you, Bailey. Have you been happy?"

She produced another fake smile. "Of course."

"How's your family?"

"Good."

She was closed up tight again. She didn't want to discuss anything personal, which normally suited him. But not now. Not with her.

"I should start playing again. I'll play two more sets."

She turned back to the piano, and Joe watched her stretch her fingers, then rotate her wrists. She turned them over, and he caught a flash of a red scar. He grabbed her hand and pulled up the sleeve.

"What's this?"

She tried to tug it free, but Joe didn't release her. His eyes traced the scar that crisscrossed the lower half of her arm and down into her palm. It was raw, jagged, and looked painful. His guess was it hadn't happened that long ago.

"What happened?" His words sounded gruff, because the thought of her in pain bothered him.

"An accident. Now let go so I can play, Joe. Your customers are waiting."

He did, and she turned away from him. When was this accident? Frustrated, Joe walked back to the bar with more questions in his head than when he'd approached her.

"She gonna stay?" Em intercepted him.

"For a couple more sets, and come back a couple of times a week while she's in Ryker."

"She's really good, Joe, and let's face it, we should know, as we've had some bad ones. Plus, there's you."

"I'm good!" Joe thumped his chest, pretending to be outraged.

"You're average. She's a million leagues better."

"There you go flattering me again. But like I told you, she's a pro, Em."

"It shows," she said, and then headed off to clear some glasses. Joe served, and watched Bailey, and wondered again what had brought her back to Ryker, and why he was so pleased she had returned when there was so much they didn't know about each other any longer, or the roads they'd taken.

To even contemplate her coming back because of him years after she'd left, he knew was a stretch, but still he wondered. And then he shut that thought away because he didn't deserve that from Bailey. Not when he'd never returned a single one of the letters she'd written him. Not when her last words to him had been, "always remember I believe in you, Joe. Be the best person you can be."

Weeks after she'd said that, and left his life, he'd failed her.

Chapter 7

BAILEY WOKE SLOWLY after sleeping deep, like she always did. Years of hotels had taught her to sleep anywhere. Pushing the curtains back, she saw the day promised to be a good one.

Maggs would be sleeping, as this was her day off, and she'd told Bailey she'd evict her if she made a noise and woke her.

Pulling on her robe, she tiptoed to the kitchen and made instant coffee, as she had no idea how Maggs's coffee machine worked. She took it to the conservatory.

Mist still clung to the mountains, and she took a few minutes to just stand there and look, knowing no one and nothing had a claim on her time today. Bailey had experienced some awesome views in her lifetime, travelling the world, but she thought this may turn out to be her favorite.

She loved Maggs's home, and the feeling of peace and solitude. She'd also enjoyed playing the piano last night, even if it was in Joe's bar. But they could be acquaintances, she reminded herself. She just had to ignore the fact that when he was near her heart thumped harder in her chest.

Their history was just that, history now. She could be friendly, and the more exposure she had to him, the calmer she would feel in his presence.

He'd called his bar Apple Sours. Bailey remembered the conversation they'd once had, where she'd said it would be a good name for a restaurant or bar.

"Let it lie, Bailey," she told herself. *There's nothing between you now.*

Deciding to walk into town to have her breakfast, and leave Maggs to sleep, she showered and dressed. Exercise had been something Bailey rarely had time for... actually, that was a lie, she'd never wanted to. Now she did.

Placing the strap of her small bag over her shoulder, she quietly opened and closed the front door.

The morning held a promise of good weather, and the air fresh as Bailey made for town. Passing the road that led to the house she'd grown up in, she walked the fifteen minutes it took to reach Ryker Falls township. It was still early, the hour just ticking over 8:00 a.m. Inhaling, she was happy the air was not filled with exhaust fumes or big city scents.

"Morning."

Bailey smiled at the elderly man who was jogging past. If only she had that much enthusiasm for exercise. She had two passions remaining in her life, horses and music; the first she seldom had time for, the second kept her sane.

"Morning."

"Phil's Place has great donuts and coffee. Cinnamon and hazelnut's my favorite. The tea rooms won't open for another hour, so that's your best bet if you're heading into town for breakfast."

The jogger was running at her side as she walked now.

"Phil, as in after the mountain, Phil?" Bailey looked behind her, and there he stood. Big and proud as he always had been, right beside but slightly back from his twin sister. She'd always thought that was because he was looking out for her.

"Roxy has her own place too. The best pizza in town."

"Nice, and thanks for the recommendation."

"Name's Mr. Goldhirsh."

Manners were something she'd had hammered into her for many years, and while she wasn't someone who liked small talk, it would be rude not to at least give him her name. It wasn't a secret, after all.

"Bailey Jones."

"You played last night at Apple Sours."

"I did, yes."

"I was there. You have a special talent, my dear. I saw you in concert three years ago in Carnegie Hall."

"Thank you," Bailey said. She had learned to accept compliments with a smile.

"I never give praise if it is not deserved."

"Thank you," she said again.

"You exercise, Miss Jones?"

"Ah—well, define exercise?" She shot Mr. Goldhirsh a look. "I mean, I walk places, and sometimes I even put in a jog." Bailey stretched the truth.

"I mean regular exercise, the kind that has you sweating?"

He was adjusting his pace and almost jogging on the spot now, hazel eyes alert as he studied her.

"I'm really not into sweating, so I guess that's a fail, right?"

"Never too late. I could take you running with me, if you like? Plus, we have the Ryker run/walk club. Meets Saturday morning. We could swing by and pick you up."

Bailey stopped and faced him.

"You don't even know me."

"I know people, and you're trustworthy. You have an honest face."

Until she'd come to Ryker, Bailey had kept to bigger towns, driving wherever and whenever she wanted since leaving Boston. She hadn't struck up conversations, or made friends, just kept to herself. She'd only been back in Ryker a few days, and already she'd become reacquainted with more people than she could remember.

"I don't trust that easily," Bailey said before she could stop herself. "So thanks, but I need to get going."

She walked on, certain that would be the last conversation she had with Mr. Goldhirsh.

Turned out she was wrong.

"Trusting doesn't come easy for people, that's true, and considering your occupation and the fame attached, I should imagine you've had your trust challenged a time or two, but if you don't allow people in, then you can't know how trusting you can be."

He was jogging beside her again.

"You don't deter easily is my guess, Mr. Goldhirsh."

His eyes crinkled.

"I was born in a concentration camp, Miss Jones. I do not have time to take offence or be deterred."

"I-I'm so sorry," she managed to get out. The horrors he must have known were nothing compared to her own. "I can't image how you suffered."

He waved her words away.

"I was but a child. It was not I who suffered, Miss Jones. I did not tell you for sympathy, just as a point of fact. Life is too short. Therefore, not trusting anyone is a shame, as it cuts you off from good people. And there are plenty of them around should you wish to look."

You trust too easily, Bailey. Remember always that gullible fools end up hurt!

Her grandfather had loved that particular set of words.

"I'll try to remember that, thank you, Mr. Goldhirsh."

"And do you read, Miss Jones?"

"Read?"

"Poetry?"

She nodded, completely at sea as to where he was going with this.

"Then should you find yourself at a loose end on Sunday at 4:00 p.m., please come to my house. Right at the end of Main Street, then right. My house is the third street off the loop road. Number four, Niagara Street. I have a reading there every week. We're into Moore at the moment."

"As in Thomas Moore?" Bailey couldn't help but ask.

"The very one."

He lifted his hand and jogged away, leaving Bailey following him with her eyes. The man made her feel old, and he had years on her.

"Poetry and walking clubs, what's next?"

Shaking her head cleared it slightly. Walking again, she saw a sign in the shape of a mountain that held a cup of steaming coffee, with the words Phil's Place.

"That's what I need," Bailey muttered. That would right her world again.

Even early, it was busy. The decor was simple and modern, with white tables and chairs. One wall held leafy green plants, another a huge framed painting that looked like it probably came from Maggie's gallery. She found a free seat at the counter.

"Morning. What can I get you?"

The woman's smile was wide and looked familiar, but Bailey didn't think they'd been introduced. Dark hair was pulled into a braid. She was tall, with a pretty smile, and

Bailey imagined she was never short of admirers, especially given the confidence coming off her.

"Coffee and a cinnamon and hazelnut donut, thanks," Bailey said, deciding to go with Mr. Goldhirsh's suggestion.

"That's my kind of morning meal."

"They were recommended."

"Mr. Goldhirsh, right?"

Bailey nodded.

"He's personally increased the sales on those donuts single-handedly."

"He's good."

The waitress smiled. "Sure is. Just stay strong when he tries to lure you into exercise. I couldn't walk for days after he caught me at a weak moment."

"I noticed he's persistent."

"He calls it tenacious, so be firm with him. He understands words like 'no' and 'never again in this lifetime,' but use stuff like 'maybe' or 'I'll see,' and he's like a rabid dog. He'll never let go."

Bailey found herself laughing again as the woman walked away to get her coffee. She'd done that a few times since arriving. It was weird how she'd safeguarded herself over the last few years from expressing or feeling emotion, but here.... In the place she'd been born, it was different.

"Coffee and donut." The waitress placed her order on the counter.

"Thanks." Bailey cradled the mug and sipped. She then ate the donut slowly, savoring the different flavors as they settled in her mouth.

"How do they rate?"

Bailey nearly fell off her chair as the deep words reached her. A large hand steadied her. Joe Trainer took the seat next to her, filling up far too much space.

His hair was damp. He wore a blue T-shirt today, and

shorts sat low on his hips. He looked vibrant, alive, and sexy as hell.

"The donuts." He pointed to her plate, and Bailey noted the wide silver band around his middle finger. "From memory, you always had a sweet tooth, so how do they rate?"

"They're good."

"Do I have to serve you again?"

Bailey looked at the waitress, who was smiling at Joe now. Another thought hit her then, one she'd never even considered. He could be married now, and possibly even have children. Why did that thought hurt so much?

"What's that look for?"

"What look?" Bailey dragged her eyes from him, and focused on her plate.

"Like you just remembered something and it's all bad."

"No," Bailey lied. Looking at the girl again, she saw something familiar in her face. "Are you two related?"

"I'm her cousin, what gave it away? The good looks, and sparkling charm? Although, to be fair, I'm more popular than Piper."

"Like hell! I'm the Trainer hottie—"

"Said no one ever," Joe drawled. He then laughed as his cousin poked out her tongue and walked away.

Bailey sipped her drink and felt suddenly uncomfortable. There had been a time she and Joe hadn't needed words, just companionship. All that had changed now.

"Where's Buzz?" Piper returned with Joe's coffee.

"He stayed out late last night, so he's snoozing in the pickup."

"That dog has a better social life than me." Piper moved on again to serve another customer.

"Piper is my Aunt Jess's daughter. Do you remember the letter you—"

"I remember," Bailey interrupted Joe. He'd wanted to write to his aunt, asking her to come and help them, and she'd helped him.

"Piper and Aunt Jess have been living with us for years."

In spite of their backgrounds, they'd once been friends. Bailey had been raised in a household where everything had to be perfect, including her, and he was the exact opposite, raised with an abusive father, and a mother who had run away unable to cope, leaving her sons at the mercy of a bully.

"I never thanked you for that. For pushing me to write that letter." His voice was low, so only she could hear.

"I-I'm glad it worked out for you all."

"Donut." Piper returned with a plate for her cousin, and broke the silence that had fallen between them.

"How are you enjoying living with Maggs, Bailey?" Joe asked.

"Bailey?" Piper Trainer studied her, then her cousin. "Bailey Jones, right?"

She nodded.

"Everyone's been talking about you since last night. A famous person in Ryker is big news."

"We get famous people, Pip, all the time."

The girl braced a hand on a trim hip while she thought about that. Everything about her said strong to Bailey's mind. Her clothes were bright, her lipstick red, and she had a confidence that Bailey envied. She'd been late to find her backbone, but it was there now, and she wasn't going back to being submissive anytime soon... if ever.

"Sure, but they never perform. They're usually up at the lodge holidaying. Any chance you could play tonight? I've got a hot date, and we're coming to A.S."

"Who is this hot date?" Joe was frowning at his cousin

now, but she waved his words away with a flick of long fingers.

"I'm coming over for a free meal."

"Why don't you pay like everyone else?" Joe said.

"Family don't pay?"

Bailey ate as they argued, intrigued that they did so openly. She'd been raised in a family that kept everything behind closed doors. To see Joe this way made her happy for him. He'd changed, and whatever path his life had taken after she left, it had directed him to the man he was today. Confident, happy, and from what she gathered, successful. Of course, she also knew how to put up a facade, so maybe he was hiding things like she was.

"Are you taking a break from performing because of your hand?"

She choked on the mouthful of donut. He pressed his palm into her back, and started rubbing circles between her shoulder blades while she coughed and spluttered.

"Here, drink this."

She took the water Piper handed her before leaving to serve another customer, and gulped it down.

"Better?"

"S-sorry," Bailey said, mortified. At least she hadn't spat it everywhere.

"Those donuts really need to be savored," Joe drawled.

"I—ah, need to go."

"You got somewhere to be?"

"No... yes, I need to get back to Maggs. We, ah, have a thing today."

"A thing, that sounds intriguing. I love a good thing."

His face was right there as she turned. Lovely forest green eyes focused on her. This close, she saw a hint of brown in the green. She inhaled a deep breath of air and Joe. It was kind of spicy, with a hint of strawberries.

"Yes, she's taking me around the town. Showing me changes."

Bailey sniffed the air again; surely she'd got that wrong, as he didn't seem the type to go for strawberry scent.

"Are you sniffing me?"

"What? No!" Bailey shook her head, horrified, but Joe laughed.

"It's my shampoo. I thought I was getting just the plain no-scent type that any man would want to use; instead I looked closer at the label, and it has strawberry extracts." His nose wrinkled. "Why the hell anyone would want to wash their hair in fruit is beyond me, but there's no accounting for taste."

She wouldn't smile.

"That looks good on you."

"What?"

"The smile. I remember those dimples." He touched her cheek again, like he had last night. It left a trail of heat. "It's sweet."

"I-I'm twenty-seven," Bailey said. "I think my sweet years are behind me."

"I don't think you could ever lose your sweet, Bailey Jones. You were special at thirteen, and from where I'm sitting you still are."

Bailey got off the seat so quick she stumbled. Righting herself, she dug into her bag and found some money to pay for her meal.

"You d-don't know me now. You can't say that."

"You'll still be the same person inside, even if the facade has changed." His green eyes were steady on her face. "Did you manage to fulfil those dreams you told me about, Bailey? The ones we shared on that winter day huddled in our secret place?"

"I'm not that silly little girl anymore, and dreams change... I'm sure yours have."

"She wasn't silly. She was kind, and loving, and one of the most amazing people I have ever met. That girl saw something in me no one else ever had."

Their eyes held for long, painful seconds before Bailey made herself pull away. She walked away from him and didn't look back, returning to the safe haven of Maggs's little house as fast as her legs could carry her.

Chapter 8

JOE FOLLOWED on Bailey's heels.

"I didn't mean to upset you, Bailey." He caught up with her as she walked out the door. His fingers closed around her wrist. "I just wanted to talk."

"There's nothing to talk about, Joe. That was then and this is now. We're different people, and don't need each other."

"I can always use a friend. How about you?"

She pulled her arm free and turned to look at him. Her face was composed, emotions locked away.

"I don't need friends, Joe, I need a job, and as you are my boss, I don't want to have this rear up between us again."

"This being talk of our past, and anything too personal?"

She nodded. "L-let's just leave it there."

"In the past?" He wanted to touch her again, see if she softened any and the chill in her eyes warmed.

She nodded. "Exactly. I'm glad that's cleared up. Bye."

Joe watched her jump down the steps to the pavement, then hurry away.

"I was never good at following orders," he muttered, turning to head back inside. His mind was full of her. What had happened to turn her into the person she was today? Where had that open, caring girl he'd loved gone? His Bailey. His savior.

"What the hell was that about?" Pip stood before him behind the counter, hands braced on top, her eyes telling him she wanted answers.

"What?"

"The chemistry between you two."

"I have no idea what you're talking about. Now bring me more food, woman, or I'll have to charge you for that meal tonight."

She didn't budge.

He sighed... loudly. "Leave it, Pip."

"We've never had secrets, Joe."

Yes, we have, he thought, *and she just walked out the door.*

"I just watched you and Bailey Jones talk out there, and the tension between you was obvious, even from here. There's something between you and her, and I want to know what."

"It's complicated." He couldn't deny it, not to someone who knew him as well as Pip did.

"Most things are, but in getting them uncomplicated it helps to share."

"When did you grow up?"

"Stop stalling, Joe."

He went for an abbreviated answer to appease her. "Bailey lived here for thirteen years of her life. Her parents owned the property we now live on."

Pip whistled. "You tell her that?"

"I haven't, no, and my guess is neither has Maggie, as

she didn't bring it up." But he should have; she deserved to know the truth.

"Is she your age?"

"Three years younger."

"How old were you when she left?"

"Sixteen."

"So if she was thirteen…." His cousin's sharp brain was moving with its usual speed, trying to connect the dots. "Surely you guys didn't have anything going on between you?"

"No!" The word exploded from Joe's mouth. "Nothing like that, we were just friends."

Pip frowned. "Was her home life crap? Was she a bad girl or something?"

Joe wished he'd just kept his mouth shut. "No, she was the only child of two uptight, rich parents."

"Then how the hell did you two become friends?"

How indeed.

"Can we just leave it that we knew each other?"

"No." Pip raised a hand to stop him saying anything else. "Sarah, I'm taking a break, call if you need me. You," she pointed at Joe, "go find a table, I'll join you."

"I don't have time for this, Pip. The story is an old one that doesn't need airing again. Plus, it's personal, between Bailey and me."

"You know I'll make your life hell if you don't tell me, and what's more, you know I can keep secrets."

"I really don't need this now."

"Sure you do, now go and sit."

He found a table and sat drinking his coffee, thinking about Bailey. She had secrets and shadows in her eyes. Why was she no longer performing? What course had her life taken since she'd left here? He knew she'd gone with her mother and grandfather when her parents separated, but nothing else.

"So, I have food, and coffee. I'm ready when you are." Pip took the seat across from him.

"Well of course, like my brothers, I live to serve you."

She smiled, flashing him a row of neat white teeth that had been cemented into braces for two years.

"I like her, FYI. She seems nice. Kind of timid, but nice."

"You've had what, a total of one conversation with her?"

"I know people."

"Do you now."

"She's pretty too."

"Aha."

And she had soft skin, and eyes the color of a cool winter sky, and something about her triggered a reaction inside Joe he wasn't comfortable with. She was scared, and trying hard not to show it. Scared, timid, hell, there was any number of words to add to what Bailey Jones had become. The hell of it was he wanted to know her story. Maybe he wanted to help her now as she had once helped him.

"So spill."

Joe twisted the wide silver band around his finger, like he always did when he was thinking. He hadn't told anyone about what he and Bailey had shared, and to do so now was to open a locked vault deep inside him—but then, maybe it was time. She was here, and stirring up things inside him; if he talked about her, it could help. He let himself go back to that day... the first day they'd met.

"This is not something I've ever talked about, Pip."

"You know I'm good for it, and maybe it's time, Joe.

Carrying stuff inside you for years isn't good. Let it out, it'll be freeing."

"Thank you, Dr. Phil."

She waved him on while she ate.

"You know the river at the back of the property? The bridge that takes you over leads to a cave in the hill."

Pip frowned. "I don't remember a cave."

"It's there, you just have to know where to look." He'd never gone back again after Bailey left.

"Okay, there's a cave, then what?"

He looked over Pip's shoulder, thinking back on that day. The memories still caused an ache, but it had dulled over the years.

"She found me there one day. Bailey. She was ten, I was thirteen. My father had just gone a few rounds with me, I was bruised and angry, and that was where I ended up. I'd found it a few weeks earlier when I was out exploring."

"Jack told me you did that a lot."

He had, because staying home was unbearable.

"He also told me you put locks on the door to their room. Locks with keys that only they held."

"They needed to have a safe place to go if he came home drunk."

Pip leaned across the table and cupped her hands around his face. "You are the best man I know, Joe."

"No." Joe shook his head. "There were times I was an asshole."

She laughed. "Oh well, sure. I know that."

He laughed as she'd wanted him to.

"Bailey walked in with a backpack on that day. She was dressed in her school uniform, hair in braids, and she had skinny legs and shoes that seemed too big. I was never sure how she got down there, as the top was quite steep."

"Your memory's good."

"I remember everything about that day, because it changed my life."

"How?"

"I yelled at her, told her to leave, even though I was on her land. She didn't, instead looking at me with those big gray eyes of hers, and then she came and sat beside me. Not too close, but close enough that I could see she was nervous. She opened her bag and gave me a cold can of soda for my eye, which was swollen."

"Oh God, Joe."

"I'm not telling you to make you cry, Pip. You wanted to hear this story, so I'm telling it."

She waved him on while blotting her eyes with a napkin.

"She then got out a ham-and-cheese sandwich and gave me half. A box of Apple Sours, and an orange. She split them in half too, placing half on my legs that were stretched out before me."

Pip sniffed while Joe lost himself in the memory.

"She took out a book, I remember the title was *Matilda*. I sat there for two hours while she read it to me that day."

"Oh God," Pip wailed, burying her face in the napkin.

"Get a grip." Joe's words were soft as he took her hands in his. "This is my story, not yours."

"It's just so... I don't know. Sweet maybe, painful to hear, but I'm so pleased you found her when you needed someone, Joe."

"So am I."

"What happened then?"

"We met there twice a week for two years. We never talked outside that place. If I saw her in the street, we walked past each other, and we both knew it was for the best, because her parents would never have allowed it, and mine would have used her against me."

"That sucks!"

"It did, but then I was older, and supposedly cooler, and hung with a bad crowd. No one would have understood what we had."

"What did you have?"

"Friendship... and so much more. When she realized I couldn't read very well, she taught me. Bullied me into doing my homework, and learning. I had to read to her for hours. And every time we met, she brought food for me to eat, and sometimes more to take home for Luke and Jack."

"If I hug her next time we meet, do you think it will freak her out?"

"Yes, and you need to keep this to yourself, Pip. I mean it."

"Okay, but tell me the rest of the story."

"It's hers too, so I'm telling you things she may not want anyone to ever hear."

Piper crossed her heart with a finger.

"One day I was waiting for her, and heard her coming. She was screaming my name, and sobbing. I ran to meet her, watched as she hurried down the hill. She fell, and I caught her. It was the first time we'd ever touched. I carried her inside and she sat on my lap and sobbed out her story."

Pip grabbed more tissues.

"Her parents were separating, and she was leaving with her mother to go and live with her grandfather in Boston. That was the last time we saw each other, until I found her in the grocery store three days ago."

"What? No." Pip shook her head. "Surely you wrote to each other. Made contact somehow?"

She wrote, Joe thought, *but not me. I was too busy self-destructing*.

"The end," Joe said, picking up his now cold coffee and taking a large mouthful to ease the dryness in his throat.

"But there's more, isn't there? Lots more."

Joe just shrugged. "Heads up, the rest of the Trainer clan is arriving," he said.

"Your secret is safe with me, Joe. But talk to her; don't let her leave without that at least. You owe each other something. A connection like that is never truly severed," Pip said before she got to her feet to greet his brothers.

She was right, of course. He would always have a connection to Bailey Jones.

"Hey, bud, that's a serious frown."

Jack was two years younger than Joe, and tall but built leaner, with hair more brown than black. Behind him came the youngest Trainer, Luke. He was the image of Joe.

"I thought you had a group to take out today?"

"They cancelled," Jack said, falling into the chair Pip had recently vacated. "One of them is sick, so they're going out next week."

"Hey, Pip." Luke threw his cousin a sweet smile that she totally fell for, and minutes later he had a heaped plate of food in front of him, as did Jack. Joe got to his feet and refilled his own cup.

"I have a lesson this afternoon with that Anderson brat. God's truth, she's the biggest know-it-all I've ever encountered," Jack moaned.

"Who are you looking at?" Piper asked, noticing how Luke's eyes were still on the door.

"That woman, Bailey Jones. I just saw her coming out of the pharmacy a few minutes ago. She looks better than the last time I saw her. She was kind of dazed then."

"What? When did you bump into her?"

"A few days ago. She was on the street and stepped off the curb and would have been hit by a car if I hadn't grabbed her."

"She did what?" Joe's heart was thumping hard in his chest at the prospect of Bailey doing that.

"Like I said, she seemed dazed. I pulled her back on the sidewalk, introduced myself, just wanted to get her talking to see if she was okay. She looked at my uniform then, and told me she was glad I was a firefighter, then walked away. It was a weird moment, I tell you."

That had to be the day they'd met in the store, Joe realized. So she'd been as unsettled by their meeting as he had.

"She's seriously hot," Luke added.

Joe bit back his irritation as Luke looked back to the door. He had no claim to Bailey, but he felt protective of her. Their history gave him that right at least, and the fact that she was running from something. He'd stake his bar on that.

"She's certainly cute," Jack said, joining the conversation now that he'd cleaned his plate. Jack took food seriously.

"She's just arrived, so give her a break," Joe said calmly. Best way to deal with his siblings, he'd learned when they were finally all back together, was not to show any weakness.

"And what the hell does that mean?" Jack scowled. "You make me sound like some kind of predator."

"A slight overreaction," Joe said. "What I mean is, she's here for a break, so don't hassle her."

"I have never hassled a woman!" Indignant now, Jack's scowl darkened. "I've never forced myself on a woman either."

"I never said you did, I was just telling you about Bailey, and that she seems a bit wound up, so give her some space if you run into her." Joe wasn't sure why he just didn't shut the hell up.

He watched the scowl fall from Jack's face, to be replaced by a smug smile.

"So you're warning me off because you're interested?"

"What? No," Joe said. "I'm just saying give her some space."

He was then subjected to a double sibling stare down. Joe was up to it, he'd spent most of the last ten years wrestling his brothers into the halfway respectable, decent humans they were today. They didn't intimidate him.

"Space, is it? Well, it's okay with us, big brother. If you want the path left clear, we'll do that for you."

"Don't be insulting," Piper snapped, returning with more coffee. "Bailey's a person, not a doormat, and you need to learn to respect women... both of you."

"How come he's exempt?" Jack glared at Joe.

"Because I like him more than you."

"Now we know that's a lie," Luke said, sending his cousin a gentle smile that never failed to make her do whatever the hell he wished.

"I'm gonna puke," Jack growled.

"There's also Angie to consider," Joe said.

Pip scowled. "You need to move on there. She's not right for you. Besides, I thought you said that was casual, and it's been, what... two months?"

"Angie is a lovely woman, Pip," Joe said, "and yes, it's casual because I've kept it that way. I made that clear from the start, just a movie or meal occasionally."

"So she knows where you stand then. Besides, there's Ted."

"Ted?" Joe looked around his family, who all seemed suddenly busy doing a shitload of nothing but avoiding eye contact with him.

"Ted?" he said again, this time louder with some steel behind it.

"You and she are just casual, you said so yourself," Luke said, looking uncomfortable. "And Jed from the station said he saw Angie with Ted from the lodge a few weeks back. They looked…." Luke waved a hand, looking, if possible, more uncomfortable.

"Happy?" Joe said. "Pissed off? Like they'd had at each other?"

"That." Luke pointed a finger at him.

"You're twenty-fucking-five, Luke, you can say the word sex," Joe teased him. It didn't bother him overly about Angie. They'd only been casual, and then not very much. He liked her, but it was never serious, even it sometimes he wondered if she believed different.

"I agree with Pip," Luke said.

"Ditto," Jack added.

"About?" Joe asked.

"Angie not being right for you. She's nice, but not for you."

"Because I'm not nice?" Joe messed with his little brother.

"Oh, lay off him." Pip stepped in like she always did. "You didn't feel a thing when you heard Angie had been seen with Ted, so that just confirms what we think. Bailey would be better for you."

"As she's just arrived back in town after many years and we've barely conversed, I'm not sure why you think that."

"Because you warned us off, and you never do that unless you're serious," Jack said.

"We're not continuing this discussion," Joe said, now the uncomfortable one. He gave his family the look.

Thankfully they let the subject of Angie and Bailey drop, and discussed business for a while. The Trainer siblings owned the cafe, several rental properties, and an industrial business in town, plus the ranch. After he'd straightened himself out, with the help of two friends Joe found he had an aptitude for playing the stock market. He'd then bought his first property, and their portfolio grew from there with the help of his family.

"I heard Mrs. Howard got into you again the other day, Joe. Why the hell do you put up with it?" Jack said. "Woman's a bitch."

"And I raised hell, so she's within her rights to make me pay," Joe said.

"You've paid already," Luke said. "More than paid, and you need to let her know it. She thinks she has way more power in this town than she actually has. Jack calls her a remora."

"Which is what exactly?" Joe asked.

"One of those little fish that sit on whales and get an easy ride."

"Nice description." Piper high-fived Jack.

"I don't need anyone fighting my battles." Joe eyeballed his siblings. "For the most this town has forgiven me. There's just a few who haven't, and I can handle them," Joe lied. In fact, they pissed him off, and twisted his gut into knots when they came at him, but he'd never let them know that.

Chapter 9

BAILEY PLAYED at Apple Sours last night. She and Joe worked out she'd come in Thursdays and Saturdays. One night was honky-tonk, the other blues. She'd never enjoyed playing more. Two weeks she'd been in Ryker, and as yet had no desire to leave.

She felt safe here, which was strange as she'd never been unsafe—no one had ever threatened her. But something about this place wrapped around her like a warm shawl.

Bailey made sure that any time she spent with Joe was in company. He disturbed her, and dredged up memories that were better left buried, so she'd tried to put contact in the polite yet distant category. She'd caught him watching her more than once, frowning, as if she was a puzzle he couldn't work out. Hell, she couldn't even work herself out, so there was no way he'd have a chance.

After Maggie had left for work this morning, she'd headed out the door. Today she would do what she'd wanted to since coming back. Bailey walked down the drive that had once held her home. She'd avoided it, and there was no reason to. Maggs hadn't brought the subject up either, which had been fine with her, but now felt the right time to let another ghost rest. Once, she'd been happy enough here; it was time to put the fear of what she'd find to bed.

The day was crisp, and a breeze played in the air. The beauty before her was breathtaking. With the twins constant companions on her right, she approached her old home. Bailey had once walked or ridden over every inch of the property she was approaching. The fences had been redone. Post and rail, they looked good. Her eyes followed the line of the drive. She'd just go halfway, so no one saw her. Close enough to see the house and look around.

Her old home was still there, and relief had her exhaling as she saw the condition of it, painted a soft gray now, with darker gray trim. Bailey released the breath she'd been holding as she saw that whoever lived there now was looking after it. The front pillars had been stoned up to halfway, the driveway still a circle, but now sealed. Flowers and shrubs planted, and the grass mown. In fact, it looked better than she'd ever seen it. Relieved, she let her eyes wander to the huge set of outbuildings in a paddock further back. The current owners were working it. Those buildings hadn't been here before.

"Hello." She approached the fence where two horses stood, holding out one hand. "Aren't you both beautiful."

One was black as midnight, with a long silken mane, the other a chestnut with soft brown eyes. Bailey loved horses.

She ran a hand down their silken necks, and leaned in to inhale their special scent as she wondered on her next move. She did love it here, but couldn't stay forever. Bailey needed to make a plan for the future. She couldn't live in limbo with no direction much as she enjoyed having no restrictions pressing down on her. Odd jobs here and there were fun, but not indefinitely, especially if she couldn't get her grandfather to release her money.

Hooking her arms around the neck of the horse, Bailey rested her head on its long forehead. Once, she'd ridden every day, and sometimes twice. Horses and music had always been her passion. She missed them both now, but it had taken a while to come to that with her music.

She wasn't sure how long she stood there, but the sound of hooves had her easing back. She looked beyond the horses, and saw a man riding toward her, but it was the dog at his side that told her who it was.

Joe Trainer wore a worn gray T-shirt, jeans, and boots. On his head was a navy cap. She didn't remember him riding, but then he also hadn't played the piano either. He sat a horse well. His tall, rangy body looked good up there.

"Hi, Bailey."

"Wh-what are you doing here? I didn't know you rode."

Buzz barked for her to notice him; she stuck a hand through the fence and scratched his head.

"We own this property now."

Shock had her stepping back.

"Y-you own this? Why did no one tell me? Maggs—"

"Was probably waiting for you to ask her about it, and as she has no idea of the history we share, didn't think it was important to mention that I now own it."

Bailey couldn't drag her eyes from him. Joe now lived in her house.

"I'm sorry, I should have told you."

"Why didn't you?"

"I don't know. Maybe because I wasn't sure how you'd react?"

Bailey didn't know how she felt.

"Talk to me, Bailey."

"I— You've made improvements, they look good." She forced herself to say the words as she turned to look again at the house. Joe lived here, on the land she'd grown up on. Why was that a struggle for her to comprehend? She'd been gone so long, and had known someone would live here... just not him.

"I really am sorry—"

"S-so these are your horses that I'm hugging?" She cut him off.

"Yes, and I have no problem with you cuddling them. Everyone needs a hug now and again, even my horses."

Bailey needed to leave. "I have to go, b-bye."

"Why are you always running away from me?"

She'd turned away and started walking; he and Buzz were keeping pace with her inside the paddock.

"I'm not running from you."

"Prove it then. Come and let me show you what we've done here."

"No, thanks."

"You just said you weren't running from me, and yet that's exactly what you're doing."

She looked up at him. The man had no right to be that hot.

"I play in your b-bar, if I was avoiding you I wouldn't do that."

"You're only around me when there's company."

Bailey didn't answer him because it was the truth, they both knew it, so she kept walking.

"Come and meet the horses. We have plenty more on the pasture out back, and stables. Let me show you around, Bailey. Please."

"I was just going for a walk, but thanks."

"Do you still ride?" he asked her.

She nodded.

"Would you like to now?"

Bailey battled down the surge of excitement at the thought of riding again. "No, but thanks."

"Why are you saying no when you clearly want to say yes?"

"I'm not!"

"You are. So unless you're out of practice or scared, what's stopping you—other than it's me who's offering."

Bailey felt heat creep into her cheeks.

"I can ride, as you very well know, and I'm not scared—"

"So that leaves me."

He was smiling at her now, teasing her.

"It has nothing to do with you, and you h-have an overinflated opinion of yourself."

Shut up, Bailey.

"Very possibly. But we're friends, so no reason at all why you can't come for a ride with your friend."

"We were friends."

He tilted his head to one side, and studied her.

"I didn't realize there was a time limit on our friendship."

"Neither did I."

"And there's the fifteen-ton elephant in the room," he said. "The letters."

"Just leave it, Joe."

"Come with me, Bailey, and I'll tell you why I didn't reply to any of the ones you wrote me."

"I don't think any good can come from discussing that, Joe." Bailey wasn't sure she wanted to know the truth.

"How about we go for a ride, and you can ask a few questions if you want, and I'll answer them."

"I d-don't have questions. I told you, the past is better left there."

"You were never a good liar, Bailey Jones. Come on, ride with me for old times' sake."

The lure of being on a horse was the only thing that had her nodding. Not the time she would spend in his company.

"There now, that wasn't hard." He moved his mount closer to the fence between them. "You climb on over, and I'll give you a ride to the stables."

"I can walk." There was no way she wanted to get on that horse with him.

"For someone who comes across as reserved, and once hated confrontation and being difficult, you surely are."

Bailey kind of liked the idea that maybe she was a bit difficult.

"Just do it, Bailey, I don't have all day."

She should have turned and walked away, but no, she let him goad her into staying. He used to goad her into most things. Gripping the fence, she climbed on top, then squealed as hands grabbed her. She was placed gently in front of Joe.

"A bit of warning!"

"I told you I was giving you a lift to the stables. Now relax, I don't bite."

"Ha," Bailey managed, her mouth now dry. One of his arms banded around her waist, hauling her closer, and suddenly she was surrounded by Joe Trainer. The solid planes of his chest pressed to her back, her thighs resting on his. His other hand held the reins and she noted the silver band on his finger again, and wondered who had given it to him.

"So you didn't write any bad stuff in the letters, but I

read between the lines. You weren't happy all the time in Boston. What was it really like?"

"Okay."

"Now tell me the truth."

"Joe, there's no point to this. Those years don't matter anymore."

"I think there is a point, and they matter to me. You're uncomfortable around me, and not for a good reason, so if we talk that may help."

"Good reason?"

"You think I'm sexy as hell and—"

"Right, got it, thanks." She cut him off.

His laugh was a deep rumble against her back.

"So tell me the truth, Bailey. Were you happy?"

"I hated it." She said the words quickly to cover her embarrassment. *But mostly because I missed you so much it was a physical pain inside me.*

"Why?"

"Just because. Tell me about the horses, Joe."

"Why, Bailey?"

"Everyone had friends," she snapped, "at the school my grandfather sent me to. I didn't, and wasn't that good at making them."

"I'm sorry."

"I did okay, and then I got a scholarship to Juilliard, and was with people like me."

"Like you?"

"Focused, dedicated... maybe a bit different."

"And you loved that?"

"Of course." She'd liked parts of it. The music and the being away from her grandfather and mother. She'd hated that Joe wasn't there, because even two years after she'd left him, she still pined for him. She'd been a foolish girl to do so, but when you were lonely, and your life not that happy, you clung to what had once made you that way.

"Truth?"

She smiled at his word. They'd spoken that way to each other once. Both knowing when the other lied.

"Partially."

He snorted at that.

"And you don't want to explain further?"

"So your family own this, and the bar?" Bailey changed the subject.

"I own the bar, but the family owns this, and the cafe, plus property in town. We started acquiring a few years after I came back."

She wanted to know where he'd been before he'd come back, but then if she asked him questions, he had the right to do that as well, and Bailey didn't want to talk about her life.

"You're a woman, right?"

"I beg your pardon?" Bailey turned to face him, surprised at his words, and there he was again. Big, sexy Joe Trainer.

"You didn't ask the question."

"What question?" She made herself face forward and look between the horse's ears.

"Most of the women I know would want to dissect where I'd been. And the girl you were would have asked at least five questions by now."

"You make me sound nosy, and I object to the general-ization that women are too."

"You were always curious. You started off shy, but that didn't last long once we got to know each other. I'd never met anyone with such an insatiable thirst for knowledge like you had."

"It's been years, Joe. I've changed, just like you. Besides, I like my privacy, which makes me respect yours."

"I can't imagine privacy was something you had a lot of while you were performing."

"It wasn't."

"Tell me about your life, Bailey. What put those shadows in your eyes? Maybe like you once did for me, I can help you?"

"Thank you, but I don't need help." She turned again to look at him and found his eyes focused on her lips.

Chapter 10

"IT'S a hard line to take to not let anyone in, Bailey. A hard, lonely road. I know, I've travelled it a time or two."

"It's better that way, you don't get hurt."

"Like I hurt you?"

"I haven't seen you in fifteen years, Joe. It would be arrogant to think I still cared, or that someone else hadn't hurt me in that time."

"Have they?"

"What?"

"Has someone hurt you?"

"I'm not discussing this with you. I want to ride, or let me down. This conversation is over."

Leaving him had hurt her, Joe knew that, because it had sure as hell hurt him.

"For what it's worth, I never meant to hurt you, Bailey. I lost my way for a while there."

She was so close that he saw the scar again. "What happened?" He touched the small indentation.

"Glass, from the accident."

"What accident? The one that left the scar on your arm?"

She nodded, her face inches from his. They simply stared at each other as every thought left Joe's head. He ran his eyes over her face, settling on that plump lower lip.

"You're beautiful, Bailey Jones."

"No."

"Yes." Joe cupped the back of Bailey's neck and held her still as he closed the distance between them.

"No, Joe."

"Yes, Joe." He brushed his lips over hers.

Sweet, he thought after the first touch, achingly sweet; his second thought was *mistake*. He had once considered this woman his soul mate, the person who understood him like no other. Then she'd been a child, now she was an adult, and he realized after that simple kiss that their connection was still there, only it was far more intense because he had a physical need for Bailey Jones now.

"I-I don't like to be kissed."

Her words brushed his lips, a husky lie. She was as touched as he by what they had just shared.

"Really, Joe. I don't want you to kiss me again, I-it's wrong."

"Wrong how?" he managed to get out around the obstruction in his throat.

"We... what we were, this...." She struggled to say what she believed needed to be said.

"It sure as hell didn't feel wrong."

"B-but it is."

"Why?"

She turned away, facing forward again.

"Too much history."

"And that makes no sense, other than we need to talk."

"No. That cannot happen again."

It would, but he left that thought in his head.

"Sure, I got it. I won't kiss you unless you ask me to. But the sparks between us are strong enough that you will, Bailey. You've felt them, I know you have, because you've been avoiding me."

"I have n-not!"

"Yes, you have. But I'll wait for you to come to me."

"That won't happen," she snapped.

"Want to bet?"

"I d-don't b-bet." She stuttered out the words.

"You never stuttered as a child. How come you sometimes do now?"

She sucked in a sharp breath and turned away from him, so he was left staring at the back of her head.

"Why the stutter, Bailey?"

"It… just happens sometimes."

"There has to be a reason. When did it start?"

She didn't want to tell him, so he left it alone for now. She'd called him arrogant for believing he was the only one who'd hurt her, and yet he had a feeling that leaving Ryker, and him, had something to do with the person she had become.

Once she'd been fierce in her determination to achieve the goals she had set for her life. *"I want to be independent and strong, Joe. I want to walk into a room and people see that I'm courageous."* He'd told her she was already courageous as far as he was concerned, but she'd dismissed his words. *"I want to be more, Joe. I want to climb mountains and swim rivers."* They'd laughed over that one, as swimming hadn't been her strength, but she'd vowed to change that.

"You ever learn to swim better?"

"Some" was all she said, so he decided to see if he could annoy her like he used to.

"So, for someone who doesn't like kissing, you have a lovely mouth."

She ignored him, her spine straightening.

"You sure grew up well, Miss Jones." He tried to tease a response out of her. It usually worked with Piper. She ignored him again, so he stopped trying, and restored peace between them with small talk.

"I'll take you on a tour if you like. Show you the changes?"

"I could get on a horse for that."

"No point, when you're already on one." He was enjoying holding her, so he wasn't letting her go until he had to.

"Piper, Jack, and Luke live in the main house. We added on a place at the rear for Aunt Jess, but she's out of town at the moment."

Joe loved that house. First, because it had once belonged to the woman in his arms, and had a very special place they'd both shared on the property, and second because it had brought the Trainer siblings together through blood, sweat, and a whole lot of swearing. They'd learned about each other, the people they really were, not the people their father had turned them into.

"It looks good, Joe. Don't you live there too?"

"No, I need my space." He couldn't live that close to someone again and not go crazy.

"Because you had to share with your brothers for so long?"

"Something like that," he said, not surprised she knew the reasons why. She'd always been able to do that. In fact, he'd once thought that Bailey knew him better than he knew himself.

"D-did you learn to ride a Harley, Joe, and get out of Ryker?"

He remembered the day they'd discussed dreams, and that had been one of his.

"Actually, I did ride a Harley for a while, but not here."

"What did you do?"

"Do?"

"Between then and now?"

"I got into some trouble after you left, Bailey. Me and some others raised hell in this town until my aunt and the Robbins sisters stepped in and sent me away to this ranch in Texas. It changed my life. Had I stayed, I would have ended up in jail."

"What kind of trouble?"

"Drink, drugs, and stealing. Pretty much anything I could find. I roped a few others in with me. One of them was Dylan Howard, which goes a long way into explaining his mother's hatred of me." He didn't add that Bailey leaving him had pretty much been the final straw for Joe. Their father was taken away for possession and put inside, and they'd never seen him again. No loss, but still a change, and then Aunt Jess had arrived. Within six months of Bailey leaving, Joe's life had turned on its head. He'd reacted with violence and a path to self-destruction.

She processed that silently for a while, trying to fill in the gaps as he did with her, about where they'd been and what had happened in their lives.

"I'm sorry things got bad for you, Joe."

"In a way maybe I had to go bad, to turn out good... or at least better."

He nudged his horse around the large stables and along another driveway through the trees, with Buzz ambling at their side. Occasionally something would catch his eye, and he'd race off, but he soon returned.

She touched his ring, one finger. "I remember you told

me once that jewelry was for girls. Did someone give it to you?"

"I bought it actually." He didn't add that it was special to him because just looking at it had reminded him of her.

They climbed, and Bailey was soon pressed into his chest, and Joe tightened the arm around her waist, holding her still as she tried to put some distance between them.

"I'm glad your aunt and the others were there to help you."

"Me too."

"They're nice, Miss Marla and Miss Sarah, and a little scary."

"A lot scary. They just give me that look and I'm back in school."

She snuffled. Not a laugh, but close.

"And that's why you taste the tea, and do whatever they ask you?"

"I like the tea thing, because with it usually comes a scone with cream and jam, plus I'm competitive, and me beating them keeps them on their toes."

"It's nice that you care about them, Joe."

"Who do you care about?"

"People. You don't know them."

He couldn't see her face, so he had no clue if she was telling the truth.

"Don't make the mistake of feeling sorry for me, Joe. I have everything I want in my life, and I don't need that from you, or anyone. Just because I'm not talkative like I used to be, simply means I've grown up."

"How do you know I'm feeling sorry for you?"

"A hunch."

An accurate one actually, but it was more worry than pity.

"I'm sorry I let you down by not returning your letters."

"I got the hint after a while, so don't worry about it."

"I know that, because my aunt stopped forwarding them to me."

He'd read each of those letters at least three times, but Joe had never replied because he'd let Bailey down, and hadn't known how to tell her. He had also believed she was better off without him in her life. However, he'd been devastated when she'd stopped writing.

Neither of them spoke again, and Joe thought that was enough revelations for one day. He held her as they reached the top of the drive, and there was his house. He loved the big house, but this... well, this was the place that held his heart. Made of cedar and stone, it was clad like many of the other houses around Ryker, but this was his haven.

"Oh, it's lovely," Bailey breathed.

Here the water from the river that flowed down from the falls, narrowed and passed by the front of his house. He'd built a bridge to drive over.

"My rooms are up there," Joe pointed to the top floor, where a window ran floor to ceiling and just as wide. "I can see the town lights, and the mountains. Sometimes when the wind is blowing the right way, I can hear the falls. It's...." His words fell away as he tried to explain what this place meant to him.

"Your sanctuary."

It was a sanctuary for him, and because she'd once lived here, perhaps that was more of a reason why.

"It must be nice to have all your family here with you?"

"Sure. When I came back, Luke had gone, but I soon found him, and Jack was in the next town over. Aunt Jess and Pip had stayed."

"Did you ever go there? To the cave?" Her words were soft, wistful.

"No. After you left, I never went back, and haven't to this day. Maybe one day soon you could go there with me?"

Her messy bun brushed his chin as she shook her head. He wondered what she'd do if he released all that blonde hair and ran his fingers through it.

"I think the past is better left there, Joe."

"Where do you call home usually, Bailey? Where is your sanctuary?" Joe wondered if she'd fulfilled that part of her dream, and found a place to lay her heart.

Chapter 11

"I'VE BEEN MOVING AROUND for a while now."

"That's got to be hard, not having your things around you?"

She shrugged. "You get used to it. When I was performing, I would live out of a suitcase for months."

"But you have to put down roots sometime, right? The Bailey I knew had one day wanted that."

"Plans change" was all she said.

"What about your brother, Beau? I don't remember much about him, as he was older, but where is he?"

"Paris. He's been there for years."

"And you miss him."

"Of course, but his life is there, and mine isn't."

"Do you think you'll go back to playing professionally? You must have plans where you're heading?"

"I don't know."

Joe just bet that was a lie. Bailey had always planned everything.

"But you have an idea, I know you do."

"I don't want to talk about it. Please take me back now."

Her back was rigid again.

"So I have to slice open a vein, but you don't?"

"Unlike your story, mine is long and boring, and I have no wish to recount it. Plus, I didn't ask you to slice open a vein, you did that all by yourself."

"I don't remember you being such a hard-ass."

She snorted. "I wish. Had I been a hard-ass, life would have definitely been smoother."

"Why was it bumpy?"

She didn't answer.

"How did you hurt your arm?"

"An accident, I told you. I fell through a window. My hand took the impact."

"It looks bad."

"It was. For a time they wondered if I'd play again."

Joe wondered who'd held her, and sat at her bedside while she recovered. Who told her that everything would be all right.

"And yet you can, so that's a relief."

She sighed, a soft little sad sound, but didn't say anything further. He didn't push, instead he said, "I have your Carnegie Hall concert on my iPod."

"Thank you."

"You're welcome," he said in the same polite tone.

He turned them round, and retraced their steps, this time heading to the outbuildings.

"I thought you might like to hug a few more horses, seeing as you're all tense again." Joe stopped inside the stables.

"I'm not tense."

"If this is you not tense, I can only imagine what you're like when you are," he said, dismounting. He grabbed her around the waist before she could argue, and pulled her down. "Funny how you used to tell me to relax, and now it's you who needs that advice."

"A little warning," she said, bracing her hands on his chest. "And there is nothing wrong with my everyday state."

Joe could feel the warmth of her palms, and then they were gone and she was stepping away from him.

"A little on the skinny side, but I have to say that your everyday state works for me." He looked over her fitted black designer jeans, and pale blue cotton shirt. On her feet were peach sneakers.

"I'm not skinny."

"You are a bit. But it shouldn't take long to fill out the hollows in those cheeks, especially if you keep eating those donuts, and a few of the teashop scones."

"Are you deliberately trying to insult me?" She dragged her eyes from the stalls, where the horses who weren't out in the fields were hanging out of their boxes.

"I'm deliberately trying to get a reaction out of you. Is it working?"

"No."

He laughed as she walked away from him to the closest horse. Buzz, he noted, had followed, which was interesting. His dog had certainly taken to Bailey.

"This place can house twenty horses in the winter." Joe kept pace with her. "We have an indoor arena through those doors at the rear. Jack mainly does the work, and from here he runs trail rides, or gives lessons, with the help of the staff. Nice shoes, by the way," he added.

"I like them."

"I guess that's all that matters then."

She stopped and looked down at her feet. "What's wrong with my footwear?"

"They're peach." Joe led her to the first horse.

"I happen to like peach."

"Well, good for you, and so do I, but I like to eat mine."

"Or wash your hair in it," Bailey said, stepping up to the stall, and holding out a hand.

"Oh now that had a kick to it. Nice work, Bailey."

She ignored him.

"That's Arthur, as in King, because he thinks he's the head dog around here."

"Or horse, as the case may be," she said. "Hello, lovely, you're definitely a big boy, aren't you."

Joe watched as she fussed over Arthur, the horse all but purring as he lowered his head and she scratched him behind one ear.

"He'll keep you there all day."

"I don't mind."

She gave him a kiss on the nose, and Joe was sure he saw stars in the horse's eyes as they left.

He took her around each horse, and she gave them the same treatment. He then showed her the tack room, the storage rooms, the indoor arena, and lastly up the stairs to the offices.

"This is the bunk room for any of the casuals who come in when it's busy. We also have a few kids in to stay and learn the ropes now and again."

"Local kids?"

"Sure, and out of towners."

She gave him a look. "Kids who need a bit of help straightening out?"

"You always were a smart girl."

"You're giving those kids what you, Luke, and Jack never had."

He was, they all were, because they'd had help when they needed it, but some kids didn't get so lucky.

"It's the right thing to do," Bailey said.

Why those six simple words made his heart feel warm he had no idea, but they did.

"We thought so. Just need to get the rec center passed now, and there will be another place for them to go."

"Maggs was telling me about that. It sounds amazing." Her eyes lit with interest. "The town should be behind it."

"Some are, some aren't. Why do you think it's amazing?"

"We would have used it back then, and it would have been warm and dry, and had adults there who maybe could have helped you and your brothers, Joe."

He nodded. Joe had thought just that when he'd started putting the proposal together. "We would have," he said, watching her walk around the space.

There were four sets of bunks, and an open-plan kitchen/dining area, with a lounge and bathroom facilities through separate doors.

Bailey came back to where he stood.

"It's like a different property to the one I grew up on. You must be very proud of what you and your family have achieved here."

"We are. It took a lot of work, especially as we'd been apart for so long, but we got there eventually."

"How long were you away?"

"Eight years on and off. I came back whenever I could."

He saw the questions in her eyes, but she didn't ask where he'd been for those years.

"I'm glad you showed me around, Joe. Thank you, but I should get going now. I'll save the ride for another day."

She went to walk around Joe, but he cut her off by stepping into her path. "Are you scared of me, Bailey?"

She looked up at him, her expression controlled.

"No. But it's time for me to leave, Joe."

"I think you are scared, but what really terrifies you is that I make you feel things you don't want to feel."

"Step aside, please."

He didn't, couldn't; instead he stepped closer.

"I'd never hurt you, Bailey, you don't need to be afraid with me."

"I know that."

"How do you know that?" He cupped her cheek, running his thumb over the soft, heated skin.

"Because the boy you were was far more dangerous that the man before me."

"That kind of makes sense."

"Plus, the anger I've carried toward you was unjustified, I know that now, and maybe I carried it for so long because I wasn't happy. Whatever the reason, some of what you explained today has helped me understand why you didn't write back."

"But only some?"

"Let me go, Joe."

Never.

"I didn't want to disappoint you," he said. "You wanted me to be the best I could be, and I hadn't done that. In fact, I'd done the opposite."

"It's done. We can move on now."

"Can we move on as friends?"

"Joe, my life is one hell of a big mess right now, and I really don't need any more complications."

"I wasn't always a complication, I was a friend."

"But you're not now. You're a man, not the boy I knew.

Not the boy who needed me. You're a man who unsettles me, and I don't want or need that."

"At least you're being honest."

"So you understand, we could never be.... Let's just be acquaintances," she said, changing her mind about the words she'd been about to say.

"Lovers, Bailey?"

"Acquaintances."

"I'm not sure I can keep my distance from you."

"Joe, d-don't...." Her words fell away as his lips touched her neck.

"I've wanted my hands on you since I first saw you in the grocery store, Bailey Jones." He whispered the words into her ear, before moving in to place more kisses on her neck. "What I once felt for you was innocent and pure; this, however, this is different."

She shivered. It rolled through her body. She arched back into the hand around her waist, allowing Joe better access to her neck. He kissed and licked, then decided he wanted her mouth.

He took it slow, but deep, drawing a response from Bailey as she opened to allow him in. Joe's head started to spin; he lost his grasp on reality, and enjoyed the feel of her.

Chapter 12

BAILEY SHUDDERED as she leaned into him. No one had held her as if she mattered for years. Not even Clark had made her feel this way with just a touch.

Her head was spinning, her body pressing into his; she wanted this, needed this, and hadn't even known it.

"God, you're sweet." His hands wrapped around her back as he pulled her into his hard chest; his lips took hers again, even deeper, more intense. She held on to him, wrapping her arms around his neck. Heat travelled through her, turning her limbs to liquid and pooling in places it had never pooled before. She had to stop—before she couldn't.

"No, Joe." She wrenched free and stumbled backward. "This cannot happen."

"Why?" He was tense as he looked at her, those green eyes darker with the flare of heat she'd put there. Ignoring the little zing of pleasure that thought gave her, she took another step back. The man radiated lust and forbidden dreams. He was the forbidden, and in his arms Bailey knew she'd find serious sexual fulfilment, but little else. She didn't need more complications in her life, especially not with him. He was experienced, she was not; if she wasn't careful he'd break her heart all over again.

"Because I don't do that," she said, crossing her arms over her waist. "It's not who I am, Joe, and you should know that about me."

"You were thirteen, Bailey, how the hell do I know who you are now? The woman before me is nothing like the girl you were."

"I'm not... loose."

"You think I am?"

"I don't know you either, Joe. How do I know if you're the type that sleeps around?"

"Well, hell."

Bailey didn't back down from the anger she saw in his face. Not anymore. She was stronger now, and she wouldn't be intimidated again.

"My life is uncertain at the moment, as I told you. I don't know how long I'll be here, but I do know that if we did this... it would change things, everything. I don't want or need that."

"And change is bad?"

He relaxed slightly, his stance easing, hands unclenching, but the bunching of the muscles in his jaw told her he was still not happy.

"Just leave it, Joe. Please. This, us, is not going to happen, nor should it."

"Why is your life a mess? What's going on?"

"That's my issue, but the point here is, you're where you want to be, Joe, whereas I have no clue. This is about me, not you."

He lifted a hand. "Oh hell no, you did not just say the standard brush-off line."

"I have no idea what you're talking about." Bailey glared at him.

"My brothers have that on the back of their business cards."

"Very amusing."

"For the record, I didn't think you were the type I'd sleep with and run from, Bailey."

"I never—"

"You did, and while I want you, Bailey, I sure as hell don't want you if that's the opinion you have of me. Especially considering our history, and how much I owe you. And, again, for the record, I don't have my life completely together."

Frustrated, Bailey walked away from him and did another circuit of the room. It was what she usually did when her emotions threatened to get the better of her.

"What are you doing?"

"Calming down?"

"Why? I'm angry, why the hell can't you be?"

She circled back to stand before him again.

"I like to be in control of my emotions."

"Emotions are real, Bailey, suppressing them is not. I'd rather see you yell and scream, like you used to, than try and control them."

His green eyes narrowed as he stepped closer. Bailey dug her toes into her shoes to stop retreating.

"I-I don't do that. Couldn't do that."

He stopped before her, close enough that she could see his chest rise and fall with each breath.

"Who told you not to do that?"

She looked away from his all-seeing eyes. "I need to go."

"Stop running, dammit!"

"You have no right to demand anything of me, Joe

Trainer. Now step aside." Bailey lifted her chin, but he simply crowded her space.

"Cutting loose now and again is good for you. Laughing like you mean it, or yelling when you're angry, is showing honest emotion and part of who we are. It's what makes us different."

"I don't want to be different, and I definitely don't want to cut loose, whatever the fuck that means." Horrified, Bailey realized what she'd said. She never used that word. "I-I'm sorry—"

"If you try and apologize for saying fuck, I'll shake you," Joe said.

Bailey pushed at his chest as he moved closer, so close she could feel his heat again, and inhale his wonderful scent.

"I'm not even sure why we are having this conversation," Bailey said. "I told myself we could be friends, or at least acquaintances, but we can't. There's too much between us."

"Yes, we have a history, but a good, warm history. What this is, between us, takes that to another level."

"No, it doesn't!" Bailey could feel the temper she usually controlled flare to life.

"Did you just shriek, Ms. Jones?"

"No!"

"Sure as hell sounded like it." He looked amused.

The heat in her cheeks grew, and she felt an uncontrollable urge to scream something at him again.

"Go on, I dare you," he taunted.

"You don't want to keep annoying me," Bailey said through her teeth. "The last person to do that was my brother, and he couldn't walk upright for days after."

He laughed at her, a loud, head-thrown-back laugh. After admiring the deep sound as it rolled through his large body, she lost it. Years of bottling up her feelings were finally finding an outlet. Heat filled her face, her head felt strange, and suddenly she was grabbing his arm, just like Beau had taught her to. She dropped her shoulder into his stomach, then flipped him. She nearly did it too, but too late she realized he knew the move, and had countered. Seconds later she was flat on her back with him on top of her. He let her down gently, so there was no pain, but she was still breathless.

"Nice try." He breathed the words against her neck.

Bailey wasn't done yet. She went limp, then tried another move; surprise gave her the edge, and she got him off her, but he grabbed her wrist as she got to her feet, and swung his legs, bringing her back down on top of him.

"You're good," he said. "What belt?"

"No belt," she wheezed. Bailey pressed a hand to his chest and tried to lever herself upright. The feel of all that muscle beneath her was good, but she didn't need good, she needed to reclaim her sanity. What the hell had she been thinking, trying those moves on Joe of all people?

"Sorry, I shouldn't have done that. I could have hurt you if you hadn't known what I was doing."

His hands gripped her waist and held her still.

"I know a few moves, and you're a lot smaller than me, so I was able to counter. Nice to know you can take care of yourself, though. Who taught you?"

"My brother." Bailey felt the hardness of Joe's body pressed into hers. "He spent four years living in Boston before heading to Paris."

"Why didn't you get any belts?"

She shook her head. "Let me up now, Joe."

"Why not?" he said, ignoring her words.

"Because my grandfather didn't want me hurt, so I

studied with my brother in his home until he left. I practice as often as I can when I have the space."

Bailey closed her eyes as he ran a finger down her cheek.

"This grandfather. Did he control all of your life?"

Her eyes shot open. "H-how d-do you know that?"

"A wild guess."

Bailey felt his eyes roam her face and settle on her lips.

"Let me up." Bailey whispered the words, but there was no force behind them; instead it sounded like she was begging him for something else.

"I like having you here." He cupped her neck and eased her closer. "Really like it."

He kissed her again, slow and sweet. Her hands dug into the muscles at his shoulder as he took it deeper. There was nothing gentle about it, it was possession, and branding, and heaven help her, she wanted that. Wanted to brand him right back.

She felt his fingers under her clothes, touching her ribs, leaving heat wherever they went. It was bliss, her body aching for more. His weight moved, and then the hand was on her breast, rubbing the hard bud of her nipple through the satin cup of her bra.

Joe stopped suddenly. Seconds later he was on his feet, and dragging Bailey to hers.

"Hi."

Bailey made herself turn to face the woman who was entering the room with Jack Trainer. She had long auburn hair, and stunning, soft hazel eyes. Her skin was creamy, with a scattering of freckles, and she looked pretty in a denim skirt and cream off-the-shoulder top.

Dear God, had they seen her lying on top of Joe?

"Hey, Angie, you're back."

"We just came from the house to find you," Jack said, his eyes going from Bailey to Joe.

"I'm just giving Bailey a tour, as her family used to own this place. She likes riding, and I said she could come here anytime she liked and we'd sort her out with a horse."

"No worries." Jack smiled. "You want a ride now?"

"Oh, I-I don't think I have time. But thanks."

Bailey wondered why she didn't feel anything when Jack smiled, like she did with Joe. But of course she knew why. He'd always been the one in her eyes.

"So how's my man?"

The ice started in her feet and traveled upward. *My man?* She watched the woman Joe had called Angie come toward him. The smile on her face suggested intimacy, as did the arms she wrapped around his neck.

Joe cleared his throat, no doubt feeling awkward because minutes before, those lips the woman wanted to kiss had been on her.

"Angie, this is Bailey Jones. She's come back to Ryker for a visit."

The woman lowered her arms, and held a hand out to Bailey. The smile on her lips didn't meet her eyes.

"Hello, Bailey. I'm Angie McGregor."

How dare he lock lips with her one minute, and introduce Bailey to his partner the next. *Bastard!*

"Hello," Bailey shook the hand. "Please excuse me, as I have to go now. Thanks for the tour, Joe."

She made herself nod in Joe's direction, then walk by Jack.

"So, Bailey." Jack followed her down the stairs. "You keen on that ride now, because I'd sure like to hear what this place was like before you left."

She wanted to ride, so why shouldn't she? Damn Joe Trainer, she wasn't letting him make her run for cover again. At least now she had a reason to stay away from him. She'd thought the man she'd seen since arriving back in Ryker was a good one, but now she knew different. He was a two-timing asshole. This should make her happy; at least now she had a reason to stay away from him.

It didn't. In fact, it hurt like hell.

"Yes, please, Jack. I'd really like a ride."

Chapter 13

JOE WATCHED Bailey leave without looking at him again. She would be justifiably pissed off and confused right about now, and thinking him the lowest life form... which he kind of was, but not really. It was complicated, but to his mind, the short version was he and Angie never had anything but a casual relationship. He'd just need to get Bailey to understand that now.

"Angie, we need to talk." He said the words because he knew it was time to stop any further contact but friendship with this woman. Not that he thought she'd mind, especially if Luke had been right and she was seeing Ted from the lodge.

If he and Bailey ended up in bed, which he'd be doing his best to make happen, he didn't want to be involved even slightly with another woman. Besides, whatever this was between him and Miss Jones, he had a feeling it ran deep, way deeper than any other relationship he'd ever had, which was a damned scary thought, but one he'd put away for another day.

"Okay, sure, but first let me tell you about what

happened while I was visiting Uncle Carl. He fell, and they had to put him in hospital, and while he was there they carried out tests. It's not good, Joe."

So maybe now wasn't the right time, he thought thirty minutes later as Angie sniffed. She was upset about her uncle, and he didn't want to talk about not seeing each other again while she was emotional.

"I missed you, Joe."

"Sure, and I'll always be here as a friend, Angie. How about we go out to dinner on Wednesday? I'll get Em to cover?"

Her smile was wide. "Yes, I'd love that."

"Great, I'll make the booking, and pick you up at seven."

She got to her toes and kissed him. It was Joe who eased back, because he felt nothing.

"I'll walk you down to your car."

"I have to work tonight, you want to come over later?"

Angie worked at the lodge.

"I'm tired, and have an early morning. I'll see you Wednesday."

"Okay, Wednesday it is. So, Bailey. You guys go back a bit?"

"Kind of. We knew each other before, but it was some time ago."

"Is she here long?"

"I'm not sure."

"It's nice of you to show her around here, Joe. Can't have been easy coming on the property that had once been her home."

He made an agreeing noise. In fact, what he'd done was kiss Bailey at the first opportunity. The hell of it was, he now wanted more of her.

He listened while Angie talked about her trip some

more, then waved her off. He then went back into the stables hoping to find Bailey, but she and his brother had gone. He was outside waiting for them to return when Fin ambled up the drive minutes later.

"I came to have a beer with your brother, but you'll do."

"Thanks. Jack's out riding."

"She must be pretty because an hour ago he told me he had a cold beer in the fridge if I wanted to share?"

"She is," Joe said without thinking it through.

"Who?"

"The woman he's out with."

"Yes, but who is it?"

He couldn't lie, Fin would know, so he went for distraction.

"I thought you had work?"

"Nope, not in till tomorrow because I swapped with Doofus."

"You know his name's Dudley, right, and if he hears you calling him Doofus he's gonna be pissed, Fin."

"Sure, just adds to the fun. You working the bar tonight?"

"Night off. Em's running things."

"Beer it is, then. Why are you frowning?

Joe didn't answer, instead he went back inside and to the fridge, took out two beers, and popped the tops. He found his friend sitting in one of the deck chairs Jack used when he wanted to clean tack outside. Buzz was crunching a biscuit.

"We discussed the biscuit thing, Fin. My dog's getting fat."

"You discussed, I didn't listen. So, Angie, she's back."

Joe grunted his agreement.

"That wasn't convincing."

"Women are confusing." Joe took a long pull on his beer. "Hell of a thing to try and get it right all the time."

"Amen." Fin lifted his in a salute. "But then I'm not an overthinker like you."

"It's called intelligence."

"Ha."

They drank in silence a bit longer. Fin was one of those people who could do quiet. He didn't fidget like Jack. Or crack his fingers like Luke. Then there was Pip, who had a foot that moved up and down. Not Fin, he just sat.

"So who is Jack riding with?"

"Bailey," Joe sighed.

"Okay, I get it now."

"Get what?"

"It."

Fin pointed his beer at Joe, and he had no idea what that meant.

"So, Angie?"

"She's a really nice person, Fin, and like I said to my brothers when they grilled me about her, we've only ever had a casual relationship, and rarely for the last two months."

"Got that, actually. And have to say, the woman is not the exclusive kind."

"You saw her with Ted too?"

"Nah." Fin shook his head. "He told me, but he's moved on now."

Joe grunted. He liked Ted, and had no problem if he and Angie ended up together.

"The fact you're not angry pretty much tells me she's not the one, Joe."

Joe let the statement settle between them while he drank some more. He looked up at Phil, and wondered way back, when he and his family had settled in Ryker, if he'd had trouble with some woman.

"So, Bailey, is she the one, Joe?"

"One what?"

He felt Fin's eyes on the side of his face.

"The one to wallpaper your lounge, you idiot. You know what I mean. Does she float your boat?"

"You did not just say that."

"Light your fire?"

"Marginally better."

"Is that Maggie coming down the driveway?"

Joe squinted. "Sure looks like it."

"Saved by the striking redhead."

"Did you just call a woman striking, Fin? Is there something you need to tell me?" Joe decided to rattle his friend's cage as a bit of payback.

"No."

"Sure you did, and if we're being honest, you and she have always had that thing."

"The hell you say!" Fin got to his feet and glared at Joe. "There is no thing, we're friends."

Joe got slowly to his feet, hiding his smile.

"If you say so, bud, but you sure as hell are pretty defensive about it, if you ask me."

"No one's asking you," Fin snarled, walking away to greet the 'striking redhead.' Joe kept pace with him. Buzz beat them both to greet Maggie.

"She's got that look about her when she walks."

"What look?" Fin asked.

"Don't mess with me, world, I'm Maggie Winter."

Fin snorted, but didn't add anything.

"Hey, Maggs. How come you're not at the shop?" Joe moved forward to kiss her cheek; Fin did the same. Maggie stiffened a bit. *Interesting*, Joe thought.

"Bill's working this afternoon, and after Bailey called, I thought I'd join her."

"They just headed out. I can help you saddle up Sandy, and you can head out?"

"Why do all your horses have female names except Arthur?" Fin asked.

"They're women that Luke and Jack have had in their lives."

"You have to be shitting me?"

Joe laughed at Fin. "No, it just kind of happened that way after the first few horses arrived with those names, so now we keep it going—unless of course they're male horses, because that would be just plain wrong."

"It would, and while this conversation is riveting, I need to get out on a horse and blow a few cobwebs out of my head," Maggie said. "Plus your sexy brother is out there with my friend somewhere, and I need to chaperone them."

Joe didn't like the flash of jealousy he felt at Maggie's words. A, because he wasn't the jealous type, and B, he was never the jealous type with his brothers.

"He's a quick worker, that boy," Fin said.

"Bailey's not like that," Maggs snapped, before Joe could. "She's not the type to get involved with anyone who doesn't mean something to her."

"I didn't mean any offence, Maggie."

She sighed. "I know, sorry, it's been a long day."

"You doing okay there, sweet cheeks?" Joe slung an arm around Maggie's shoulders.

"Sure."

"Bailey's an old friend, right?" Fin asked.

Maggie nodded. "And it's awesome that she's back."

"But?" Fin said as the three of them headed back to the stables.

"But nothing."

"There was definitely a but in there, Maggie."

"Stop hounding the woman," Joe said, because he could feel the tension in Maggie, and while he wanted to hear more about Bailey, he didn't want to do so if her friend was upset. "Seriously, what's with you today? Thinking of auditioning as the next Oprah?"

"Just gentle curiosity and nothing more. You're my friends, I'm just checking everything's going okay." Fin gave Maggie a smile that reached his eyes, and made Joe wonder if in fact he'd been on to something before.

"Gentle, my ass," Joe snorted.

"And what a nice ass it is," Maggie said as she always did, but this time it didn't hold its usual kick.

"Yours too, sweet cheeks."

"If we're done butt admiring, shall we saddle you up a horse, Maggie?"

"I got it, Fin, but thanks. You two go back to your beers, and I'll head out."

They sat in silence, picked up their beers, and drank.

"She's off today, it's not like her," Fin said quietly, so Maggie couldn't hear.

"Probably that needle-dick she's dating. Guy's a loser."

"Then why is she dating him?" Fin asked.

"She likes losers, is my guess. Damned if I know."

"That makes no sense."

"Okay, I didn't realize you wanted sense, because let's face it, anything to do with women and their love lives is black and white, right."

"Fair point."

They fell into companionable silence again.

"I sometimes wonder about big city life, and then I look around me and...."

"You think no."

Fin grunted his agreement.

They turned to watch Maggie come out. She had just put her foot in the stirrup when they heard the noise.

"Was that gunshots?" Joe got to his feet.

"No one should be shooting around here, not without permission," Fin said, doing the same.

"I'm taking the horse, Maggs." Joe took the reins she handed him, and vaulted on its back. Seconds later he was galloping away. "Hold on to Buzz!"

Chapter 14

BAILEY WAS ENJOYING THE RIDE. The tension of the kiss with Joe, and then seeing Angie, was still there, a tight little knot in her chest. How could he do what he had to her, when he obviously had a girlfriend?

"So you used to ride all over this place alone?"

"We had farm hands, and they sometimes came with me. Plus Maggie, when she was allowed. But for the most, yes. This was my playground growing up."

Jack smiled. "Awesome playground, it has to be noted."

"No complaints here."

They headed into the forest, the air cooling as the leaves formed a canopy overhead. Dappled sunlight played on the ground as they moved deeper. She could hear the river that ran past Joe's house and down from the falls as they approached.

"While I'm here, Jack, if you need any help with rides, or the stables, I'd love to help."

"Really?" His face showed surprise.

"Really. I miss this, and being around horses." As the last word left her mouth, she heard the first gunshot.

"Christ!"

Turning at Jack's anguished cry, she watched his horse rear, and him fall off the back. Bailey dropped her reins and quickly dismounted. The second shot had her dropping to all fours, and scrabbling through the dirt as she made her way to Jack.

"Jack?" She kept her voice low. "Are you all right?"

"My side," he rasped. "I've been shot. You need to head back, Bailey, and get help. There's no cell coverage here."

"I'm not leaving you out here alone." She reached him, and moved the hand he had pressed to the wound. Raising his shirt, Bailey saw blood, lots of it. She took off her own shirt, and reached for his belt buckle. "I need to use this, Jack."

He edged forward, and she forced the leather through the belt loops. Folding her shirt into a pad, she strapped it to his side. Taking his good arm, she pressed the hand against the dressing to hold it in place. "You have to keep the pressure on now, Jack."

"Y-you need to go for help, Bailey. I mean it. One shot could be a wild one, but not two. I think someone's d-deliberately targeting us. I'll hide." His voice was strained, and she knew he was in danger of losing a significant amount of blood.

"No, I'm not leaving you here exposed. We have to get back, Jack. To do that, I need to get you on my horse."

"Bailey, just go for help, please. We can't risk whoever is shooting seeing us."

She ignored him, and brought her horse closer. Jack's horse was standing a few feet away, wild-eyed. No way did she want to attempt to get on her.

"Right, up you get now."

"Bailey—"

"Now, Jack!" The tone of her voice had him struggling to his feet. She put her arm under his shoulder and helped him rise. His legs were shaky, and the hiss of breath told her he was in pain. Shock, she realized, and blood loss were very real problems. She had to get him help now. Had to get him back to safety.

"Hold out your leg, I'm going to give you a boost up."

"I'm too big, Bailey, and my side is burning like fuck."

"Jack, shut up and do as I tell you!"

He did as she asked, and used one arm to pull himself up onto the horse. He was pale and sweaty now, blood flowing over his fingers and onto the ground.

"Move back and stick out your foot."

Again he did as she said, and seconds later she was seated before him. "Now I'm bending forward, you bend over me, Jack."

"Jesus, Bailey!"

"Just do it, damn you!" Fear put strength into her words. Seconds later she felt his body hunched over hers.

She directed the horse through the trees as fast as she could, all the while listening for movement, or gunshots. Nothing happened, and then she was out of the forest.

"Hold on!"

He did, one arm wrapped around her waist. Bailey galloped as fast as she could.

"Stay with me, Jack!"

The relief when she saw someone coming toward them was immense.

"It's Joe," Jack said.

"Thank God."

He was low over his horse, galloping hard, slowing only when he reached them.

"It's Jack, Joe! Someone shot him, we have to get him help." She galloped by him, and soon he'd turned and was passing her. He reached the stables first; she charged in seconds later.

"Call for an ambulance!" Joe was roaring orders.

He came to her as Bailey pulled her horse to a halt. "Take him, Joe. Help him. I-it's his side."

Joe's face was fierce as he reached her side.

"H-help him." Bailey could hear the hysteria in her words. "So much b-blood."

He lifted one arm and wrapped it around her, easing her to the ground so he could get at his brother. "Thank you." He crushed her to him briefly as he whispered the words into her hair before letting her go.

"You take his right, Fin."

Bailey watched as they lifted Jack off the horse; his eyes were glazed with pain now, and he moaned as they carried him gently to a bench and lay him down.

"Bailey!" Maggie came running, with the phone still in her hand. "Are you all right?"

She nodded, and then shook her head. "M-Maggs, J-Jack was shot."

"Shit!"

Her friend wrapped Bailey in her arms and held her tight. Bailey burrowed into Maggie and held right back.

"I need to get you a blanket, Bailey. You're shivering. Sit here now." She was nudged into a seat, and sat shivering, watching as Joe and Fin leaned over Jack and worked on him.

Maggs came back with a blanket and wrapped it tight around her; the warmth was wonderful, but she was still ice-cold on the inside.

She kept her eyes on Fin and Joe, and Jack's feet. When the fear inside her got too much, she moved closer. Maggs held her hand.

"Is h-h.... Is he going to be okay?"

Joe looked up at her; his eyes were greener than she'd ever seen them. Green, and rage-fueled. He nodded, and then returned to looking at his brother, his hand holding the dressing in place, and applying pressure. Jack was almost gray now, his breathing shallow, eyes closed.

"Bailey?"

She dropped down beside his head as he called her name.

"Thanks."

Bailey leaned down and kissed his cheek. She took his hand and squeezed it, then held it until the ambulance and police arrived.

"I'm Deputy Steve Sanders, and this is my colleague, Deputy Rollins." Two officers approached.

"Someone shot at Jack," Bailey said, her voice raised. "You need to go out there and find them!"

"It's okay now, Bailey," Joe touched her cheek briefly. "Jack's safe."

He was just saying that to calm her down, she knew it, but she latched onto his words, wanting to believe them.

"Maybe you should go on out and look for leads while they're fresh, Steve. The shooter could still be around," Fin said. "I'll take Bailey into the station, she can give Chief Blake her statement."

"It'd make sense to do that, Fin. I'd be obliged if you got her there sooner rather than later."

"As soon as the ambulance leaves we will too."

The officers nodded, and then they left. Jack was put into the ambulance, and with Joe at his side, they soon departed too.

"Okay, Bailey, we'll go see Chief Blake now, and tell him what's happened," Fin said. Like Joe, his face looked like it had been carved in granite.

"Okay." She looked up at the sound of a horse approaching, and saw Jack's mount trotting back inside.

"Let me unsaddle her, and put her in a stall, then I'll come too," Maggie said.

Soon they were in Fin's cruiser, Bailey wrapped in a blanket, as her tank top was covered in blood. Maggs sat in the back seat with her.

"I'm okay now, really. It was just the shock."

"Humor me, okay. I need to know you're warm and right here beside me. I've heard about shock, and maybe you don't have it, but I sure as hell do."

Bailey leaned into her friend and let her hold her. It felt good. She hadn't leaned on anyone in years... if ever.

"Okay now, Bailey. Let's get this done, then Maggs can take you home," Fin said as they pulled up outside the Ryker Falls Police Department.

It'd changed some since she was last here. Then it had been a small shed-like building; it was now long and low, and made of stone. Beside it was the fire department, and she imagined Luke had left there in a hurry already.

She got out with Maggs.

"Okay, let's go."

They walked her inside between them, and Bailey was grateful for the support. In fact, it felt good to have them watching over her.

"Jonas, is the chief in?"

The man behind reception nodded, then lifted his phone and spoke into it.

"Go on through, Fin, you know the way."

She saw desks with phones and computers. Trays with paper, and passed a room that had a coffee machine that made her desperately want a cup to steady her nerves.

"Chief Blake."

"Come on in, Fin."

They entered a large office that had an equally large desk, two chairs, and a long squishy-looking black sofa.

"This is Bailey Jones, Chief, and you know Maggie."

"Course I do, how's my favorite art critic doing?"

"Good thanks, Chief Blake."

The man who came around the desk wasn't overly tall or big, but she knew he was fit. Bailey pegged him as late fifties, with short spiky hair and hazel eyes. She shook the hand he held out to her.

"That blood yours, Miss Jones?" He looked at her hands and arms. "And have anything to do with that ambulance call out at the Trainer ranch?"

She shook her head, and then nodded, and he waved her into a seat. Maggs took the one beside her, and Fin stood at her back.

"Not injured, are you?"

"No, but Jack Trainer is."

"Like those Trainer boys," Chief Blake said, moving back round his desk. "Be mighty unhappy if they're hurt through any fault but their own."

"I sent Steve and Jed out to take a look around, Chief. Thought it best while the trail is warm. They agreed after I told them I'd bring Bailey in here so you could get her statement down," Fin said.

Bailey watched Chief Blake hit a button on his phone.

"Always thought you'd make a better cop than ranger," he said. "Coffee, Jonas, now!" he then roared into the phone, while winking at Bailey. "Important they fear me a little bit, Miss Jones, even if everyone knows I'm a teddy bear." He turned to his computer. "You go on and tell me your story now."

She did, with as much detail as she could.

"And you say the second shot came as you dismounted?"

"Yes."

"Did you hear it hit something near you?"

"I d-don't know, I-I just wanted to reach Jack." Bailey laced her fingers through Maggie's, glad of her friend's support. Funny, she'd never reached for someone before returning to Ryker.

"Now there might be something else you remember, Bailey. Anything, and you call me."

She took the small white rectangle of cardboard he handed her.

"What you did today took courage, Bailey, especially as we don't know what was going on out there on Trainer land."

"I think it's fair to say someone was shooting at Jack."

Fin had been quiet until then, but she'd felt his anger, just like she'd felt Maggie's.

"Now, Fin, I understand your anger, but we have to follow a process here to come to the correct conclusion."

"Process, my ass! Jack was shot, then Bailey heard the second shot nearby. No one makes that mistake twice. And let's not get started about someone shooting on private land. What the hell would they be shooting at anyway? Bailey said she saw no elk, or anything else, did you?"

She shook her head.

"Like I said, Fin, I'm not jumping to conclusions until I've checked all the facts. First off I'm heading out to the Trainer land to look around myself. Can you tell me exactly where you were, Bailey?"

She could and did, as she knew the land intimately. "My family owned that land fifteen years ago, Chief Blake."

"Must have been just before I arrived here, then. Nice piece of dirt."

It was, and it now had Jack's blood on it. The thought that what happened could have been much worse made Bailey shiver.

Chapter 15

JOE LOOKED DOWN at his sneakers. Beside him Luke and Piper sat silently, all of them thinking about what was happening somewhere in the hospital.

"He'll be all right," Joe said for the fifteenth time. He was the oldest, and meant to reassure his family, but it was a hell of a job—because while his brother had been talking before he was taken away, maybe he wasn't now.

Fear was so thick in the room, he could taste it. Fear, rage, and helplessness.

"Motherfucking son of a bitch!" Luke got to his feet and started prowling again. He'd been doing that on and off for the last two hours. "I'm gonna kill someone."

Luke was the gentle Trainer—until he was riled, then he was mean.

"No one is killing anyone," Joe made himself say, when deep inside he was in total agreement. "Get your shit together, and stay calm. We don't know anything yet, so let's focus on Jack."

Luke stalked to where Joe sat, his eyes narrowed, and

Joe stood. He saw the fear and pain, and simply wrapped his arms around his little brother.

"It's okay, Luke. He's going to be okay." *Christ, let him be okay.*

He felt Pip's hand in his, and clenched it hard while he held his brother.

"I brought coffee."

Joe let Luke go as Angie walked in. She had a tray of coffee and bag of food.

"Thanks."

"I won't stay, I know you don't need that, but call if you need anything."

She hugged and kissed all of them, and Joe got an extra squeeze. He wished all over again that he could love this woman. They thanked her, then it was the three of them alone once more, but now they had coffee. The food bag remained unopened.

Bailey slipped into Joe's head as the fourth hour ticked over, and he wondered if she was okay. He had a feeling he and his family now owed her a debt of gratitude, and he'd be sure to tell her. That was, if she would talk to him again.

He'd been a dickhead kissing her when he and Angie were still seeing each other. The hell of it was she made him lose his head. He wanted her, there was no getting around that fact. But it was more; he just couldn't put his finger on what that more was, and wouldn't until he'd closed things off with Angie.

All eyes went to the door as it opened, and in walked Dr. O'Roake. He smiled as the Trainers stood and met him in the middle of the room.

"Jack's doing good, he pulled through surgery well. The bullet went through the fleshy part of his side, so he was lucky as it hit nothing vital. He's lost a lot of blood, and like I said, he's a lucky boy."

"Is he awake?" Pip asked.

"Yes, and someone will come and get you when he can be seen."

"Thanks, Dr. O'Roake." Joe shook the man's hand. Then he and his siblings sat again, but this time it was easier, because they knew that Jack would live.

HE WAS pale from blood loss and pain, and his eyes were closed as they stood around Jack's bed. But on the day following the shooting he looked a hell of a lot better than he had when Joe had pulled him from Bailey's horse covered in blood. They'd only been able to see him briefly last night, so they'd arrived at the hospital early.

Luke was still pacing the room, away and back to his brother's bed. Pip sat in a chair, still looking pale, holding Jack's hand. Joe just looked at his brother lying there and kept repeating over and over inside his head that he'd be okay.

"Thank God Mom's away," Pip said.

"Aren't you meant to be talking in hushed voices around someone who's near death?"

Joe reached for Jack's hand. His eyes were open and bloodshot. Pain was etched in the lines of his face, but he still managed a smile as he looked at the worried faces hovering over him.

"I'm okay."

The breath exhaled out of Joe like a balloon deflating. He lowered his head and hugged his brother gently. Jack gripped his shoulder and held on.

"Jesus," Joe whispered, "you scared me, little brother."

"Scared myself," Jack said as Joe eased back to let Luke in.

After the hugging was done, Joe took the seat beside him.

"You up to telling us what happened?"

"We were just riding, and Bailey was telling me about living there, and how she used to ride all over the place on her own, even as a child."

Joe knew this, but nodded.

"She'd just offered to work in the stables if I needed her, I remember that part, and we'd entered the forest and were near the river, then the bullet hit me. Beccy got spooked and reared, and I fell. I roared at Bailey to ride for help, she refused, and then the second shot was fired. She hit the ground and crawled to me. Took off her shirt, and my belt, then made a dressing."

"Nice work, Bailey," Luke said.

"I told her to go again, she said no again. She's a lot tougher than I thought. Then she bullied me into getting up on her horse. She got up in front, and we left. We kept low through the forest and then we were galloping, and that's when you found us, Joe. After that everything became pretty hazy."

Joe had to find Bailey and thank her for saving his brother's life.

"Do you think it was deliberate, Jack?" he asked.

"I don't know how it couldn't have been, no matter how much I've tried to convince myself otherwise. The second shot was close to Bailey and me. Once is a mistake, but twice...."

"Well, fuck," Luke snarled.

"Trainers." Fin walked in with a bag of food, which he lowered to the bedside table, and more coffee. "How you doing, Jack?"

"Okay, if you discount the red-hot poker in my side."

Fin looked like he wanted to spit tacks just like Joe, but he simply leaned in and hugged Jack.

"Glad you're okay."

"How's Bailey, Fin?" Jack said the words as he eased into a more comfortable position, which caused him to grunt in pain.

"Haven't seen her today, but spoke to Maggie, who said she's shaken, but holding up well. Me and Maggie went to the police with her yesterday. She told Chief Blake every-thing she knew, and didn't derail once. No hysterics, no crying. I seriously thought about proposing then and there. A calm woman in a time of crisis is a rarity."

"I'm sure I should be insulted about now," Piper said.

"Bailey said you were just having a nice ride and then the bullet hit you, your horse threw you, which by the way is going to give me some serious mileage," Fin said, to which Jack rolled his eyes. Joe didn't have an eye roll in him, in fact what he still had was a red-hot burning rage that someone had shot his brother. A few inches the other way and he'd be dead. Bailey could have been shot too, and until now he hadn't allowed himself to focus on that. The thought was a chilling one.

"She said she got off her horse, and came to you, then bound your side, and you headed back."

"Yeah, I was just telling these guys that I told her to go but she refused, then bullied me up on her horse. That's pretty much all I remember."

"Chief Blake's been out at your place twice now, scouring the area. He's gonna take Bailey back at some stage to go over things."

They talked until Jack fell asleep again. Joe told the nurse to call him when he woke. He then left the hospital and went to find Bailey. He needed to check on her, make sure she really was holding up okay, and he refused to acknowledge just how much seeing her meant to him right at that moment. His world had just been rocked and it was to her he wanted to go to steady it again.

Chapter 16

HE'D BEEN to her house, then his, but came up empty-handed. Finally he decided on heading to the bar, and it was there he found her. She was in the utility room staring at the washing machine, muttering to herself.

"It can't be that hard to use."

He stood in the doorway watching her. She was dressed in denim shorts that looked like they'd recently been a pair of jeans, and a pale gray fitted long-sleeved T-shirt. On her feet were the now slightly grubby peach trainers. Her hair was in the ever-present messy knot. He followed the length of two long curls that had made a break for freedom, and fell to below her shoulders, and felt something heavy settle in his chest. Why those two locks of hair made her appear vulnerable, he had no idea.

"You're an intelligent woman, Bailey Jones. How hard can it be to operate?"

She bent, and he admired her ass, and the length of her legs. Then straightened, and braced her hands on her hips.

"It's a washing machine."

She yelped, turning with a hand now pressed to her chest.

"I-I didn't hear you."

"You were too busy talking to the washing machine."

Color filled her cheeks and she looked away.

"How's Jack?"

"Better, thanks."

"I'm pleased. It was scary not knowing how bad he was."

"Very scary. Now tell me why you are standing here looking at my washing machine?"

"I came in to see if Em needed me to play tonight, and she was flustered because someone didn't turn up for work today to clean. I offered to help, and she asked me to put the bar towels on to wash."

"And you don't know how?"

"I'll work it out."

"It's a pretty standard model."

"I'm sure it is."

"What kind do you have?" Joe said. "I'm sure it's not that different."

She muttered something, so he moved to her side and looked at her. "Sorry?"

"I've never used a washing machine! All right, are you satisfied?"

"Why would you not using a washing machine satisfy me?"

She turned to face him again. "Because it just proves what a spoilt, self-indulged person I've been my entire life."

He wasn't sure how not knowing the workings of his washing machine pointed to that, but he'd run with it.

"I don't know how to look after myself, but damn you, Joe Trainer, I'm learning!"

"Because you've lived your life in hotels, and with your grandfather's staff looking after you?"

She nodded. "A washing machine shouldn't be that hard, right?"

"Sure, but they have these things called Laundromats now so it's really not a big deal."

She sighed. "I can't even use a coffee machine. Cell phones are a wonder of modern magic, and when I ran out of fuel on a road, after leaving Boston. I had to learn that a car needs to be refilled and have its oil and water checked... actually I knew that, I just didn't fill up in time."

Joe wanted to rub the pain in his chest; instead he smiled.

"Poor little rich girl."

"Don't make fun of me!" She was glaring at him again. "I performed, I practiced, and I didn't learn basic life skills. But I have been over the last year, and I will master this washing machine!"

"Good for you. Want me to teach you?"

Her eyes narrowed as she looked at him, waiting to see if he was messing with her. When she realized he wasn't, she nodded.

"The powder goes in here." Joe explained the workings, and then made her run through them manually. When it started, she clapped her hands like a small child, and the pain in his chest intensified.

"I need to write this down."

"Why?"

"Because then I'll remember it for next time," she said, looking at him. "I have a small book with these things in."

Joe had to clear his throat.

"Bailey, I need to thank you for what you did when Jack was shot."

"I'm just glad he's okay."

"You didn't panic, and did everything exactly right. The Trainer family is in your debt."

"I don't want you in my debt. I did what anyone would."

"Are we going to argue about this?"

She shook her head.

"How's Angie?"

And there it was, the little extra tension that was in the air between them.

"Bailey, I need to explain to you about Angie. I don't want you to think—"

"I don't want to hear it, Joe. What happens in your life is none of my business, as what happens in my life is none of yours. What h-happened between us was wr-wrong, especially considering you and Angie have a thing, but let's put it down to insanity and move on."

"It wasn't." He grabbed her as she tried to leave. "Nothing that good could be wrong or considered insane. Angie and I don't have a thing either."

"Don't lie to me, Joe!"

"I'm not. We're—"

"I saw her. Saw the way she walked up to you with that secret smile, and wanted you to kiss her. It made me feel terrible. So I won't be a party to that again, even if you will."

"What the hell are you implying?" Joe felt his anger climb. She wouldn't give him a chance to explain, wouldn't believe him.

She pulled her arm free and left without answering. Joe stared at the washing machine until his blood had cooled. How was he supposed to get her to listen?

"Jesus, women drive me fucking crazy," he muttered, then kicked the washing machine for no other reason than it felt good.

"You got a minute, Joe?" Em poked her head around the door.

"Sure." He left the room, and followed his manager. Of Bailey there was no sign, which pissed him off, because in his current mood, he'd been ready to pick her up and lock them both in his office until she listened to him.

"I've put Elijah Neil in your office, Joe. He said he needed to speak with you urgently."

"Thanks." Joe headed up and wondered what the man wanted. They'd run together for a while as teenagers, and then Elijah's family had stepped in and banned him from having anything to do with that bad Trainer boy.

"Elijah." Joe walked in and shook his hand. Buzz was snoring softly in his bed, no doubt thinking of his next dog biscuit and whom he could fleece. "What can I do for you?"

He sat behind his desk, and Elijah took the chair.

"How's Jack doing?"

"He's coming along well, thanks."

"I was up on the trails yesterday, Joe. Went for a quick hike at lunch."

Elijah was someone who enjoyed nature. There wasn't a week went by when he wasn't out hiking, and usually dragging his wife and four children with him.

"Good day for it."

"It was. But that's not why I'm here."

The man's face was serious, not an expression he usually wore.

"I saw someone as I passed the lodge, Joe. He was lurking around the outbuildings. There was something about him that triggered a memory in my head, so I moved closer. He got spooked and ran."

He wasn't sure why ice was suddenly slithering down his spine, but Joe felt cold.

"It was your father, Joe. I'm 100 percent on that, because he recognized me just as I did him."

He couldn't speak for a few seconds. His father was back in Ryker, and his brother had been shot. Coincidence? He didn't think so.

"I'm obliged to you for coming to me, Elijah. But I'd be grateful if you didn't tell anyone else what you saw for now."

"I have no issue with that at all." Elijah got to his feet.

"And let me know if you see him again."

"I will, and you take care now, Joe. This business with Jack is nasty."

It was, Joe thought minutes later as he sat in his chair staring at the wall. Work forgotten, he wondered what the hell his father was doing back in Ryker, and what connection his appearance had with Jack's shooting. One thing he knew for certain was that he'd be finding out, and if Tim Trainer was in any way involved, he'd deal with the man himself.

When Angie walked in twenty minutes later, he was hard at work trying to put the morning from hell behind him, and failing.

"Hey there, lover boy."

For some reason that made him wince. Maybe because of what Fin had told him.

"I thought we were seeing each other tonight?"

"We are... were, that's why I called. I have to work tonight. A few staff are down with a virus. Can we rain check?"

She was in the Falls Lodge uniform of deep gray skirt and white shirt. The fitted lines of the clothes suited her, but he felt nothing when he looked at her.

"Sit down, Angie, we need to talk."

"Sure. How's Jack?" She watched him walk around the room.

"Better. They're letting him out as soon as all the tubes and wires are removed. He can then come home as long as he takes things easy. The bullet went through the fleshy part of his side. He was lucky." Joe felt the relief again that his brother had survived, and would show no lasting effects from what happened.

"Have the police found any leads?"

"None. A few tracks, but nothing concrete."

"Maybe it was someone illegally hunting?"

"I don't buy that. The first shot took Jack down, the second was aimed at Bailey, according to him."

"She seemed nice, Bailey."

She is.

"Angie, I know what we've had is casual, but I'm going to have to stop seeing you." He looked at her, but she'd turned away so he couldn't read her expression.

"Why?" She looked back at him, and he couldn't read anything in her face. "I thought we had fun? No strings, no hassles?"

"Sure we did, but it's over for me now."

"It's Bailey, isn't it? I felt something was going on between you in the stables that day."

"No, I just think it's time." Joe wasn't bringing Bailey into this.

"I like what we had, Joe." She got to her feet and headed his way. Joe evaded her hands and went to sit behind his desk.

"I want us to be friends, Angie."

"Friends." She laughed, and he saw no anger, which was a relief. "Okay, I can do that, but if you change your mind, you know where you can find me."

"I won't."

She gave him a gentle smile, and left before he could say anything else. Joe did something he hadn't in years. He had a drink before the bar opened.

Chapter 17

"HEY THERE, Bailey. You come to watch the parade?"

"Hi Fin, yes I have. Maggie's meeting me here."

"You did good the other day, Bailey Jones. Just need you to know that."

"Thanks, but I'm sure most people would do the same thing."

His smile was slightly lopsided.

"Well, you'd like to think so, but to be fair not everyone has smarts, Bailey. In fact, for some it's a daily struggle not to show their stupid."

She laughed.

"I hear you've been helping out at the bar, and the stables, while Jack's laid low, and Joe's spending time at the hospital."

"I don't have anything else on." She shrugged.

"Not comfortable with praise, are you, which to my mind is weird considering it has to have come your way a lot in the past."

Bailey found the conversation awkward. "I took that

praise because I deserved it. I tried to be the best, and often I was."

"I like a woman who speaks the truth. So going with that logic, it would suggest because you're not the best at helping out in the bar, and stables, you can't accept the praise?"

Bailey narrowed her eyes at Fin in the hope he'd shut up. He simply smiled back.

"Is there a reason we're having this intense conversation right here on the main street of Ryker Falls, with half the town around us?"

"I like to debate, Bailey. It adds spice to your day."

"Good for you."

"Now that there was sarcasm, and I don't mind some of that too."

"The Fall Parade is a lot bigger now than it was in my day." Bailey changed the subject."

"You were what, thirteen when you left?"

She nodded, looking around her at the smiling faces and fluttering flags. "There were two or three floats, and a handful of sweets. The crowds weren't this big either."

"Well, you're in for a surprise then."

"It should be interesting, that's for sure. How long have you lived here, Fin?"

"About eight years. I arrived with Joe when he came home, and never left."

He wore denim shorts and a faded black T-shirt, and on his feet were sneakers. The few times she'd seen him, he'd seemed relaxed, but after the conversation she'd just had with him, she knew this was a facade. Plus, he was the head ranger around here, not a job for a clueless person.

"So you and Joe met away from here?"

"We did."

Fin didn't elaborate, so Bailey didn't ask, but she

wanted to. She'd tried to push thoughts of Joe aside since their conversation over the washing machine, but hadn't been entirely successful. His kissing her while involved with Angie had disturbed her, because she'd believed him a better person than that—and she still did.

"Come on, the parade is due to start, and I have a spot being saved in the front row."

Bailey started to protest, but Fin simply took her hand and towed her behind him through the crowds. Bailey smiled, offered apologies as they weaved around people.

"I can stand back there," she tried to protest. Fin ignored her. Finally, he stopped when they reached the very front. Bailey looked at the people standing behind her, some four deep. "Maybe I should just—"

"This is Cindy, Bailey."

She nodded to the tall, leggy brunette who wore the shortest shorts she had ever seen. Her top looked like it had been sprayed on, and Bailey wondered if it restricted her breathing in any way.

"Hi." Cindy flicked candy-pink nails at her, and skimmed her eyes over Bailey's simple lemon shift dress. *No competition here, Barbie*, Bailey thought, and then felt ashamed. Jealousy was an ugly thing. "So, Bailey, how are you enjoying your time back in Ryker so far?"

"Good, thanks. A lot has changed, but all for the good." She'd given up wondering how people knew so much about her. Small towns were like that. News spread like wildfire.

She let her eyes roam up and down the street. There were people lined on both sides. Kids chattered in excitement; parents tried to keep them in check. It was close to dusk, and someone had strung up yards of fairy lights that were starting to twinkle, along with the old-fashioned streetlamps. It was a beautiful setting, Bailey thought, especially when you added in the quaint shop fronts.

"There is no place quite like Ryker Falls," Fin said. "You want a soda?"

She looked at the cooler bag at his feet and shook her head. "I'm good, thanks."

"I made it."

Bailey looked at Maggs as she arrived. Her usual smile wasn't in place, and she seemed flustered.

"Hi, Maggie, you okay?" Bailey asked.

"Sure, just a busy day."

Beautiful as always in an off-the-shoulder top and short skirt, teamed with a pair of high wedge sandals, Maggie looked her usual glamorous self. Bailey wasn't sure why she thought something wasn't right with her friend, but she did.

"Hi, Cindy, Fin," Maggie said.

"You want a drink?" Fin waved at his cooler again, but Maggie shook her head.

"It's starting now."

Bailey turned at Fin's words, and looked up the street.

"They start from the school," he added.

"So the head ranger doesn't have to be on a float?"

Fin shuddered. "Hell no. They've tried, but I pulled rank and told the others to do it."

"He's thinks he's too cool," Maggie said.

"No I don't, I just don't want to do it."

"The others don't have a problem."

"Well, I do." Fin's eyes narrowed as he frowned at Maggie. Maggs was doing the same. *Interesting.* There was definitely some tension there, but as she didn't want people prying into her life, she didn't say anything.

"Where's that loser you're dating?"

"Fuck you!" Maggie snapped, and then she turned away to watch the parade.

Bailey shot Fin a look; he was staring at the back of Maggie's head.

The music started to increase in volume then, so talking became difficult as the first float arrived. Bailey pushed her friend's behavior aside until later.

"Look," Cindy said, "it's the police department."

"The one with padding down his front and dressed in black and white stripes—which, if you didn't already guess, means he's a criminal—"

"No, I got that, actually," Bailey said.

Fin nodded. "Nice work. Well, he's Harry, one of the deputies. He wasn't on duty the day we went in to report the shooting. His wife is Gail Pedderson, and she designs the float, much to the distress of the entire staff."

"I've met her, actually." Bailey remembered the small birdlike woman with bright eyes who seemed to never stop talking.

"Harmless enough, but not someone I'd want to be stuck in an elevator with."

"Right, got it."

Fin explained who was who on the floats, and Cindy added comments about personalities that had Bailey laughing and revising her opinion of the woman. *Don't judge a book by its cover*. Maggs however, stood silently and watched the parade. Bailey shot her looks, but her friend didn't return any of them.

"Cindy's a biochemist."

"Congratulations, that can't be easy," Bailey said, now well and truly ashamed.

The woman shrugged. "I was gifted with a good brain, I like to use it."

Bailey liked her more and more with every word she spoke.

"Would you look at the Tea Total float this year," Fin said, laughing.

The Robbins sisters were sitting inside a big yellow teacup. The saucer had large scones with jam and cream around it, and Mandy, their niece, was dressed as a spoon. Miss Marla and Miss Sarah were tea leaves.

"That's their best so far," Cindy said. "Last year it rained, and their float disintegrated."

"Hello, Bailey!" Miss Marla threw a small bag at her. Fin caught it and handed it to her.

"Is that tea?" Maggs leaned over Bailey's shoulder to look.

"It says, calming, rejuvenating blend."

"Well I certainly need that," Maggs said, taking it, and turning back to watch the parade.

"Now there's a surprise," Fin drawled. "Mr. Goldhirsh is in his exercise gear."

A group of people, all middle aged or older, were jogging alongside the floats. All wore green shorts, and white T-shirts with the words Ryker Roadies in red across the front. They were throwing candy to the kids.

"I want some," Maggs moved to the front.

Fin caught several pieces and handed them to her. Bailey then watched her open two at once, and stuff them into her mouth. Something was off with her friend, Bailey just didn't know what.

"And here's the float I've been waiting for, along with half the female population. Although we weren't sure they were going to run it without Jack. But apparently the hospital let him participate, as long as he sat in a comfortable chair."

"I'd say the whole the female population have been

waiting for this float," Cindy said, puffing out her ample breasts. "You know the deal with them, don't you, Bailey?"

"Who?"

"The Trainer males."

Bailey shook her head.

"A Trainer male is for a good time, not a long time. So remember that and you won't get your heart broken like some of the other silly women in this town."

Too late. She wasn't sure why the words slipped into her head, so she chose to ignore them. Obviously they weren't true.

"That goes for most men in this town," Maggie added, sending Fin another dirty look.

"Ignore them, Bailey," Fin said. "Jack refuses to date Cindy, and she's pissy about it, and your friend Maggie... well, she's just pissy."

"Am not," Cindy said, but there was no animosity in her voice.

Maggie just raised her middle finger.

"The Trainer float has all of them on it. Jack is a cowboy because of the trail rides, Piper is the barista, and Joe sits at the piano, and Luke dresses in his fireman gear, even though there's a fire float. Never fails to get the crowds going," Fin said. "Especially as Buzz is on there too. All the eyelash fluttering nearly causes a mini tornado."

"Should Jack even be out of hospital? I mean, it's only been ten days since the shooting."

"He's tough, but not stupid. He won't do anything that is a risk to his recovery."

Bailey stood on her toes, eager to see the Trainers. The float stopped beside them, as the ones before had come to a halt, so she was able to have a really good look. Joe wore a cap with A.S. on it, and looked sexy as hell in a black button-down shirt. Piper looked cute in a white shirt, with her hair loose, standing behind a chrome coffee machine making it steam. Jack wore a cowboy shirt, hat, and carried a rope in one hand. He sat in a big comfortable chair and smiled, which only amped up his level of handsome. Luke was leaning on the piano in his uniform, smiling also. Bailey giggled as the two women to her right started waving and calling out his name. Buzz had a black silk ribbon around his neck, and lifted a paw to acknowledge people.

"Damn, that is a fine-looking family," Cindy sighed, and Bailey had to agree.

"I'm not gonna lie, I've had a crush on Jack for years," Fin drawled.

Joe found her then, and his smile grew. She lifted a hand in acknowledgement, and told herself she was waving to Luke, Jack, and Pip. He was just so male in every way, and even if she was pissed with him for his behavior, he had once been her friend.

"Oh lord, not another one."

"What?" She looked up at Fin after he whispered those words into her ear.

"You. I can see that look on your face, I'm just not sure which Trainer it's for."

"Don't be silly, they're my friends."

"Of course they are." He winked at her, so she rolled her eyes and looked away, and of course straight back at Joe.

He talked, dressed, and walked like he was comfortable in his skin, something so foreign to Bailey she couldn't fathom the concept. Everything about him seemed comfortable. She just bet he got out of bed and knew instantly what he wanted for breakfast, unlike her, who struggled with that decision daily.

"Joe wants you to join him."

"What?" Bailey shot Fin a look. "No way." She started backing up, but as there was a wall of people behind her, there was no escape.

"It'll be good PR for the bar."

"I'm not working in that bar anymore," Bailey lied quickly.

"Sure you are, we just discussed it."

"She doesn't want to go up there, Fin," Maggie snapped.

"I definitely do not want to go up there!" Horrified, Bailey shook her head at Joe. He simply nodded, then looked at his friend. The next minute, Fin had her in his arms and was lifting her onto the float. Bailey squealed, the crowd roared, and there she was standing with hundreds of eyes on her.

"So for those of you who have been living under a rock, and have not heard her play at Apple Sours, this is the wonderfully talented Bailey Jones," Joe said into a microphone. "Cheer if you want her to join me!"

Bailey felt hands nudging her to where Joe sat. Looking left, she found the smiling eyes of Luke Trainer.

"Sit right there, honey, and make him look good."

She sat, because she was too numb to do anything else. One of the reasons she'd left her life behind was the lack of control she had over anything, plus she'd often suffered from crippling stage fright. People were always making decisions for her, from her clothing to what she ate, and where she'd play next. Bailey had decided to wrestle that control back when she'd recovered from surgery.

She'd vowed never again to let anyone tell her what to do, or take choices away from her. This was minor, the rational side of her knew that, and in fact it should be fun, but Bailey had never been good with surprises, or losing control, and this had both elements. Plus, it was Joe. She wasn't rational around him either.

Her hands shook as she placed them on the keys beside Joe's. She'd play, because she could do that without thinking, but when it was done, she'd tell him what she thought of him, then she'd hand in her notice and leave Ryker. Coming here had been a mistake. It was time to go. Time to get away from all the emotion this place was stirring up inside her. Time to run away from Joe, and this time she wouldn't come back.

Chapter 18

JOE FELT the tension in Bailey, and realized he'd made a mistake by having Fin lift her up here. It had been an impulse, and he'd thought she'd find it amusing. It seemed he was wrong. She wasn't happy with him, and he guessed this business with Angie still had her pissed.

"I'm sorry," he said. "I didn't mean to upset you by getting you up here."

Her eyes turned briefly to lock on his, and he had a feeling that when the parade was done, he was going to hear just how pissed she was with him.

"It's just a bit of fun, Bailey."

"It's not my kind of fun."

"Performing in front of people is not your kind of fun?" He tried to tease her out of her mood. She ignored him.

For now, he'd just enjoy having her thigh pressed to his. Enjoy the contact with this woman who could make his body hum with a single look.

She was a dream to play with, following wherever he led, her hands flying over the keys in perfect harmony with his. Joe had to admit to leaning into her every now and then to touch her, or inhaling her perfume.

"Jack's just lassoed a woman," Joe said as they finished a song, drawing Bailey's eyes up from where they'd been focused on the keys.

"I'm sure that's not what the doctors meant by taking it easy."

"He's all right, Bailey. I wouldn't let him do anything to hurt himself further. He needs the release."

"A Trainer male is for a good time, not a long time."

"Pardon?" Joe leaned closer, sure he'd heard that wrong.

"I was told that a Trainer male is for a good time and not a long time. Considering your behavior, this is accurate, I'm guessing."

"Who the hell told you that?" Joe felt his anger rise.

"Can you deny kissing me while you are in a relationship with Angie?"

"Yes, because we've never had a relationship, me and Angie. We went out casually a few times, nothing more. Angie and I are done. Which I would have told you if you'd let me the other day while you were talking to my washing machine."

She didn't speak again, just launched into another song, and he followed, frustrated and angry again. He'd been even-tempered before Bailey arrived in Ryker; now he was anything but.

When he'd seen Bailey in the crowd beside Fin, dressed in that shift that floated round her body and rested midthigh, he'd felt his pulse spike. Her hair wasn't in its usual messy bun, but hung over one shoulder and down her back in golden curls, He wanted to thread his fingers through it, preferably while he was kissing her senseless.

The more he learned of Bailey, the more intrigued he

was with her. The small insight she'd given him into her life, when she'd told him she hadn't learned life experiences, little things he took for granted, like cell phones and washing machines, had only made his curiosity climb.

She'd also possibly saved his brother's life, and that had shown courage. Bailey Jones was a complex mix of so many things, and Joe wanted to know her better. Know the woman his thirteen-year-old Bailey had become.

"You play well, Bailey." He thought he'd get her talking by flattering her. He was wrong; she ignored him, so he tried something else.

Joe placed and arm around her and played.

"What are you doing!" She stiffened; the crowd cheered.

"Stop it!"

"Relax, Bailey, I won't hurt you. It's just a bit of harmless fun for the crowd."

"I-I d-don't...."

He watched her suck in two deep breaths.

"Please remove your arm."

He did as she asked, because that stutter told him she was upset, and he had no right to do that to her. He'd always vowed never to frighten or intimidate this woman.

Joe didn't say anything further. Now wasn't the time. He left her alone until the float finally stopped at the hospital, behind the others. His siblings were laughing and slapping each other on the back, talking about the fun they'd just had. Jack greeted the hospital staff who had come out to check on him. Joe got to his feet, and turned to help Bailey. She ignored the hand he held out to her, and got to her feet. She then made for the edge of the float, and jumped down.

"The street party starts now, Bailey."

"Thanks, Luke."

She waved at his little brother, then started walking. Joe followed, catching her when she rounded the building away from prying eyes.

"It was a bit of harmless fun, Bailey, what's the problem?"

She jerked out of his grip, and stepped back away from him.

"I-I don't like surprises, nor do I like people making me do things I don't like."

"Sorry. I didn't realize the great Bailey Jones couldn't stoop so low as to play on a float in a town parade with her old friend." He shouldn't have said the words, they were ugly and uncalled for, but his anger had begun to climb right alongside hers, and he'd spoken without his usual filter.

"Is that what you believe this is?"

"What the hell do you expect me to believe? You won't let me explain about Angie, and then tell me that shit on the float about Trainer males. You expect me to just sit there and take that?"

"You think I was angry you got me on that float, because I wasn't playing to a crowd of my choosing? That I would b-be s-so indulgent I c-couldn't lower myself to play for those people?"

He reached for her as she stuttered, but she slapped his hands aside.

"Maybe you're right and it was harmless fun, b-but all my life people have judged me, and told me what I should think or feel. Maybe I was just angry you took my choices away by not asking me, not because I c-couldn't lower myself to perform in front of your hometown."

"You're judging me!" He roared the words. "You thought I kissed you while I was committed to Angie."

"I don't care if you have five girlfriends! You and I are

oil and water, and what we once shared is d-dead and buried."

"Because I'm not good enough for you?" His old insecurities rose, and with them stupidity. He knew she wasn't like that, but the words came spewing out of his big mouth anyway.

"And that comment just confirms how little we know or mean to each other now." She gave him a final look that he felt to his toes, because her face was tight with the emotion she was trying to shut away, and then she turned and ran. He followed with Buzz on his heels, but soon she'd reached the crowds and he lost her.

"Fuck!"

"Problem?"

"I'm an idiot, Fin," Joe said as his friend appeared at his side.

"Am I supposed to be surprised?"

"I need your help to find Bailey."

"Okay."

They searched, he and the man who had played a hand in straightening Joe out when he needed straightening. But they didn't find her. It was hard going, because there were people everywhere, and most wanted to talk to him, or pat his dog, who was lapping up the attention.

"That dog's a serious babe magnet. I never really realized it until now."

"Yeah, every woman but the one I want seems to gravitate toward him." Joe ran a frustrated hand through his hair.

"She's not here, bud."

"Fuck," Joe said again, because nothing else fitted the moment, then went to the bar to get a drink. He'd call on her later when she'd calmed down, and apologize again. And he'd get her to talk to him about what was going on inside her head, while he attempted to get her to listen to what was inside his. Because one thing he did know was that whatever shit was between them, it had seriously derailed him, as was evidenced by his recent dumbass behavior.

BAILEY RAN the entire way home. Shutting the front door, she slumped against it breathless.

"That you, Bailey?"

"Yes. How come you're not still at the parade?" She found her friend in the conservatory. "I thought you were meeting Ben later?"

Maggie sat with a glass of wine and a tub of Ben and Jerry's in front of her. The combo made Bailey wince. If the bottle had been full when she started, her friend was now halfway down it.

"Are you okay, Maggie?"

"Ben dumped me."

Bailey stepped closer and saw her friend's eyes were red, makeup smeared.

"Why didn't you tell me at the parade?"

Maggs shrugged.

Bailey had zero experience with consoling friends who had been dumped, because she'd never had any close ones, or been dumped herself. She went on instinct and took the seat beside Maggs. Placing an arm around her shoulders, she then went in for a hug.

It wasn't the most natural thing to her, but when Maggie slumped against her and started sniffing, Bailey thought she'd done something right. They sat in silence for a while, with Bailey making soothing noises and stroking Maggs's hair. It was surprisingly comfortable, even considering her friend's obvious distress.

"I hope he eats something rotten and spends a week with a vile stomach bug."

"Nice." Maggie sniffed again. "Who knew you could be mean."

"I can be mean when my friend's been hurt."

Maggie started crying again.

"I'm sorry you're hurting, Maggs."

"Thank you, and thanks for being here."

A knock had them both looking at the door.

"Who the hell is that?"

"I'll go and get rid of them." Bailey quickly got to her feet as someone knocked again, this time louder. "Don't you worry about it. Just get another glass, and we'll drink our way down the rest of the bottle."

She ran to the front door and opened it, hoping that Joe Trainer didn't stand on the other side. She wasn't ready to face him again right now.

"Stand aside, I have supplies." Piper gently pushed Bailey to one side, and entered with a bag over one arm. "I just saw the shithead Ben, and he told me he was single again, which lead me to believe a certain redhead may be heartbroken, as she was his other half until recently."

"He didn't?" Bailey whispered the words. "What a loser."

"Yeah, well he's got a nice bruise right in the middle of his foot now, because I stomped on his sneaker before walking away."

Bailey looked down at the spiky heel of Piper's boot.

"Good, and I hope you told him he was a loser as well?"

"And more," Piper said. "Now I'm missing the party, but this is more important. Plus, if we cheer her up, we can head back in when things rev up later, and hopefully that dickhead will be gone."

"Ah... sure," Bailey said.

"Lock that sucker," Piper threw over her shoulder. "We don't want interruptions."

Bailey clicked the lock on the front door.

"Jesus, Maggs, you look like a panda with those eyes."

Bailey heard these words as she entered the conservatory. Maggie snuffled, which better than the weeping of before.

"Sit, Bailey. We have some drinks to consume. I also brought my first aid kit," Piper pulled out chocolate, "to eat while we crucify men in general. It's part of the process."

"Is it?" Bailey took the glass of wine Maggie handed her.

"Of course. We tell stories about men, and being dumped, etcetera." Piper waved a hand about. "Not that there have been many," she added.

Bailey took a large gulp of her wine, and listened as Maggs told the tale of Ben's dumping. The fruity flavor was nice, and had her taking another.

"H-he played that card, 'it's not you, it's me.'"

"Bastard," Piper said around a mouthful of chocolate. "I hate that line. It's a massive cop-out in my book."

Maggs waved her wineglass at Piper as she spoke. "'I'm just not ready to commit,' he said."

"Did you ask him to?" Piper asked.

"No, we never even touched on it."

"Bastard."

Bailey listened as Piper and Maggie talked, but she didn't add anything, because she had no experience to speak from.

"But here's the thing, Maggs, you knew he was a bad boy when you started dating him," Piper said. "I told you that, as did others."

"I like bad boys," Maggs wailed. "Really like them, and that's the problem. A good one would probably hang around longer, but I've never found one I like that makes me want to…." She waved her hands about, but Bailey had no clue what she was getting at.

"Jump them, Bailey. Hell, girl, get with the program." Piper waved her chocolate at Bailey.

"But surely there's more you want from a potential boyfriend than to just jump him?" Bailey had to admit that she had a slightly fuzzy head now. She'd never been a big drinker, and she was now halfway down the next glass.

"I start with the physical," Maggs said.

"She's shallow, Bailey, and proud of it."

"Like you'd ever date anyone you didn't want to jump, Pip, so don't give me that."

Bailey let them debate that topic while she drank more wine. When they were done, she surprised herself by saying, "I can't tell you any stories because I've never been dumped."

"Oh God," Maggs wailed. "She's famous and never been dumped."

"No, no." Bailey shook her head. "I've never been dumped because I've never had a man. I haven't had any friends either… not real ones like you were, Maggie."

Bailey hadn't realized she'd silenced the room until she looked at the two women, now silent, both with their mouths open.

Chapter 19

"YOU'RE A VIRGIN?"

"No. I had sex once, it was horrible. He was there, I was there." Bailey waved her hand about.

"Once?" Piper asked.

"Yes. I didn't enjoy it, and left while he was sleeping."

"N-no friends b-but me?" Maggie was crying again.

"I didn't tell you to make you sadder, Maggs."

"She'll be fine." Piper topped up Bailey's wine. "How come you've never had a man in your life, when you're hot, smart, and talented?"

Bailey shrugged; her head felt full of cotton wool. It was nice. The swirling thoughts had eased, and she was pleasantly mellow now.

"I didn't have time, and I never really met anyone. My grandfather had me dropped off and picked up when I attended Juilliard, and I was never left alone at any of the parties we attended later when I was performing."

"So he kept you a prisoner?" Maggie whispered.

"No. How could I be a prisoner, travelling the world? Although I did say to Joe the other day that I was inexperienced about the ways of the world because I'd never really had to do anything for myself... which just makes me sound pathetic," Bailey added.

"Joe?" Piper looked even more interested.

"I was trying to work the washing machine. He taught me."

Piper and Maggs exchanged a look that she had no idea how to interpret.

"Why did you let your granddad control you like that, Bailey?" Maggs asked her.

She'd thought about that often since she'd walked away from him. Why had she let her grandfather control every facet of her life? She was no closer to an answer yet.

"It just sort of happened, I guess, and he always told me he wanted the best for me, and I wanted to be the best pianist I could be, and to do that I didn't need distractions."

"So I need clarification here," Piper said, handing Bailey chocolate, which did actually go surprisingly well with wine. "Trips to the mall, movie nights with friends, slumber parties, and the other prerequisite teenage stuff that helps you become a well-rounded adult... supposedly."

Maggs snorted.

"You had none of that?"

Bailey shook her head.

"She never had birthday parties, either, because I would have been invited," Maggs said.

"It wasn't so bad." Bailey felt embarrassed now. "Really, I've had a great life."

"Tell me what cake you wanted as a child, and don't lie. I bet you dreamed about it like everyone else."

"Cake?"

"You know, the cake every little girl dreams of. Pink frosting, fairy dress, unicorn?"

"I don't—"

"Yes, you did, so tell us," Piper demanded.

She saw it in her head like she had once dreamed it would be. "I wanted a Mickey Mouse cake. Red and white spots and a set of black ears on the top. I saw it once, in a magazine my mother had, and it just kind of stuck with me."

"You should have had it." Maggs looked defiant. "Damn it, Bailey, you should have had it!"

"We can't have everything we want, Maggs, and I had it good, believe me. And this is about you, not me."

"What about Beau. Where was he?"

"Beau?" Piper looked at Maggs.

"Her brother. He's six years older and lives in Paris."

"He was around to start, then left to study and never really came back."

"But you talk with him, right?"

Bailey shook her head.

"What?" Piper shook her head as if to clear it. "Why not? You should be Skyping him from your laptop regularly."

She realized then how utterly pathetic she must sound in the eyes of these modern women. Bailey tried to explain how her life had been. "Practice just took up a lot of my time, so I never really got around to getting a computer. My grandfather didn't have one, and I didn't see a need for one either. Mostly I used the ones in the hotels. A lot of my time was spent travelling, doing promotions, or playing shows. When I had downtime I read books mainly. I liked not being able to read reviews and have people contact me."

"But you could have communicated regularly with Beau, Bailey?" Maggie persisted.

"I-I… no I haven't." Putting her head in her hands, she cried. "I-I never cry!"

"You should, it's totally cathartic," Piper said, thrusting tissues into her hands. "You can't beat a good cry for release. Other than sex that is, that works too."

"Gr-grandfather told me that Beau had said I was a spoilt brat and wanted nothing more to do with me. When I rang Beau to talk about it with him, he had no time for me, which confirmed it."

"Confirmed how? He may have been working, or sick… or having an off day, Bailey. I cannot believe you just called him once!" Maggs looked angry.

"I've spoken to him a few more times since then," Bailey rushed to add. "But it's stilted and both of us are uncomfortable."

"That's just bullshit, and I bet it's your grandfather who caused the rift between you," Piper added.

She tried to lighten the mood. "But I did spend my twenty-first birthday in Paris."

"Okay, so I'm not feeling sorry for you after hearing that," Maggs said. "When did you last speak to Beau?"

"I can't remember."

"Do you want to speak with him? Does he know you've run away?"

"I haven't run away!" Bailey looked at the two women. "I had an accident, and after, I just didn't want to do it anymore. The punishing schedules and living out of a suitcase. I wanted it to stop, so I walked away to have some breathing space."

"Nice," Piper said.

"Pass my laptop, Piper, it's in that red case." Maggs pointed to the small side table. Bailey watched Piper do as she was asked. Maggie got the computer out and opened the lid.

"What's Beau's full name?"

"Why?"

"Just give it to me, Bailey," Maggie said.

"Beauregard Winston Jones."

"And he lives in Paris?"

She nodded.

"What are you doing?"

"Finding him on Skype. We'll send him a friend request, and see if he replies, although he's not likely to remember me."

"Really?" The thought of seeing her brother was terrifying, and yet exciting too. "But he may not want to speak to me."

Maggs looked up briefly and shook her head. "I can't believe the girl I knew let someone steamroller her like you have."

"I didn't... not all the time. It wasn't all bad." She felt the need to defend herself.

"No, I get that, but not having a phone, or a laptop. How the hell does that even happen? Then this shit with Beau, Bailey. It's BS is what it is."

Taking a breath, she told them the rest. "He controlled my money. I-I have none."

"What?" Maggs's shriek made Piper wince. "That bastard!"

"It's complicated," Bailey said, then swallowed more wine, as she wanted to keep the mellow feeling going, if only for tonight. "But when I started performing he set up a bank account, and gave me money. I then set one up, and he paid it into that. I thought it was sorted and I had control, but it wasn't until I left I realized that wasn't the case."

"But it's your money, surely?" Piper asked.

"It is, but he won't release it to me until I return and start performing."

"The scars on your arm?" Maggs asked. "That's the accident?"

Bailey nodded.

"He's accepted!"

"What?" Bailey moved to sit beside her friend and look at the screen in her lap. "How could he do that so soon?"

"The wonders of cyberspace, sweetie."

Bailey held her breath for tense seconds, and then her brother appeared.

"Beau!"

"Bailey?"

His hair was longer, and his face more lined, but there he was. Her big, beautiful, older brother. She started crying again.

"Hey there, Beau. You probably don't remember me, but I'm Maggie Winters."

"I remember you, Maggie. You and Bailey went to school together."

"That's right. Well, your little sister has found her way to Ryker, and she's had a few wines, so go easy on her."

"What happened, Bailey? What did that bastard do to you? Jesus, look at you, you're so beautiful."

The siblings looked each other, seeing the changes the years had put on their faces.

"How long has it been since we've seen each other, Beau?" Bailey heard her friends leave the room, but didn't look up. She kept her eyes on her brother.

"Years... hell, I don't know. We talked, but even then not much, and there was so much between us."

"I'm sorry, Beau, that things got complicated between us. I never meant that to happen, but wasn't sure how to fix things."

"Me too, Bay... so sorry. I should have tried harder."

"No, I'm to blame too, I let him control me. I should have pushed harder to speak to you, but he told me some things you'd said, and then when I called you, you seemed distant."

"I'm a guy, we're distant." He made her laugh. "But I never said anything to him about you, Bailey, I promise. I missed you."

"I missed you too. I'm sorry we didn't try harder, Beau, and sorry we drifted apart."

"That's in the past now. Tell me what's going on with you, Bailey. Why are you back in Ryker Falls? Fill me in on what I've missed."

Beau's hair was darker than Bailey's. He had a square jaw, cheeks you could cut glass on, and piercing blue eyes. He'd been her idol until he left home and never returned.

"I called Mother, and Grandfather was home, about six months ago, but neither of them would talk about you, other than to say you were fine. What's the real deal?"

"I had an accident, Beau. I fell through a window. My right arm and hand were damaged."

"No one told me." He looked shattered. "I would have come, and to hell with work."

"No, I didn't need someone else looking after me, Beau."

"But my love is unconditional, Bailey. That's where I differ from him."

"I didn't know that, though."

He nodded. "I understand that, and like I said, I should have tried harder."

"I had an operation to repair the damage, it went well, but then after rehab, I didn't want to go back to playing. I'd had enough. I didn't know who I was anymore. I suddenly wanted to experience what other people did."

Her brother's face was so serious, she wanted to reach through the screen and soothe away the worry lines.

"Jesus, Bay." The breath hissed from his throat. "You should have told me. Should have let me come to you, bring you home with me."

"It's okay, Beau."

"It's not!" The words exploded through the screen. "How long?"

"How long what?" Bailey said, knowing exactly what he meant.

"How long have you felt like this? That you wanted to give it up."

Her silence was enough.

"So you've been miserable for years and couldn't find a way out?"

"Don't be dramatic, Beau. I loved what I did, I've just been feeling the restrictions he put on me lately. The accident allowed me to change things."

"Dramatic! Jesus, my baby sister has an accident, and has been living in hell, and she couldn't tell me. The one person who should always be there for her."

Bailey struggled to fight back the tears.

"Don't cry, sweetheart."

"I-I'm okay. It's the wine."

"I'm glad you found your way to Maggie. I always liked her."

"M-me too."

He talked gently until she was in control again. Telling her he loved her, and always had, and it was a wonderful feeling, to know that she had a person in her life who cared solely about her.

"Where have you been since leaving Boston, Bailey?"

"I took to the road. Moving from town to town."

"Alone?"

"Of course alone. I just told you I wanted to do that, find myself, and try and survive on my own."

"I just went cold," Beau muttered. "The thought of you taking care of yourself for the first time at your age is terrifying. I don't think you even know how to boil water."

"I do so... well I do now, anyway. It's true that it's been hard, but I've enjoyed learning things. I actually went into a bank and opened a separate account, and then transferred money into it."

"What do you mean? Why haven't you had a bank account before?"

"I had one, Beau, and thought I was in control of my money, but turns out he is."

"Bastard! Controlling, manipulative—"

"He loved me the best he could, Beau," Bailey interrupted her brother. "But his way of loving is controlling, and I just couldn't handle it anymore. Especially when Clark joined in."

"Clark?" Her brother frowned.

Bailey sighed. She needed to tell him everything; he was her brother, and deserved to know.

"My agent. The man Grandfather wanted me to marry. For a while I thought maybe... then I realized I didn't want that."

Beau swore long and loud, and Bailey found herself laughing.

"God, Bailey, I've just realized that's the first time I've heard you really laugh in years. Shall I send you a ticket so you can come to Paris, and I'll look after you?"

"I can take care of myself," Bailey said.

"Really? Is this a new thing, because from memory he kept you in a bloody glass cage."

"Which is why I have now broken out of it, Beau. I wanted to have some say in my life."

"Well hallelujah. Don't tell me you finally developed a backbone after all these years."

Bailey snorted.

"Come to Paris, and live with me."

She could do that. Go there, and Beau would watch out for her, but wasn't that moving from one support system to another? Granted, this one would be nicer, but still....

"No, I don't want you to watch out for me. I need to find myself first, Beau."

"I have absolutely no idea what that even means," her brother said, sounding frustrated.

"It means I love you, but I don't want you looking out for me until I've learned to look out for myself."

"Do you have enough money?"

"I'm working here."

"That bastard isn't allowing you any money, is he? You worked for it, and he's keeping it?"

"Yes, but I can manage. So please don't worry, and now I can Skype you."

"I wish I could hug you."

"I wish it too." Bailey swallowed. "But for now this is enough. I love you, big brother."

"I love you, Bay."

She blew him a kiss, and closed the screen. She found her friends sitting on Maggie's bed.

"You look happier," Piper said.

"I really am, thanks to you," Bailey said.

"Right. We're going out to celebrate the liberation of Bailey Jones. I'm choosing what you wear," Maggie said.

"But you're heartbroken," Bailey said.

"Kind of, but not really, so I'm ready to party now, which I know makes me sound shallow, but possibly the wine may be helping there. Tomorrow I'll be heartbroken again I'm sure."

They left the house twenty minutes later, and Bailey wasn't sure what the future held, but she knew it would have friends in it, because she now had two—plus a big brother.

Chapter 20

"ABOUT BROKE MY HEART," Jack said.

"What about broke your heart?" Joe was seated outside his bar in the street. It had been closed off for the parade and following street party. Apple Sours had set up a bar outside, and a DJ played music. He was seated with Jack, Fin, and someone called Claudia who Fin had just met. She didn't speak a word of English, but Joe was pretty sure that hadn't been the drawcard as far as Fin was concerned. The woman was stunning, especially her long legs in that short skirt.

"Bailey."

"Why did she break your heart?" Joe let his eyes move over the crowds. He was not looking for her, he assured himself.

"I saw her trying to figure out how to get the music running on my iPad at the stables. I let her go for a while, then stepped in and gave her a lesson. She's one of the hardest workers I know, but a total innocent, who has no everyday smarts. It's like she's lived in a bubble."

Joe knew what his brother meant. He'd seen her with the washing machine. Her grandfather had kept her prisoner, was the best Joe could come up with. She'd had all the trappings and no freedom. The thought made him want to get on a plane and go find the bastard.

"How's she working out in the stables?" Fin said.

"Really good. The horses love her, and she's a fast learner."

"And Buzz loves her," Joe added, still searching the crowds. "He's real picky about his women."

"Where is he?"

"I took him home. He needs a solid eight hours or he gets cranky."

"Hey, Joe."

"Hi, Angie. You having a good time?"

"I really am."

Her smile was genuine, much to his relief. It seemed she'd moved on and there were no hard feelings between them.

"A group of us are going down to the boardwalk. Do you want to come?"

"No, but thanks for the invite. You have a good time."

She lifted a hand and was soon swallowed up by the crowds.

"That was awkward," Fin said. Claudia had disappeared, so he could focus again.

"No it wasn't. We never had anything to make it awkward between us. Things are amicable."

"Amicable, my ass," Jack scoffed. "No woman likes being dumped, even if you 'never had anything.'"

"True that." Fin raised his glass.

"Speaking of Joe's woman, will you look at Bailey," Jack said.

Joe's head turned so quick at Jack's words, his neck

made a cracking sound. She was standing in a group of people behind him. Maggs and Pip were there, but it was Bailey he saw. She wore a short pink skirt with a flirty hem that he knew would kick up when she moved, and black wedges that showed off her sexy legs. Her top was white and off-the-shoulder, and hugged some serious curves. She was laughing, head thrown back. A real laugh, not the tight smiles he'd been the recipient of. Her hair was still loose, and she looked seriously hot.

"Your woman's hot, Joe."

"She's not my woman," he made himself say, but the words came out gruff.

"Sure she's not," Jack drawled. "But just so you know, if she does become your woman, I'll kill you if you hurt this one."

Joe dragged his eyes from Bailey to rest them on his brother.

"She saved my life." Jack shrugged. "Plus, she's sweet, innocent, and lost. She's also a really nice person I would hate to see hurt, because I think she may have suffered enough already in her lifetime."

"Nice words, bud, and also true." Fin raised his glass.

They both looked at Joe.

"I would never hurt Bailey."

"I figured that, but what I can't figure is why." Jack spoke, his eyes thoughtful. "There's something between you, a history that has this tension… I can't put a name on it, but it's there. Care to enlighten us?"

"No, but yes, there is history," he added.

"And?"

"And it was innocent, and she was a friend when I needed one. We lost touch after she left, and I never saw or heard from her until she returned to Ryker."

Jack studied him. "I don't remember her."

"I do," Joe said slowly as he got to his feet. "And now I'm going to talk to her."

He made his way to where Bailey stood.

"Here's my handsome cousin." Piper wrapped an arm around his waist. "Hey, Joe."

"Hey." He kissed the top of her head. "You seem happy."

"We are. Me, Maggs, and Bailey have been drinking and eating chocolate."

"Who dumped who?" Joe knew the ritual. Pip had cried all over him enough during breakups, while Jack or Luke went and got her a supply of wine and chocolate.

"Ben of the flaccid dick dumped me," Maggie said as loudly as she could.

Joe looked around, but didn't see her ex. He wouldn't mind bumping into him and giving him a lesson in manners.

"He was a loser, Maggs. A hot woman like you doesn't need someone like that in her life. You're worth ten of him."

"I love you, Joe." Maggie walked into his arms after he'd released Pip.

He hugged her hard. "He seriously doesn't deserve you, sweetheart."

"I know," she sighed. "But it still hurts."

He kissed the top of her head.

"Want to come and dance with us?"

"Sure."

Bailey hadn't looked at him yet.

"But I get to partner the pretty pianist first."

"Good move," Maggs whispered loudly, releasing him.

"And I'll take the angry redhead." Fin arrived. He then wrapped an arm around Maggs's waist and nudged her through the people.

Joe clamped his fingers around Bailey's wrist and followed.

"Joe, I don't think—"

"Don't think." He leaned in and kissed her, just a brief brush of his lips over hers.

"Wh-what are you doing?"

"Shutting you up, which will give me a chance to apologize for being an asshole earlier."

"We both behaved badly, which tells me we should keep our distance. This… you and me, it's too complicated, and I can't do complicated right now."

He'd like to do her, but kept those words to himself.

"I don't buy that. We have a connection, Bailey. You know it, just as I do."

"Maybe we once had that… but not now. We're different, Joe, and tonight I turned another corner in becoming who I want to be."

He drew her in closer, wrapping an arm around her waist and pulling her into his body. He thought she'd resist, but instead she rested a palm on his chest, leaving a few inches between them.

"What drove you round this corner?"

"Friends, and maybe two glasses of wine, but the point is I have a long way to go to become the person I want to be. I can't complicate that with… with you."

Someone bumped into her, sending her into Joe.

"We can't talk here. Let's go." Joe took her hand in his and began walking through the crowds, towing Bailey behind him. He walked around the back of the bar and let himself inside, closing and locking the door behind them.

"Piper and Maggs will wonder where I am. Plus Maggie's nursing a broken heart. I should be with her."

"He didn't break her heart, Bailey. He was a loser, and she knows it." Joe led her through the room, which was lit only by security lights. Reaching the bar, he grabbed Bailey and lifted her onto a stool.

"I can't see, Joe."

"I can, and you look seriously hot tonight."

"Joe, what are you doing? I thought you wanted to talk?"

"We'll get to that." He held her face, looking into her eyes. "Right now I really need to kiss you again."

"No." She shook her head, but leaned closer so they were only inches apart. "I don't think we should."

"Yes, you do." He kissed her softly, giving her a chance to pull back. When she didn't, he took it deeper.

"This is real, Bailey." He eased back a little. "We owe it to the people we were to pursue this."

Her fingers shook as they touched his jaw.

"I'm a mess, Joe. I've never lived like others. I'm.... I let someone else run my life for me. I don't even know the person I am or want to be, and my friends made me realize how much growing I have to do."

"Friends. I bet that feels good?"

"So good," she whispered. "I didn't realize how good until I came back here and found some."

Joe cupped his hands around her face, holding her eyes on his. "I'm not going to stop you growing as a person, Bailey. Not going to stop you from doing what you want. I simply want to get to know you, and if in the course of that I get my hands on you... well, that would work too."

Her giggle was sweet. She then traced the line of his cheekbone tentatively, before moving to his hair, where her fingers stroked. Joe was already hard with wanting her; her touch ignited him further.

"I don't know how to do this."

"This being?"

"Flirting, interacting, being a woman with a man she feels something for."

His heart kicked at her words.

"You'll learn, and if you keep touching me, that education will come sooner than you expected."

"I know what happens, the sex part, and yes, I've done it once. But I wasn't very good at it."

"How did we jump from flirting and interacting to sex?" Not that he minded.

"Because the wine has loosened me up, and because when I'm around you I feel this ache deep inside me, which tells me I want you, Joe."

"I have that ache too."

"But it's not right. We're strangers now, we can't do this."

"We could never be strangers." He kissed the side of her jaw. "You're a part of me, Bailey Jones, and you always have been."

"I shouldn't want this, Joe."

"This being?"

"You. Your lips on mine," she whispered the words against his mouth.

He slid his hands up the outside of her thighs and stepped between her legs, closing the distance. Their kiss was hot and wet, and in seconds he was too far gone to pull back, and expected she was too. She was like kryptonite to Joe. The feel and smell of her, the smooth texture of her skin beneath his hands, it all drove him crazy. He wanted her with a desperation that had built steadily since he'd seen her in the grocery store, and he was done fighting.

Joe kissed the line of her jaw while his hand stroked her thigh, moving slowly up her body. Teasing the lines of her ribs, he found what he sought next. Her breast was the perfect size for his hand, the nipple hard and pressing against the sheer cup that restrained it.

"I want to see you, Bailey. All of you."

Chapter 21

HE WAS close enough that Bailey could see his features clearly. Behind them the music from the street party was loud, and only the front of the bar kept them from the hundreds who were out there enjoying it. Bailey's heart thumped, her breasts felt full, and Joe's hand felt so good cupping one. He stroked her nipple, and her breath grew choppy.

"Take off your top, Bailey."

Her fingers fumbled as she drew it over her head. This was Joe, she reminded herself. Her Joe, one of the few people she had ever loved in her lifetime.

"You're beautiful," he rasped.

Bailey could do nothing to stop the moan as his finger traced the satin edge of her bra. He then picked up her locket. The gold oval had been a gift from her father when she was five, it now held something special that she'd carried close for years.

"Who gave you this?"

"My father."

Releasing it he then lowered a satin bra strap, exposing her nipple.

"Joe," Bailey whispered as her body arched into his.

"Right here."

He licked her then, one hot stroke from his wet tongue over her nipple, and her body shuddered. He steadied her, and then continued to caress her with his mouth. Bailey could hear the sighs and moans she made, but could do nothing except hold on as he continued the sensual torture. By the time he'd moved to the other breast, she was wet and aching.

His hand began moving too, tracing the edge of her panties. He stood between her legs, his body holding her thighs open, exposing her, and she could do nothing to stop him easing a finger under the elastic and touching the wet heat… not that she wanted to.

"Oh Lord, Joe."

"That's it, baby, just feel."

He kissed her as his finger stroked the soft folds. He found the tight bud between her thighs, and the tension inside Bailey tightened to an almost unbearable point. He then took her nipple and pushed a finger deep inside her. She came apart in a shuddering climax.

"I… I've never experienced anything like that."

"Good," he whispered against her lips. "I want to be the first."

Bailey wanted to touch him, make him feel what she was. She opened his shirt, and slid her hands inside. Joe moaned as she explored his chest, tracing each muscle and rib. She'd never been this close to a man before. So close she felt a part of him.

"You have a lovely chest, Joe." Her nail scraped a nipple, and the breath hissed from his throat, so she did it again.

"So good," he whispered. "Your touch is exquisite, Bailey."

She leaned forward and kissed him. His breathing quickened, so she licked him.

"I want you now, Bailey. Tell me you want this too?"

"Yes, I want it, Joe."

He stepped back, and she watched as he pulled out his wallet and removed a condom. He unbuttoned his jeans, and sheathed himself.

This wasn't like last time, Bailey knew. That had been a slaking of lust on the man's part, and curiosity on hers. This was hot, sensual, and achingly sweet. Feeling Joe's skin, having his hands and mouth on her, it was beyond words.

He stepped between her spread thighs again, and she felt him there at her entrance, the thick, hard length of him moving slowly forward. Their gazes caught and held as he eased inside her. His kiss was slow, their lips clinging, as he took her with a slow, deep thrust.

"Are you okay?" His arms held her tight.

She nodded, her head burrowed into his neck. She felt stretched, and possessed. She'd never experienced something like this before, and because it was Joe, it was so much more, almost too much emotion to handle.

"Bailey?"

"I'm okay, please don't stop."

He lifted her face to meet his. "Never."

He started to move, his rhythm slow at first, helping her adjust. The feel of his body leaving and entering hers tore a moan from her lips. She wrapped her legs around his waist and held on.

"Let go for me again, baby."

She did with another moan, and it was deeper and

more shattering than the last time. It robbed her breath and made her light-headed. Joe followed.

He stayed there, between her legs, holding her against his body, as if she was the most precious woman in the world. One hand on her head, the other wrapped around her.

"Are you all right, Bailey? I didn't hurt you?"

"No. It was wonderful."

He snorted. "It was beyond wonderful, and yet I knew it would be with you. Only you have ever been able to make me feel things more intensely than anyone else."

"It's the same for me."

His kiss was so sweet it made tears sting in her eyes. Leaving her briefly, she heard him go to the bathroom, and Bailey tidied herself and followed.

"We have to go back now, or they'll come looking for us, Joe."

"I know, but tomorrow we talk, Bailey."

She nodded. "Yes, I want to talk now. There is so much to say. I-I spoke to Beau tonight."

"And you haven't for a while?"

She nodded. "Maggie helped me Skype him."

"Go, Maggs."

She laughed, and leaned into him. He held her close, and Bailey was pretty sure she'd never been happier than she was right at that moment.

He unlocked the door and they stepped outside.

"Bailey?"

She looked at the man standing there. Tall, smooth, and dressed in a suit that cost more than an average family's weekly wage. Her heart sank.

"Clark?"

"Bailey, who is this?" She felt Joe's eyes on her.

"I'm her fiancé."

...

Sweat dripped off the end of Joe's nose as he bent to tie his lace. The ball hit him in the head.

"Fuck! Time out already!" he roared, looking at Luke, who was smirking, which told Joe he was the thrower.

"You're testy today. Don't you think he's testy?" Jack said from the sideline where he was watching with Buzz, who was leaning on his legs, no doubt cutting off the circulation with his bulk. His side was better, but it still ached, and he still needed to take things easy.

Joe ignored his brothers and Fin, who was also dripping sweat and had a smirk on his face.

Three days ago he'd had the best sex of his life with Bailey. *Not sex, Joe, we made hot, incredibly sweet love.* He'd never felt closer to anyone than he had in that moment. He'd thought this was it, the one, the moment when his life changed. But in fact she'd be hiding a fiancé. Which just went to show what a fool he was to believe all her BS about Angie, and how hurt she was he'd kissed her and still supposedly been in a relationship.

Fucking woman! He absolutely refused to acknowledge the pain in his chest as anything but a stitch. He did not care about that lying, cheating woman.

"He's been dark for three days, and hiding from everyone. Even Pip, who he usually talks to, hasn't seen him."

"I'm not dark, and I have not been hiding, I've been working," Joe gritted out between his teeth. To make matters worse, he didn't know where his father was, and no one had been arrested for shooting Jack. He was edgy, there was no other word for it. Shit was pissing him off, and that wasn't a good thing, because he couldn't sleep. Then there'd been the dream he'd had about Bailey last night, which had aroused him to the point of pain. "You fuckers know what that is, right?"

His words were greeted by a series of whoops.

"Work? I've heard the word a time or two," Luke needled him.

They'd been shooting hoops for an hour, and he was about done. In fact, he was about done on a few things. Like why the hell Bailey hadn't left town yet.

His family had tried to talk to him, but he'd been too busy, and yes... he was avoiding them. But he knew Bailey was still working for Jack, because his brother never shut up about her!

"Real testy," Luke drawled.

"I'll show testy, you little shit." Joe bounced the ball toward his brother, who dodged, and stole it from him.

"Slow and testy," Jack said as they watched Luke jog to the hoop and throw the ball up. Of course it went through.

"I've been working hard," Joe snarled.

They were at the outdoor courts down by the sea, where they came as often as they could. Looking at the empty space that he wanted for a rec center, he wondered if he'd succeed in getting the locals on side at the upcoming town meeting. With that thought came the memory of his conversation with Bailey. *We would have used it back then, and it would have been warm and dry, and had adults there who maybe could have helped you and your brothers, Joe.*

"It's a woman. He gets this way when he's involved. All moody and consumed."

"The hell I do." Joe glared at Luke.

"It's not Angie, because I know that's done," Fin mused, scratching the chin Joe wanted to plant his fist in.

"It's Bailey, because Pip said she's all sad and quiet too, and has been since the parade and street party," Jack said. "We're just not sure why."

"I'm sure her fiancé will cheer her up!" Joe hadn't meant to roar, but he had anyway.

"They're not engaged," Jack said calmly.

"Right. That's why he introduced himself as her fiancé, is it? Because he's not?"

Joe started pacing, dribbling the ball backward and forward as he worked out more of the rage and hurt he thought he'd just eradicated from his body. Yes, it was hurt. She'd sucked him in, and he'd fallen for it. Bailey had misled him. Bailey, of all people. The one person he'd believed in unconditionally.

"I can explain, Joe." What a laugh. She'd followed him when he'd stalked away that night, firing more lies at him until he'd turned on her and said he didn't want to hear them. He'd thought her different, but she wasn't. Joe refused to acknowledge the pain his words had obviously caused her. She'd deserved it.

"Maggie told Piper, Bailey was upset but wouldn't talk about that night, or the new guy who'd arrived. But she thought him being here and Joe suddenly hibernating were connected."

"What new guy?" Fin asked.

"The new guy. Classy Clark of the Dior suits and handmade Italian loafers," Jack added.

"I've been on three ten-hour shifts, so maybe I haven't seen him yet."

"Maybe. Anyway," Jack continued, much to Joe's distress, "Pip went round to Maggie's last night and sat on her."

"Pip sat on Bailey?" Fin asked Jack, who nodded. "My eyes just crossed at that vision."

"Gross, that's my cousin, Fin."

"Not my cousin, though." The park ranger had his eyes closed as if savoring the vision.

"The point here is that he, Classy Clark, was Bailey's

fiancé, according to Pip. But she broke it off, and he won't accept her answer."

Joe stopped walking, clutching the ball to his chest. He'd never once doubted the man was her fiancé, because... shit, because he'd got in so deep so quick with her, he'd panicked.

"Did Pip believe her?" Joe said.

Jack look confused. "Of course. Bailey would never lie to someone she cares about."

"How could you know that, when you've only known her briefly?"

Jack shrugged, then winced as his side pulled. The gesture brought back just how close Joe had come to losing him. They better catch the culprit soon, or he was starting his own investigation.

"Bailey's just one of them," Jack said.

"One of what?"

"Someone you trust instinctively. She's sweet, and innocent as a baby lamb, and wouldn't hurt a fly. Hell, the other day I watched her spend twenty minutes fishing a moth out of a puddle it had fallen into. She then put it on a piece of wood to dry out. Didn't have the heart to tell her it wouldn't survive. She's one of the good ones, Joe. You have to know that surely, especially considering this history between you?"

Joe walked away slowly, dribbling the ball. Did he know that? Was he so caught up in emotion that he'd forgotten that Bailey was one of the good ones? Had he misjudged her without even giving her a chance to explain, because he was scared?

"She told me he wasn't her fiancé and I didn't believe her." He said the words to the wall he now faced. The men behind him heard.

"Why?" Luke's voice reached him, so Joe made himself turn to face him.

"Because... ah hell, because she's special, and always has been to me. The thought of her lying to me made me go little crazy and irrational."

"What a dickhead." Jack threw the ball at Joe, and winced. Buzz barked and charged at him.

"For an intelligent man, you keep behaving like an idiot. Jesus, Joe. Anyone can see that woman's a good one," Luke added, looking disgusted.

He looked at his brothers, who were shaking their heads. Dropping to his haunches, he gave Buzz a good scratch.

"You're lucky he's too dumb to understand, or he'd be giving you hell too," Jack said. "That dog loves Bailey."

"If I may interject, I know you said there's shit between you and Bailey—how about you come clean and tell us about it now?" Fin said.

"It's complicated."

"Okay, there's a story there, like I said, and now's as good a time as any to tell it. Then we can work out a plan for you to grovel."

Chapter 22

FOR TWO DAYS Bailey felt as if someone had taken a club and battered her heart. It was bruised and empty. She'd known pain when she left Ryker all those years ago, but this was different, more intense. By day three, she was done hurting, and woke angry—a much better emotion. How dare Joe Trainer treat her like he had. He hadn't given her a chance to explain about Clark. He'd simply wanted to believe her in the wrong.

They'd made love, and she'd never experienced such emotion, and to have that dashed in cold water immediately after had been shattering.

She'd given Clark a piece of her mind too, which had shocked him, and told him to take himself out of Ryker Falls and not return. She also told him to tell her grandfather she was not coming back anytime soon.

According to Maggie, Clark hadn't left. He'd rented a room at the lodge. She hadn't seen him, and had no plans to. He'd tried to talk to her though, calling at the house, but she'd told Maggs to send him away. She'd seen him in town yesterday, but hid in the tea shop until he passed.

Miss Marla had then insisted on the blindfold test, which she'd failed, but still, it had kept her busy.

Working with Jack kept her sane, and she'd made sure to arrive and leave when Joe wasn't around. If she heard a car, she ducked in the tack room, or a stall. Her newfound strength was tentative at best, she had no wish to test it with exposure to Joe. Of course, this was his town, and she would see him again soon, but not now—not yet.

Today was Saturday. Maggs had gone to open the gallery, and Bailey had decided to stay in bed. She had a cup of coffee, toast, and one of Maggs's books. It was bliss. Her body ached from the work at the stables, but it was a good ache, because she had pushed herself hard. A worthy ache, she thought. She'd put up a temporary wall around the crack in her heart, and so far it was holding—as long as she kept her anger close, and didn't see Joe.

The knock on her front door was loud. Four sharp raps. Throwing back the covers, she pulled on her robe and went to answer it. Peeking out, she saw the bright eyes of Mr. Goldhirsh.

"We can give you six minutes, Bailey. Hustle now, the rest are waiting for us at the end of the road."

Bailey opened the door a bit wider and looked to where he was pointing. She saw a group of people all moving from foot to foot, but not going anywhere.

"Ah... I'm not quite sure I follow."

"Walking club," he said. "Remember we discussed it when you arrived. I think it's time for you to start exercising now, you've been here a few weeks. Now get moving, young lady, we have to be on our way before the sun gets too high. Some of the oldies are a bit fragile."

"B-but I get exercise."

"Not enough, now move it. This will clear your head."

"How do you know my head needs clearing?"

"Piper told me."

She'd get hers when they next met, Bailey thought, as she watched Mr. Goldhirsh leave, striding down the path pumping his arms.

"But I wanted to stay in bed," Bailey muttered, running to her room. Digging through the drawers, she found her stretchy exercise pants and sports top, which were new because she'd rarely worn them. Pulling on underwear so fast she ended up hopping across the room and nearly face-planting into the bed, Bailey was dressed in two minutes. A glance in the mirror showed hair all over the place, so she found a band and pulled it back. Running to the bathroom, she cleaned her teeth and washed her face.

"Running shoes!" She ran back to the bedroom and found her sneakers. Seconds later she was out the door.

"Of course, I could have just been brave and said no," she muttered, hurrying down the path and along the road to where the group stood. She was the youngest by at least ten years.

"Morning!" everyone greeted her with a sunny smile. Most wore caps and shirts with the words Ryker Roadies on them.

"Right, let's be off then!" Mr. Goldhirst announced. He lifted a whistle to his lips and blew two sharp bursts. Everyone fell into two lines, and started walking.

What the hell have I got myself into?

She counted twenty people. She was paired with Miss Sarah and Mrs. Lowens, who as it turned out knew every-one, and everything about everyone.

"Bernie's had his second hip replaced and came back stronger, and Maddie has just had her tenth grandchild. Delivered the wee boy herself, as the husband's useless."

Bailey must have issued the appropriate response, as Mrs. Lowens continued.

"Are you still practicing each day, Bailey?"

"No, Miss Sarah, I'm taking a break."

"Seems a shame. Perhaps Joe would let you use the piano?"

She wasn't going there, so she made a noise that neither agreed nor disagreed.

"It's important to keep those fingers limber, dear."

"Yes, ma'am."

"That's enough now, Sarah, our Bailey is looking quite peaky." Miss Marla appeared before her, walking backward of all things, looking fresh and neat. Bailey wanted to bare her teeth. "Deep breaths now, dear."

"The youth of today have no stamina," Mrs. Lowens stated from up ahead.

Bailey was wilting, and they'd only been walking fifteen minutes, but she was damned if she was stopping now.

A younger woman dropped to Bailey's other side when she slipped back, the Robbins sisters powering on ahead. She thought briefly about slowing, then simply turning and running back to the house, but wasn't entirely sure they wouldn't come after her.

"How you doing?"

"F-fine," Bailey panted.

"Takes a few times to get used to it, but you'll feel better for it. I've been doing this for a year now, and wouldn't miss it for anything. My husband says it's improved our sex life."

Luckily, Bailey didn't have any water in her mouth, or she'd have spat it out. She choked though, which was surprising because there wasn't a drop of saliva left in there.

"Name's Jane."

"Bailey," she wheezed.

"I heard you play twice now, you're good."

"Thanks."

"My husband heard you in New York. His aunt dragged him to the concert, but he said he was glad he went."

"Oh... ah, I'm glad your husband enjoyed the concert, but equally glad that you've enjoyed hearing me play at A.S." It was the truth, actually. It had always been about the music for Bailey, and giving people an experience they remembered.

"I hope to hear more of you."

Not happening, Bailey thought as Joe stepped back inside her head. She was not playing there again.

Jane talked for a while more, then others dropped in when she sped up, and on it went until they'd been walking an hour. Bailey's shirt clung to her, and her face was slick with sweat when finally they reached the main street of Ryker. She was the runt of the herd, no doubting that. The lame gazelle who the others came back to check on. It was pathetic, and she was disgusted with herself.

That was changing now too. She'd get fit if it killed her... which was a possibility if she did it with these people.

"Right now, dear. We will all have a nice breakfast at Phil's place."

Bailey looked at the Robbins sisters, who were now standing before her. They looked fresh, and not red-faced. Clothes still immaculate on their trim figures. Sneakers white with no scuff marks.

"We can have coffee now?"

"Yes, and you did well, my dear. It's never easy, especially as we've been doing this for many years now. But given time, you'll be just like us."

"W-we're done?" Bailey tried not to let the elation show too much.

Mr. Goldhirsh patted Bailey's shoulder and pulled out his whistle. He gave a sharp blow, which made her wince, but everyone else relax. They then all filed into Phil's.

"I'll be right in," she said. When she was sure they'd all gone, Bailey bent at the waist and braced her hands on her hips. "Mother of God, I'm out of shape."

"I'd have to disagree with that."

The deep words had her snapping upright. Turning, she found Joe Trainer behind her. His eyes were doing a leisurely study up and down her body, heating her more, if that was possible, which Bailey reminded herself it was not. He was nothing to her. She did not think he looked like sin standing there, hands at his sides, in a white shirt, sleeves rolled, top buttons undone, worn jeans, and sneakers.

"Go away."

"I just want to talk, Bailey."

"No."

"Remember when you didn't believe me about Angie? Isn't this the same thing?"

"No, it's not, and I don't want to talk."

He was below her, so their eyes were almost level. *Walk away, Bailey. Place one foot in front of the other and leave.*

"Sure it is. I reacted to what Chip said because it hurt to think you'd made love to me while engaged to him."

"Clark!" Bailey snapped. "And you should have known that I wouldn't behave that way."

"Like you knew me?"

Bailey remained silent.

"You didn't give me a chance to explain about Angie, Bailey, just like I didn't let you explain."

She battled down the guilt, because he was right, but she wasn't acknowledging that.

"This was different. We...." Bailey couldn't say the words out loud.

"Had the best, mind-blowing—"

"Stop!" Bailey hissed, looking left and right. "You can't talk like that out here where anyone could hear you."

"Admit that you misjudged me as I misjudged you, then."

"We're not children anymore, Joe. This entire situation between us is out of control. We should not have done what we did, and this discussion is over."

"And you like to be in control, don't you? Because for so long you weren't."

Bailey didn't answer him, but they both knew his words were right.

"Don't try and analyze me, Joe."

"I'm not, I'm saying that I understand, and...." He blew out a breath. "I just want to talk, Bailey. No more misunderstandings. Just you and me, and we clear the air between us."

She looked down at the toe of her sneaker.

"This is uncharted territory for me too, Bailey. What I experience and feel for you is totally foreign. I reacted like any man would when Chet appeared and declared himself your fiancé."

"Clark!"

JOE WATCHED as Bailey exhaled slowly. "Why do you believe me now?"

"My siblings bashed it into my head."

"Piper," she said. "She sat on me until I came clean."

"I know. Fin said it was a vision that he'll carry with him for some time."

"Stop that!"

"What?" Joe gave her an innocent look, then swept his eyes over her body. Those exercise clothes really did something for her. Especially her butt.

Her eyes went from right to left again. "Y-you were...."

"Totally checking you out?" he added. "Sorry... not sorry." He gave her a slow smile. His black mood of the last few days had lifted just seeing her. He wasn't about to examine that too deeply. "You been walking with the Ryker Roadies?"

She nodded. "I wasn't given a choice."

He laughed. "Yeah, Mr. Goldhirsh can be persuasive when he wants. But it will be good for, you obviously need to get in shape."

"Will you stop," Bailey hissed.

He let his eyes run over her again. "I've tried, but it's not working."

"What's not working?"

"Me not wanting you, it's not working. Even after two days of anger and one of self-reflection, I still do."

"I can't believe you just said that right here on the street."

"I learned long ago to seize the moment. I saw you all hot and sweaty, then you bent over in front of me——"

"I didn't know you were there!"

He wanted to laugh at her agitation. She looked cute all hot and messed up. Joe was keeping it light, instead of following through with his instinct to grab her and ravish her in the street. She hadn't run away, so he thought she was coming round to accepting his apology. He hoped so, because he'd been miserable the last few days.

"Aww, now that's a shame, I thought you were putting on a show just for me," he teased her.

Her hair was pulled back in a tail that was off-center. Her shirt clung to her and had damp patches, her exercise pants were like a second skin, and he thought she looked sexy as hell. He also remembered the naked parts of her he'd seen, and what it felt like to sink deep inside her wet heat.

"Who'd have thought it, the prissy piano player looking all hot and messy," Joe drawled as he battled with the lust raging through him.

"I'm not prissy."

"Sure you are, that just adds to your hotness."

"I'm sure that should be insulting. I'm equally sure I shouldn't want to stand here talking like this with you. Especially as I'm not sure I forgive you."

"But you do, because whatever the hell this chemistry is, it's riding you too. Especially now we both know how good it is between us when we give in to it."

Her face was already flushed, but it deepened.

"I'm not used to this." She looked around her again. Nervous, yes, but he also thought excited. "I've never done this before, Joe. The laughing, and innuendos, the talk. I don't get it."

"You're a natural," Joe said gently. "But right now I have to get back to the bar and do inventory for tonight. Otherwise, I'll give in to the impulse and drag you into the nearest dark corner and have my wicked way with you."

Her eyes looked left and right again. "You shouldn't be talking like that, not here on the street. Especially as you're on the town council."

"You make me think bad thoughts." He shrugged. "I can't help it if you do it for me."

She let out a strangled moan.

"So, we good?" He moved closer, and reached up to tug on a damp strand of hair. "I'm really sorry, Bailey. More than I can say, for the way I behaved. It's not like me to react without facts, but you have me all over the place."

"But—"

"How is it I know what you're thinking?" Joe tugged her face closer.

"What am I thinking?"

"No more misunderstandings. From now we listen to each other, and ask questions."

She nodded. "But, Joe, I don't know where this can go."

"Me either, but it will be fun finding out."

He kissed her, right there on the street, and hoped Clark saw it.

"Bye."

He watched her walk away, and sighed. The woman had him tied in knots, and this was a problem because A, he couldn't concentrate for thinking about her, which B, pissed him off because that messed with his work schedule, which was totally unacceptable and led to C, he had to get Bailey back into his arms, and hopefully bed, ASAP.

Chapter 23

"SO LOOK AT YOU," Piper said, handing Bailey her coffee. She was in Phil's for dinner. Maggie was working, and then going to the town hall for a meeting, so she'd decided to treat herself.

"What?" Piper looked down at her sundress.

"You look fit, and healthy. You have spunk in your step, and just yesterday I heard you tell Jack to pull his head out of his ass. I like it."

Bailey returned the high five before Piper walked away to serve another customer. She had changed. In the weeks she'd been back in Ryker, she'd made inroads into becoming the woman she wanted to be.

Peace had been restored between her and Joe, and while she'd not slept with him again, he occasionally caught her when she wasn't looking and dragged her into the nearest isolated space and kissed her senseless. It was like some kind of evil mating ritual that left her feeling hot and edgy. She loved it.

But she wasn't lowering her guard enough to get physical with him again yet. Bailey had stuff to work through, and he messed with her ability to do that.

"I just want to talk, Bailey."

Clark slid onto the stool next to hers. He was tall, with smooth good looks, although on closer inspection, Bailey thought he looked a little dog-eared. His hair needed a trim, and he had a shadow on his jaw from not shaving. Which was pretty shocking, considering the man she'd known never left the house looking anything but immaculate. He also wore jeans and a shirt. Bailey couldn't remember seeing him in jeans before.

"Go home, Clark. I can't imagine what is still keeping you here. I don't want to perform again, nor do I want to go back to Boston or the control my grandfather had over me. Go back to your clients."

"You've changed." His brown eyes studied her. "You look good... happy."

"I am, and I'm also getting to know the person I can be, Clark. I can't return to what I was. That's no longer a fit for me."

"What'll it be?" Piper appeared to serve Clark. She wore a fierce frown.

"Pip, it's okay." Bailey patted the hand her friend braced on the counter to make herself look intimidating.

"It better be, or I'm personally running him out of town."

"Just black coffee, thanks."

Clark's eyes followed Piper as she went to fill his order.

"You have friends here, Bailey. Protective friends."

"I never had them before."

"Friends?" He sounded surprised.

"Maggie, you've met her."

"The fierce redhead who said she'd turn me into a eunuch if I upset you?"

"That's her." Bailey smiled. "When I lived here, she was a friend. I never made any more when I left. Acquaintances, not friends."

He sipped the coffee Piper placed before him with another scowl.

"I'm not your enemy, Bailey, and I never wanted to be."

She sighed. "I know that, and also that we're both just products of my grandfather. He's a master manipulator, Clark."

"Your grandfather only wants what is best for you. I thought that was coming back to Boston, and performing again."

"It's not. I don't want that anymore. I did enjoy it, but not now. Now I need to do things for myself, Clark."

"Why did you never tell me you were unhappy, Bailey? You were always so calm and composed; not once did I see you any different."

"I was calm and composed, but also unhappy. To be fair, I didn't realize how unhappy until I had the accident. I had time to think then."

"I'm sorry that you didn't feel you could talk to me about it, but of course our disastrous engagement played a part in that."

Bailey looked at Clark. He was a good man, just not the man for her.

"We should never have allowed him to talk us into that either."

He shook his head. "No, but I got swept up in his plans, and for that I'm sorry, because you deserved more."

"*We* deserved more, Clark."

"We're closing in five," Piper said. "Then heading to the meeting. You want to come, Bailey?" She didn't include Clark in the invitation.

"That woman's terrifying."

"She's wonderful," Bailey said, getting to her feet. "And everything I want to grow up to be."

He laughed at that, and Bailey thought it suited him. In Boston, he'd been serious whenever they were together.

"Mind if I tag along?"

"Why haven't you left, Clark?"

He stood and dropped money on the counter. "Actually, I'm not entirely sure, but for the first time in a while, I feel as if my stress levels have reduced. I even went for a walk yesterday. A strange gray-haired man accompanied me, and we discussed poetry. Very odd."

Bailey laughed this time. "Don't let him con you into anything, he excels at that."

"GO GET 'EM."

"Yeah, thanks." Joe slapped hands with his brothers as they all entered the town hall. It was already full, and he nodded and smiled as he walked down the aisle, leaving his brothers to take their seats.

"You're all over this, bud."

He gripped Fin's hand briefly, and then moved on.

"We're proud of you, Joe, don't forget that."

"Thanks, Miss Sarah, Miss Marla."

"'To begin, begin,' Joe."

"I'm guessing seeing as Wordsworth's on your mind at the moment, this is from him, right?" he said to Miss Marla.

She nodded and blew him a kiss. Joe moved on. They were here for him, and that thought was a humbling, if terrifying one. What if he messed up? What if he got up there and froze while delivering his speech? *Shut it down, Joe. You got this.*

He climbed up to the stage, and took his place beside Mayor Gripper, Mary Howard, Mr. Goldhirsh, and the other council members. He'd run because the younger proprietors in Ryker Falls felt they didn't have a voice, and decided he should be the one to speak for them. He hadn't wanted the job, but he'd taken it. Mary Howard had fought his election every step of the way, but she'd failed, so here he sat.

Running his eyes over the people seated in the hall, he knew most of them. Ryker had a growing population, so he didn't know everyone like he once had. Most of the work here was seasonal, except for the school and hospital, fire and ranger stations, but the nearest big town was only ninety minutes away, so some new residents commuted.

"You're late!"

"No, he's not, and you can button up that mouth of yours, Mary Howard, as no one wants to hear any more of your venom."

Mr. Goldhirsh winked at Joe after he'd spoken, and while he appreciated the support, he didn't want the elderly man in the woman's firing line. The Howards were wealthy, and had been in Ryker since the beginning. They believed they had rights far and above everyone else. Add to that the bad blood between Joe and them, and you had a nice little volatile cocktail going on.

Mary Howard still held Joe accountable for the mayhem he'd created—with help from her son—when he'd been one hell of a bad bastard. Unlike some of the other locals, she wasn't about to change that viewpoint anytime soon.

Mayor Gripper was reading his notes and hadn't heard a thing, because he couldn't focus on more than one task at once. Not overly tall, the mayor tried to hide that by wearing hats. It didn't work, but people didn't tell him that.

He was an eccentric soul who everyone liked, so they kept him in office, and his councilors kept him on track. Tonight he'd dressed for the occasion in salmon-colored fitted trousers, and a salmon-and-gray checked shirt. For some reason he could get away with dressing like this. If Joe tried it, he'd be laughed out of town.

"If I may have your attention, please."

Joe looked over the crowd. The place was full, with some people even standing at the rear.

The hum of voices stopped. The mayor then tapped the mic, as he always did. It shrieked, again as it always did, and everybody winced.

"We are assembled this evening to discuss the board-walk, and proposal of a recreation center down there." He adjusted his glasses and looked down at his notes. "This will be a facility to benefit the residents of Ryker Falls and the tourists."

Mary Howard snorted. She wasn't for the proposal; in fact, unless it was something she came up with, she vetoed it. They usually outvoted her, and the only reason she still sat on the council was because of her core group of buddies who got her back in.

"It will be aesthetically pleasing, and designed by the local architecture firm of Grey and Hinders. The costs are outlined in the handouts you received upon entering. We will be fundraising also, to assist with this cost."

"I object!"

Joe watched one of Mary Howard's cronies raise her hand.

"I haven't opened it to the floor yet, Penelope, so you'll have to wait."

The woman lowered her hand, and Joe knew what followed was going to be a shit fight. Some locals didn't want change, some did. Some wanted money spent on other things, others didn't.

"Joe, as this is your baby, you stand up and explain why you think it will benefit the town of Ryker."

He'd written notes, and memorized them, but he didn't need them now. This was a passion project for him. Had there been a rec center, or somewhere he and his siblings could have gone as children, then maybe... just maybe their lives would have been easier. Ryker was growing, and with it more families with young children arrived. They needed a focus, and he wanted to give it to them.

He climbed to his feet, moved to the edge of the stage, and looked at the people. He found her then, Bailey, wedged between Piper and Clark. He saw the nod, and smile of encouragement she gave him, and suddenly he felt stronger.

"I was a wild child," Joe said. "Trouble was something I relished because that was the only way I could get attention."

Chapter 24

BAILEY COULDN'T TAKE her eyes from Joe. He stood up there, confident, eyes connecting with people as he told them why he believed the rec center was important for the community.

"I had no one to turn to, and neither did my brothers."

Bailey found Luke and Jack, seated across from her. Both looked calm as they watched and listened to their brother.

"He's good," Clark whispered to Bailey. "I'm sorry I told him we were engaged."

She waved him to silence, not wanting to miss a word of Joe's speech. The man before her was so far removed from the angry young boy he'd once been. Pride nearly choked her.

He spoke from the heart, and she felt it. He had everyone right there with him. He spoke of budgets lastly, and his vision for what the center would look like and be used for. "It would," Joe said, "benefit everyone."

"Excellent, Joe." The mayor got to his feet again as

everyone clapped after Joe's speech. "Now, we will open it to the floor."

There were plenty of people for Joe's proposal, yet there were plenty against it too, starting with Mary Howard.

"It's a waste of money, and I for one have no wish for these kinds of adolescents to have a place to congregate and plan what mayhem they will wreak on the innocent tourists and residents of Ryker Falls."

Bitch, Bailey thought.

"She seems a pleasant sort," Clark whispered in her ear. "There's always one in every town who would fight change even if it was for the better."

"She hates Joe."

"Ah, well that makes more sense then. She's doubly committed to making sure he fails."

She was. She had plenty of supporters too, and there was no doubting she had whipped them up.

"I run a business, I don't want those delinquents causing trouble!" She couldn't see the face of the man who spoke. But the murmurs following his words told her he had support.

"It won't be just for those children who are without parental support or going through a rough patch," Joe said calmly. "It will be for all children. We will run weekend events, like concerts."

"Why would other children need or want a place like that, where they will come in contact with those types of kids? No way I want my children learning to hot wire a car!"

"It will be used for other things, Mr. Tailor. There will be a gymnasium, and we are hoping to get indoor swimming facilities eventually. There will be programs for school holidays——"

"Parents should care for their children, not strangers!"

"But there are many families who need a double income. Often, both mother and father have to work," Joe said in that same steady tone. "This would allow those parents peace of mind that their child is being cared for in a stable, secure environment while they are working."

"My children are well behaved and have no need of any rec center, as they amuse themselves," a woman said. "It's a waste of our money."

Bailey watched Joe's hand curl into a fist. He was getting riled, his patience nearly out. Getting to her feet, she raised her hand to speak.

"Go ahead." He nodded to her, his eyes steady on her face.

"I-I was raised in this town, and while some of you will believe I have no reason to be involved in this discussion I believe differently." She spoke to Joe, because if she was looking at him she wouldn't give in to the panic clawing at her throat. "While I was here, I was often lonely and confused. I would have loved a place to go like the rec center. A place to feel part of something, and be with others my age. I would have loved to have things to do, and adults who showed interest in me. I did not go without the material things, but what I really craved was support and friendship."

She sucked in a deep breath, and gripped Piper's fingers tight, grateful for her new friend's support.

"It's not just children who are going down the wrong path, and failing at school who need this center. There are plenty of straight-A students, who would use it too. A place to play, a place to be a child. Add music to the mix, and I assure you it will be a place that attracts a great deal of interest for a diverse group of children. Thank you."

Bailey sat, and let Piper wrap an arm around her

shoulders and hug her. Clark patted her hand. She was shaking, but she felt good. She'd spoken what was in her heart and that was a rare thing for Bailey. Usually she swallowed those thoughts back down.

The mayor called the discussions to a halt ten minutes later, and a vote was called. Minutes later, it was confirmed that Joe would get his rec center. After saying goodbye to Piper, who had a date, she and Clark headed out of the hall, and into the cool night air. It felt good after the heat and tension inside.

"You were amazing, standing up there like that and speaking of your childhood. I never knew things were hard for you, Bailey. We never really talked about each other, did we?"

"No, but it's okay, Clark. I think we'll be better friends than husband and wife."

His smile was wry. "I think you could be right. Will you let me buy you a drink?"

"Not tonight, but thanks. I worked today, and I'm tired."

"I still can't get over the great Bailey Jones working in a stable."

"Neither can I. When are you leaving?"

"I'm not sure yet, but I'll let you know when I decide."

He walked off toward Apple Sours, and Bailey thought even his walk was different now. Looser, and that made no sense. *It's this place*, she thought, following behind him slowly. She walked down the street, listening to the conversations taking place around her.

"You had no right to speak as you did in there!" Mary Howard caught her. Her face was tight with anger as she grabbed Bailey's arm.

"I have every right to speak as I like, Mrs. Howard, just as you do. That's the wonderful thing about democracy.

Now please remove your fingers from my arm so I can leave."

"Just because you're some hoity-toity piano player doesn't mean you're special. And throwing your lot in with that piece of filth just confirms to me what type of woman you really are."

"Oh hell no, you did not just call Joe a piece of filth!" Bailey felt the wonderful heat of rage.

"He's filth!"

"Joe is a wonderful man, and I don't want to hear you state otherwise in my presence again or you will be very sorry, Mrs. Howard."

"He's nobody and nothing," the woman snarled, and that for Bailey was about the final straw. She battled the red haze that filled her eyes, and lost.

"Joe has made good on his life and come back to the town he loves to live with the people he loves. He runs a successful business and is highly respected. So whatever this crap is that's crawled up your behind and lodged there, I suggest you get it surgically removed, because I can tell you now this is one argument you will not win when it comes to a popularity contest. Let the grudge go, Mrs. Howard, because it's making you look a fool, right along with your silly friends!"

The woman's mouth fell open.

"Good evening," Bailey said, walking around her and off down the main street.

"IF YOU DON'T WANT that woman, then I'll take her."

Joe was still trying to process what Bailey had just said to Mary Howard, right here on the main street of Ryker. The verbal battles he'd had with the woman had always been conducted in private. People knew, but he rarely let anyone else get involved—but now Bailey had laid it all out there. He should be pissed, but what he felt was a steady build of heat in his chest.

"What?" He looked at Fin.

"Are you going to just stand there like an idiot, or go thank her for defending your honor?"

Joe looked down the road to where Bailey was fast disappearing. He started running. Dodging around people, some of whom called out to him. Ignoring them, he caught her at the end of the street. Grabbing her hand, he pulled her into a shop doorway.

"Bailey." Her name was a sigh. "God, Bailey." He touched her chin, lifting her eyes to meet his. He then kissed her until he couldn't breathe. When they came up for air, Joe's hands were in her hair, his body pressed into hers. Their breath mingled as both tried to inhale.

"J-Joe." She looked and sounded a bit dazed.

"Thank you."

"Sh-she's a horrible woman."

"No arguing here," he whispered against her lips, before leaning in for another kiss. This one was gentle, a soft brush and nip of her bottom lip.

"I know how hard that was for you to do... both of those speeches, Bailey. The one in the hall, and the one outside it. That you did so in support of me makes me feel like I could scale the tallest mountain—twice, about now."

"I'm not sure how that happened. I mean, the hall thing that had to be said. Those people are wrong, Joe, in thinking only those children who have nothing or come from abusive families need a rec center."

"I know, baby."

"I had to speak up then. Someone had to say it."

"You did, and we got the vote, and to my mind part of that is down to what you said."

"I'm glad." Her smile was sweet. "Glad that those kids will have a place to go instead of a cave in the side of a hill."

He snorted. "I liked our cave."

"Me too."

Joe pushed hair from her cheek, then slid his hand around the back of her neck and hauled her closer. She rested her cheek on his chest. It felt so right, it should have scared him.

"While I don't like the idea of Mary Howard having you in her sights, it felt surprisingly awesome to hear you tell her she needs to have whatever is lodged up her ass surgically removed."

"I can't believe I said that." Bailey pressed her forehead into him, moaning. "I don't lose control, Joe, but I just did, and people saw."

"You did, and it was a nice touch. It's fair to say no one will mess with you now—or me, for that matter."

"I'm glad you find it funny." She looked up at him again.

"Not funny, baby. It felt amazing, wonderful, and several other words I can't think of right now, but I'm sure they'll come to me."

"What's the deal with that woman and you, Joe?"

Joe couldn't seem to keep his hands from moving over Bailey. Stroking her hair, touching her cheek; he needed the contact, but only with her.

"Her son and I used to run together as children. He broke into a store one night, and stole money and supplies, and she blamed me, even though I wasn't there. Jay was then sent away to military school and has never returned. My guess is she blames me for all of it."

"What a foolish woman."

"So, you think I'm a wonderful man?"

"Don't let it go to your head."

He buried his face in her hair and then placed a hot kiss on her neck. She shuddered. He'd held her eyes as she spoke in the hall, looked at her standing there uncertain, and yet determined, looking so fucking sweet in that lilac dress, and thought, *Christ, I am so gone.*

"Come home with me."

"A-aren't you working?"

"Shit!" He'd forgotten he was to take over from Em tonight. "Come with me, and then we'll go home."

"I'm tired, Joe."

"I'll give you a sugary drink, it'll pick you up."

Joe kissed her again, and this time he slid his hand up her thigh under the hem of her dress. She shivered.

"All right, but I know it's just your way of making me work for you for free."

"No, it's my way of not letting you out of my sight." He kissed her again.

Chapter 25

A.S. WAS BUSY, and most people wanted to congratulate Joe on getting the rec center passed.

"Well, if it isn't little Miss Feisty."

"Ha," Bailey said as Luke, Jack, and Fin approached.

"Nice work there, Miss Jones." Luke kissed her cheek. "I've never seen Mary Howard speechless. It's a moment I'm not likely to forget anytime soon."

"Thanks, sweet cheeks, for having Joe's back." Jack kissed her next. "Don't tell him I said this, but he's special to us, and he's never let us get into it with Mary Howard, but you... well, you just did it right there in the street."

"Did many people hear?" Bailey looked around, hoping they hadn't.

"Plenty." Fin hugged her hard. "And that's a good thing, Bailey, really. She needed it, and maybe it will have her backing off, but I doubt it. The woman's full of anger."

More people arrived, and she was soon talking with the Robbins sisters and Mr. Goldhirsh. After a while, she started moving through the bar collecting glasses and bottles, wanting to help Joe and the staff, as the place was busy. Looking around, Bailey realized she knew so many people in Ryker Falls now, and liked it. Liked that she could walk down the street and people would call out a greeting. Liked that she could talk with friends, real friends, like she'd never had before.

She found Joe behind the bar, his hands moving everywhere while he smiled and listened as people talked at him. As if sensing her, he looked up, their eyes caught and held, and she felt his smile right to her toes.

Deciding she'd take out some of the bottles to the recycle bin, Bailey headed out the back. She'd reached the door when Clark joined her with his hands full of bottles too.

"What are you doing?"

"Hell if I know?"

"Did you just say hell, Clark Munro?" Bailey looked at him, and noted a sparkle in his eye. "How many have you had to drink?"

"Not many, and don't be a nag, Bays."

"Bays?"

"The woman who stood up in front of all those people tonight, and again on the street, deserves a nickname."

"Not you too. I've had people talking about that since I arrived."

"I'm proud of you," Clark said, then reached around her and opened the door.

A man was standing beside the recycle bin when Bailey reached it. He was doubled over, so she couldn't see his face. She lowered her bottles inside as she said, "Can I help you?"

He straightened, his eyes running over her face. She thought he smiled, but it was hard to tell in this light.

"I don't feel so good."

"What's wrong?" She moved closer as Clark dumped

his bottles. Bailey wondered if the man had drunk too much. The knife appeared in his hands seconds later, and he swung it at her face. Bailey leapt back.

"What the hell!" Clark charged forward. "Don't touch her!"

Bailey kicked out and knocked the knife from his hands. The man raced off into the shadows.

"What the hell was that about?" Clark said.

"I-I don't know."

"Come on, we need to tell someone there's a madman out here."

Shaken, Bailey found Fin, and told him. He called the police.

"Are you all right? Fin just told me what happened." Joe arrived at her side minutes later, while she collected more glasses. He held her, hauling her close with everyone watching on. "What the hell were you thinking, kicking that knife from the lunatic's hands?"

"I don't know, it just happened."

"Well don't let it happen again. Jesus, you start finding yourself and then suddenly you're doing crazy shit like speaking to a room full of people and taking on crazy knife-wielding men. It's enough to make me gray."

She laughed.

"Oh, so it's funny, is it?" He cupped her cheeks.

"Laughing stops the panic."

His eyes sobered. "I don't want anything to happen to you, Bailey Jones. I want you to sit at the bar and not move. I need you to be safe."

"I'm okay, Joe. It was scary, but it's okay now. The man was obviously high or drunk."

He was about to say something, but stopped, his gaze now focused over her shoulder.

"Officer Martin has just arrived, so you go on and take him to my office, and make your statement."

"Okay, but Clark needs to come too."

"Why?"

"We're friends, Joe. Besides, he was there, and rushed in to stop the guy, so he needs to talk with the officer too."

"Yeah?" His brows rose.

"He totally did."

"He totally did," he mimicked her. "You're losing your prissy-girl edges, baby." He kissed her softly. "Go. I'll send a drink over when you come down."

"Who is playing for sing-along night?"

Joe winced. "Me."

"I'll do it." His relief made her laugh.

"You sure you're up to it?"

"Yes, and playing helps me relax."

"Strange, it makes me tense." He kissed her again, right there in front of anyone watching. "Now go before I drag you into the nearest empty room."

She spoke to the officer with Clark, telling him everything they knew, and then she went to the bathroom. Angie was in there.

"Hi." Bailey gave the girl a smile, wondering what reception she'd get. Surely Angie had seen what had just happened between her and Joe.

"Hi, Bailey."

Angie turned away from her.

"Good, thanks. Listen, Angie, about Joe——"

"It's done, Bailey, I don't want to talk about it."

"Okay, sure," Bailey said, feeling uncomfortable.

Angie brushed by Bailey and left. Seconds later, she followed and joined her friends.

"Hey there, Supergirl."

"Hi, Piper."

"What's up? Don't tell me you went at it with someone else tonight?"

Bailey shook her head. "No, I just saw Angie, and she wasn't happy to run into me."

"They were never serious, her and Joe. Plus, she was seeing someone else.

"Really?"

"Really, and I'm telling you the 100 percent truth, Bailey. Friends don't lie to each other."

Relief flooded through Bailey. "Thank you, Piper, I needed to hear that. I'm not sure what's going on, or where this thing with Joe is heading, but I didn't want that worry hanging over us."

"Nothing to worry about there. And for what it's worth, you and Joe were made for each other. I've never seen him with anyone like he is with you. You're driving him crazy, it's a wonderful thing to see."

"Thanks... I think." Bailey laughed. She then headed to the piano, and Joe joined her. Handing her a soda, he took over the microphone.

"So it's sing-along night. Let's have your requests, because Bailey has offered to play."

This was greeted with a round of applause, and several whistles. Bailey laughed her way through several badly sung songs, and even sang herself. When Joe called it a night, she was exhausted, but happy... really happy, she realized.

"You ready to go home now?" Maggs came to where she stood with Joe.

"She's coming home with me."

Bailey felt Joe's hand on her spine.

"If I want to?"

"Do you?" He held her eyes.

"Yes."

Maggie accepted with a knowing smile. "About time, if you ask me."

Her friend hugged her hard, and then left with Luke and Jack. As everyone was aware of what had happened to Bailey earlier, and no one was leaving solo until that man had been caught.

After the last customer had gone, she went with Joe to his pickup.

"Did you recognize that man at all, Bailey?" he said as they drove down the main street.

"No, he was in the shadows, plus his face was lowered." Bailey had heard something in his voice that made her look at him. "Why do you ask, Joe?"

He hesitated.

"Tell me."

"My father has been seen around Ryker."

"But he would have no reason to attack me, surely? Besides, how did he know I'd be out there at that time?"

"I don't know. Maybe he knows about us, and recognized you."

"What us? We've barely spent any time together."

"I can't be within a foot of you, Bailey, and someone not know what I'm thinking, and tonight you stood up for me in public."

She didn't want to feel the slither of fear that crawled up her spine, but it was there nonetheless.

"I won't let him hurt you, Bailey."

"I can look after myself, Joe."

"Sure, kick-ass chick is what you are, but I have your back too, just like you had mine tonight."

She thought about that as they drove through Ryker, and liked the idea that someone had her back.

. . .

BAILEY WAS silent as he pulled his pickup into the garage. Switching off the engine, Joe got out and came round the hood to join her.

"What is that noise?"

Joe listened as Buzz's yowls increased in volume.

"Buzz is letting me know he's not impressed that I left him home alone. With, I might add, a large rawhide bone, and soft bed, which he won't use, as he will have slept on the furniture, and his favorite music playing."

"Wow, it's really loud."

"This is the side to that mutt that the townspeople don't see. He sulks, spits up on things, and chews my shoes."

"He's the best dog I've ever known."

"Not you too," Joe said, brushing a kiss over her hair. "Come inside and be quiet, I want you to see the treatment I get from him when he's pissed off like he is now."

Joe opened the door and led Bailey though the mudroom, and down a hall, into the living area.

"Hey there, Buzz." His dog was sitting with his back to the door Joe and Bailey had just entered. "Come on, bud, don't be a baby, come and greet me."

Buzz yowled out a chorus of what Joe liked to think of as insults, and refused to face him. Beside him, Bailey giggled.

"He's so cute."

The dog turned so fast, his neck had to have cracked. He then got up with a loud, joyous woof, and ran at Bailey. She dropped to her knees and hugged him.

"Hello," Joe said. "Owner here. You know, the one who feeds and puts a roof over your head," he said, and was ignored by those participating in the mutual admiration festival taking place before him.

"Be nice to your daddy, Buzz."

The dog looked up at him, and gave him a small tail wag.

"Gee, thanks, Buzz, I'm overwhelmed. Now you're going outside for a run."

Joe took the dog out, leaving the door open for when he was ready to come back in, which he knew from experience would be some time. When he came back inside she was looking out the windows.

"This is amazing, Joe."

The main feature in here was the floor-to-ceiling windows that looked out at the mountains. The moon was bright tonight, and showed off the view.

"It's so beautiful."

It was, he acknowledged, looking at her. The room was pretty awesome too. He'd lived here for long enough that the thrill should have passed, yet he still felt it when he realized that this was all his. When you came from nothing, you tended to love what you eventually got. Joe loved this place.

The cream walls held artwork he'd picked up on his travels. Each had its own memory.

"That's one of Maggie's."

Bailey walked to where a miniature bronze statue of a man stood. His hands were spread wide, and his face could only be described as elated.

"What is it called?"

"Freedom." He'd had to have it the minute he'd laid eyes on it.

Bailey traced a finger down the arm.

"It's beautiful."

"I thought so," Joe said. In fact, what he'd thought when he saw it was that it symbolized the man he now was. Free from his past, and living life as he wanted.

"I understand how he feels."

Joe slipped his arms around her, and she turned to face him.

"Do you feel free now, Bailey?"

She nodded. "Since coming to Ryker I've felt freer than I ever have before. Just as you do." Her fingers traced the lines of his forehead and then down his nose. Just the lightest of contact, yet Joe felt it through his entire body. She rose to her toes when her hand reached his lips and replaced her fingers with her mouth.

He let her set the pace, let her kiss him, explore him. Joe knew she was inexperienced, he also knew she needed this, to find the confidence to take things further. His body went up in flames with the first tentative touch of her tongue. Innocent, yes, but so goddamned sweet she had him hard in seconds.

He cupped the back of her head and angled it, allowing her better access, then gently took it deeper. Joe felt her hands on the buttons of his shirt. With each one she opened, her fingers brushed the skin beneath, and he was an inferno as she reached the last, then pushed the edges open and slid her hands inside. The breath hissed in his throat as she touched him. She turned him inside out, and made him feel things he'd never felt.

"I love your body."

He managed a strangled groan as she leaned in and kissed his exposed skin. Her lips then trailed every inch of his chest, leaving him reeling. The breath rasped in and out of his throat as her hands moved to the buttons on his jeans. Flicking each one open, she slid a hand inside and caressed him. His body was rock-hard, and her touch was exquisite torture, but he made himself stand still, made himself let her do what she wanted. When her finger traced the band of his shorts, he nearly expired.

"Bailey, you're killing me here."

Her hand stopped. "Am I doing it wrong?"

"No... hell no," he managed to get out. "You're doing it right, and because I want you so much that right is driving me crazy."

"Oh." She liked that idea, he knew because a sultry little smile played around her mouth.

"Oh, indeed." He kissed the smile away, and didn't let up until she was sagging against him. He then stroked her dress up her lovely body, and stripped off her bra and panties.

"Sh-should we... your bed?" She sighed as he picked her up and walked backward.

"I won't make it." He settled her on the cabinet, and braced his hands on either side of her. "You know that orgasm you had the other night?"

She nodded.

"We're going for round two." Joe kissed his way down her body, spending time on her breasts, teasing, nibbling, and then sucking a nipple into his mouth. Moving lower when she was panting, he placed hot, openmouthed kisses on her stomach, then moved lower.

"Oh my." Her hips jerked as he stroked his tongue over the soft, wet folds between her legs. "That's...." Her words fell away on a long, soft moan. Joe had never heard anything so erotic. He teased her, pushing her forward to a climax, then swept his tongue over the hard bud, and she lost it.

"Jesus, you are one sexy woman." Joe looked at her. Hair now loose, breasts full, a heavy-lidded look in her eyes.

"I want to do that to you."

"Not tonight, I don't have that much restraint."

The thought of her mouth on him had him ripping open a foil pack and sheathing himself. Joe stepped between her legs, and slid home. It was slow this time; he eased out and then back in a few times.

"More," she begged as he pulled out again.

"Seeing as you asked nicely," he managed to get out. Thrusting back in harder this time, he set the pace, and was rewarded with her body tightening about him. Their breathing became labored, and she called his name as she came in a shuddering rush. Joe followed seconds later.

Once their breathing had slowed, and he thought his legs would hold, Joe lifted her into his arms and carried her to the door.

"Buzz, get your ass in here!"

The dog galloped inside and straight to the kitchen. Joe shut the door, then hit the lights, and headed up the stairs; he had just enough energy to make it to his bed. Pulling back the covers, he lowered Bailey onto it, and followed. Hauling her back into his arms, he closed his eyes. She was slumbering before him.

Chapter 26

BAILEY WOKE with her back pressed to Joe's front, and his hand around her waist. She felt surrounded by him, and having never slept with a man the entire night before, she thought it was something she could get used to. The night had been a revelation of feelings and emotion. He'd wrung so much out of Bailey she wasn't sure she could put herself back together the way she'd always been, contained, unemotional. He'd demanded she participate, demanded she tell him what she was feeling, and she had. She wanted to purr as his hand stroked her thigh.

"I stood at the end of the main street the day you left, and watched you drive away. I remember thinking, there goes part of me." He spoke the words into her hair, his face resting there. "The pain in my chest was physical, and I'm ashamed to say I went a bit crazy. I wasn't strong enough to cope with how I felt losing you, Bailey."

"I cried for hours," she said. "My mother got angry with me, and said I needed to grow up, but I couldn't stop. The sadness and desperation gripped my entire body. It was like I couldn't function without you." Maybe because she wasn't looking at Joe, Bailey could say the words. Whatever the reason, it felt good to finally let them out. "At the time it hurt so badly to leave you that I wondered if I would carry that pain forever."

His lips settled on her shoulder.

"You'd asked me to be the best man I could be for you, Bailey, and I failed for a while. I lost my way totally after you left."

"Oh, Joe, I'm sorry." Bailey had to face him now. She rolled onto her back and looked up at him. "That must have been a terrible time for you all."

His lips touched hers in a kiss that was so sweet she felt it through her entire body.

"I rebelled against Aunt Jess and the rules she wanted to put in place. In fact, I pretty much rebelled against everything and everyone. I missed the one person who I felt knew me... understood where I was coming from. You were mine alone, Bailey. I had to share you with no one, and suddenly you were gone. I'm ashamed to say I became a bad person."

Bailey cupped his cheek. "But you came through it, and that's what matters, Joe. I just went further into myself. I never wrote to you about how I really felt, just kept it light—"

"I know. I read about where you lived, the city, and what you were doing, but never a word about how you were feeling."

"I couldn't put that on you."

"I wish you had, maybe then I wouldn't have been such an ass, and picked up a pen and written back. But one thing in all those letters that never changed was the closing line."

"I miss you so much, Joe." Bailey remembered writing the words over and over again.

His smile was sad. "I read those letters so many times, trying to read between the lines."

"I thought you were throwing them away."

"Never."

"I'm glad you turned things around, Joe. Glad I came back here and found you happy, because I always wondered."

"Is that why you came back?"

"I don't know... maybe, or maybe I just came here because it was somewhere that once, for a brief period of time, I actually felt like I belonged. Both you and Maggs gave me that."

"I'm glad you came back, and for now that's enough."

Joe kissed her again, long and slow. He then picked up her hand and kissed the scar that ran down her wrist and into the palm.

"Does it still hurt?"

"Sometimes, just an ache, but it's better."

"How did it happen?"

"I was running, actually, down some stairs, because I was late for practice, and I tripped and fell through the window at the bottom."

"Christ, you're lucky these were all you ended up with."

"I was. The surgeons said that."

"And you spent time in hospital?"

"That was where I did some thinking, and realized I needed to change my life. Grandfather wasn't happy, but I didn't care. I did rehab, then told him I wanted a break. He refused, we argued, so I left. I simply packed up my things, and walked out the door."

"I hate that you were in pain, Bailey, but I can't be

unhappy about the fact that you came back to me. I'm just sorry that your accident was the catalyst."

His smile was gentle, as was the kiss he placed on her lips. It grew deeper, and when he slid inside her, Bailey was soon lost to all thought but him.

WHEN BAILEY ARRIVED at the stables, she found Jack in the office. He swiveled in his chair to look at her.

"You have the same smile on your face that Joe had when I saw him earlier."

"No, I don't."

"Sure you do. The 'I'm extremely happy with myself' smile."

Bailey wasn't used to people speaking like that, especially about personal stuff.

"Bailey, Bailey, Bailey," Jack said, rocking back in his chair as color filled her face. "You need to harden up to that kind of thing if you and my brother are in a relationship. You'll get a bucketload of teasing from the others, believe me. I'm just warming you up."

"We're not."

"Not what?"

"In a relationship." *Are we?* The thought of being in a committed relationship with Joe was both terrifying and exciting.

"So it's just sex then?"

"Jack!"

"Sorry, I couldn't resist." The smile fell away. "But for what it's worth, Bailey, I like the idea of you and my brother being together. The history between you also supports that."

"Joe told you?" Bailey wasn't sure how she felt about that, because for so long it had been their secret.

"Some, but not all. And thanks for watching out for him when he needed it, and we couldn't."

"He watched out for me too."

"Good to know. Now, I need you to ride Rae and Lou, then lunge Jacqui. I'll take Sandy and Beccy when I get back."

"Should you be riding?"

"I'm better." He dismissed her words. "But I have to go to the hospital for a checkup, and then meet this guy who wants to sell me his horse."

"I'll take Sandy and Beccy out if I have time and you're not back."

"Are you sure? It'll be just you here."

"Do I look soft or something?" She narrowed her eyes at Jack.

"Wellllll, you do have that Boston rich-girl look, and those soft hands."

"Which have been working for you for a while now, so watch it, buddy, or I'll demand a pay raise."

He laughed, then ruffled her hair. "Can you feed Kimi too? She's about ready to have her kittens."

"You guys and your female animals. It's really unsettling," Bailey said, following him from the room.

"We like to be surrounded by females, what can I say. Plus, we have Arthur and Blue, so that evens the numbers some."

She swatted his shoulder, and he laughed, heading out the stable doors.

Bailey saddled Lou first, after they'd had a cuddle, and headed outside. The horse was a big baby, and loved to be hugged. Buzz had decided to stay with her today, and ran alongside as she took the horse on a slow canter over the paddocks.

Looking around, she still couldn't take it in, that Bailey

Jones, concert pianist, was riding a horse for a living, and mucking out stables. She loved it. Playing the piano was in her blood, but for now this was something she wanted to do. If she could also play at A.S., then she was happy.

"Joe," Bailey sighed.

What she felt for him scared her, there was no getting around it. Last night had been one of the most wonderful nights of her life, but what now?

To blow away the thoughts tumbling around inside her head, Bailey urged the horse into a gallop. Muscles bunched beneath her as he sprang forward, and soon the wind was in her face, and she was smiling. Turning when they were both breathless, she headed back. Buzz was waiting for her in the doorway.

"Did we go a bit fast for you, boy?"

He gave her a woof, and a tail wag. Bailey rode into the stables, and dismounted. After rubbing the horse down, she gave him some food, then saddled Rae.

When she was done with the horses, Bailey put the tack away. She got a dog biscuit for Buzz, and topped up his water, then fed Kimi, who was settled in a stall in a pile of hay. Her belly was big now, and Bailey thought the kittens would be arriving any day.

Back in the tack room, Bailey took a soda out of the fridge, then sat in a chair and drank until her thirst eased. She'd never guzzled in such an unladylike manner before, and the thought of what her grandfather and those she'd mixed with while playing concerts might think made her giggle. When the tack room door slammed, she rolled her eyes. Jack must have come back early. Getting to her feet she tried to open it but it wouldn't budge.

"Very funny, Jack, now open up."

She waited, but nothing happened.

"Open up, Jack." Bailey was about to give him a piece

of her mind, when she smelled the smoke. "Open up!" Rattling the doorknob produced nothing. She leaned on it. It moved, but didn't open wide enough to get out. There were no windows in here; she was trapped. Smoke meant fire, and if she didn't get out and rescue the horses, Kimi, and Buzz, the smoke would cause panic and they'd hurt themselves. Looking up, she hoped the sprinkler system kicked in soon.

Buzz started to yowl.

"It's okay, boy, I won't let anything happen to you."

Grabbling a cloth, she found some water and wet it, if the smoke got thick, she'd wrap it around her face. She then ran at the door. It moved, but didn't open. So she did it again. By the fifth time, she was losing her strength.

"Open, damn you!"

It did, and she fell face-first on the ground, just as the smoke detectors started blaring. The sprinklers followed seconds later, soaking her and Buzz. Getting to her feet, Bailey looked around. Whoever had lit the fire had shut the main stable doors. Searching for the source, she found a pile of horse blankets beside the tack room that were still burning, and the flames were now climbing the walls. She grabbed the fire extinguisher with Buzz on her heels. Jack had taught her how to use it.

"Move away, Buzz!" She waved a hand at him, sending him back several feet. "Pull the pin, and aim." Bailey recited Jack's instructions. "Aim low, and sweep from side to side." She did as he'd told her, using it until her arms ached, and she was sure the fire was out.

The horses were getting restless with the noise and water. Bailey could hear them snorting, and pawing the ground with their hooves, but she could do nothing about them yet. She ran to the stable door, but couldn't budge it.

"The office, Buzz!" She sprinted up the stairs and threw open the windows, inhaling deep breaths of air.

"It's okay now, boy." She patted a chair beneath the window, and Buzz jumped up. Once he was there, and she was sure he was getting fresh air, Bailey picked up the phone and punched in the only number she knew well.

Chapter 27

"APPLE SOURS." Joe answered the phone. He'd spent the morning smiling, and hadn't been able to stop. He'd woken with Bailey in his arms, and the scent and feel of her was etched in his head. They'd talked too, only briefly, but it was a start.

"Joe! Come quick. Fire at the stables. It's out, but hurry, the stable door is locked!"

"Are you safe?" His heart pounded as he heard the fear in Bailey's voice.

"I-I think so. Hurry!"

Joe ran down the steps, yelling at his staff that he had to go. He was dialing Jack as he jumped in his pickup.

"Get home, there's been a fire." He then called Luke with the same message.

The thought of Bailey anywhere near danger was making his heart pound out of control. Reaching his driveway in record time, he looked for smoke as he pulled up outside the stables, but to his relief found none.

"Bailey!"

"Joe!"

She was standing on the other side of the stable door. Someone had bolted it from the outside. Buzz was with her, yowling loudly.

"I'm opening the door now, Bailey."

She didn't answer. He got it open seconds later. Her face was white as she stumbled toward him. Joe opened his arms, and she flew into them.

"God, you scared me." She was wet from the sprinklers.

"Me?" she croaked.

"I asked if you were safe, and you said I think so." He couldn't stop kissing wherever he could reach. Couldn't make himself ease the punishing grip he had on her.

"S-sorry, I didn't know what I was saying."

She was shaking, her hands clutching his shirt as she tried to get closer. Fear, Joe thought. She'd been terrified. He'd think about that in a minute, and the fact that someone had locked her in there with fire. For now he'd focus on her.

"I have you, sweetheart. Take some big breaths for me."

Lowering a hand, he dug his fingers into the fur of his dog's wet head, reassuring him that he was safe too.

Bailey did as he asked while his hand ran up and down her spine. She pulled back as they heard cars.

"I'm okay now, Joe."

"No, you're not, but at least you've stopped shaking." Some of the color had come back into her face too.

"We need to get the horses out, and stop the sprinklers and fire detectors."

"Luke and Jack are here, they can help," Joe said still holding her close.

"What happened?" Jack got to them first.

"Come inside," Bailey said, reaching for Joe's hand.

"First we need you to get the horses and Kimi out, then I'll explain what happened."

Luke took care of the horses, and Joe released Bailey reluctantly so she could go and get on some dry clothes, and then rescue Kimi. Jack and Joe dealt with the smoke detectors and sprinklers. They then investigated the fire.

"Diesel." Jack looked up at him.

"No fucking way!" Joe's blood ran cold as he realized his brother was right. "Someone lit this deliberately." He'd known it, but having it confirmed forced hot, seething rage to overtake the cold fear he'd experienced when he knew Bailey was in danger. She could have been killed, and it had been deliberate.

"I was in the tack room with Buzz. I was having a soda, and him a biscuit," Bailey said from behind him. "Someone closed the door, and jammed something against it."

"You were locked in the tack room?" Jack went to inspect.

"I'm going to kill someone. Christ, Bailey." Joe stepped closer, and held her face.

"I'm all right, Joe."

"I need to get you to the doctor."

She shook her head. "I don't need a doctor, because I got out before the fire really took hold." She held out her hands. "See, no burns."

Fin walked in with Chief Blake.

"I called him," Luke said, returning. "He needed to be here."

Joe nodded.

"This is becoming a habit, Miss Jones," Chief Blake said.

"And what the hell does that mean?" Joe demanded.

"Simmer down, Joe. I just meant there was the business

with Jack being shot, then the man in the bar, and now a fire has been deliberately lit. Miss Jones was there for each."

"She had nothing to do with it."

"I can figure that out for myself, Joe." The chief of police sent him a steady look. "Now, are you all right if I ask you some questions while the incident is fresh in your head, Miss Jones?"

"Of course."

Joe let her go, but only because she was going to be a few feet away where he could see her. He then formed a huddle with Fin and his brothers.

"Chief Blake's just doing his job, Joe," Luke said.

"I know, I'm just so fucking angry. Someone is either out to get us, or her. My money's on us," Joe growled. "And I'll double that bet by saying that piece of shit who donated sperm to get us here is involved." He'd told his siblings about Elijah's sighting of their father.

"I changed my plans this morning. I was meant to be here with her, so my guess is you're right," Jack said. "But why does he want to come at us? We're his children, for Christ's sake!"

"He asked me for money six months ago. Rang the bar. I refused, and he said he'd make me pay, and I thought it was just his way of blowing smoke out his ass. Now I'm wondering."

"And you didn't tell us?" Luke didn't look impressed.

"Tell you what? That your father's an asshole? You know that already."

"So what? Bailey and my horses were just going to be collateral damage?" Jack looked mean, his eyes narrowed, face rage-fueled.

"Okay, you both need to calm down now," Fin said.

"Calm down!" Joe roared. "My woman was nearly

burned to death, and you want me to calm down. First someone shoots Jack, now tries to burn the stables down. Both times someone I love could have been killed!"

He realized what he'd said a second after the L word left his mouth. "Fuck," Joe growled.

"Nice." Luke nodded. "About the love thing, but this other shit's seriously disturbing. We have to find him, our sperm donor, before he does anything else."

"No disagreement there," Jack snarled. "And ditto on the love thing."

"I actually came here for another reason, before I heard what had happened from the chief after we pulled up at the same time," Fin said. "Still pissed, FYI, that no one called me."

"Excuse the fuck out of me for upsetting your delicate sensibilities," Joe snapped.

"As you should be, but because you're all over the place, I'll let it lie... for now."

"What's the reason you came by, Fin?" Jack asked.

They heard another car speed up the drive. A door slammed, and in seconds Piper had arrived.

"What's happened?"

Joe filled her in, as Bailey was still being questioned. He could see her from where he stood. Her hair hung in a long, damp braid down her back. She was leaning on one leg, the other foot turned in slightly, peach sneakers resting one on top of the other. Having changed into them out of her wet riding boots. Her black jeans were snug, and the shirt she wore was an old denim one of Jack's. Just looking at her was messing with him. Looking, and knowing that she could have been taken from him today.

"I don't understand why this is happening. First Jack, and now Bailey."

"I know, Pip, but this latest incident confirms someone's targeting us to my mind, and that means we have to be diligent," Joe said. "Always in pairs, and eyes open."

"Okay, listen up." All eyes turned as Chief Blake left Bailey and addressed them. "Fin and I need to speak with you."

Bailey moved to Joe's side, and he wondered if she realized she'd even done it, or the fact that she stepped in front of him so he could wrap his arms around her and hold her close.

"Helen Neil called me this morning. Elijah went up the mountain yesterday for a quick hike, told Helen he'd be three hours, no more, and home in time to help get things ready for little Sally's birthday party today. He hasn't returned."

"He does go up there for a couple of days at a time though, Chief," Luke said.

"Sure, but not when he promised Helen he'd return for the birthday. Elijah loves those kids."

No one disputed that.

"We need to get a search going. So all of you who can, saddle up and meet me at the ranger headquarters. It's a big ask, I know, considering it's obvious that someone is deliberately targeting you all, and you have a mess to clean up—"

"We can do it, the mess will be here when we get back. We'll be sure to stay in pairs." Joe spoke for his siblings.

"I'll call in a few casuals, they can watch over the ranch, feed the horses, and start the cleanup," Jack said.

Chief Blake nodded. "Knew you would, and nothing I said would deter you, but had to say the words just the same. I'm heading there now, and will coordinate the search from the station. It's my hope Elijah's injured and holed up there somewhere waiting for us, because no other scenario is comforting me."

Joe wanted that to be the case too. He watched as Pip hauled Bailey out of his arms and hugged her. She still looked pale, and her eyes big in her face. Fear, Joe knew, affected you for a while after the event.

"I'll go bring in the horses with Luke," Piper said. "You get the tack and supplies we need ready."

"I'll take the quad up," Jack said, much to Joe's relief. He hadn't wanted to come down hard on his brother if he decided to ride.

Joe moved to where Bailey stood watching Fin and the chief leave.

"I don't know what time we'll be back, but I want you to go find Maggie, and stay with her until I do."

"I'm coming."

"No." Joe shook his head. "You've had a shock, and you don't know about search and rescue."

"I understand your words are motivated by worry, Joe, but I'm fine, and the more eyes out there, the sooner we'll find Elijah. Plus, I'd rather be busy."

"No, absolutely not."

"Problem?" Jack asked.

"Bailey's not experienced enough for this."

His brother gave him a steady look. "She rides better than any of us, and has proven she's tough, so if she's fit enough, let her do it."

"She's just been through hell!"

"And come out of it fine. I want to come, Joe. Need to keep busy."

"Be reasonable here, Bailey. You have no idea how to do search and rescue, and haven't been in those mountains for years. We've been doing it, winter and summer. You're a city girl; this is not for you. It'll be rough going and dirty out there—"

"And I'm too soft to handle it?" She hadn't raised her

voice, but he wasn't fooled, and neither was Jack, because he winced.

"Yes... no, I mean, *shit*. This is for people who have experience, Bailey. People who have competence...."

Jack groaned as Joe struggled to come up with the right words.

"And because I'm smaller than the strapping Trainers, I'm weak?"

"You're misunderstanding what I'm trying to say. We know how strong you are, you've proved it continually since you arrived, but—"

"I don't need your permission to do this, Joe. And while I do understand what is motivating your words, they're pissing me off. I'm not weak!"

"Goddammit, I don't think you're weak—"

"Nor do I need you, a big strong male, looking out for me."

That entire conversation had come out wrong, Joe knew it, Jack knew it, because he rolled his eyes, and Bailey definitely knew it, because hers narrowed. He was rattled, no other word for it, or he never would have spoken that way.

"Be reasonable, Bailey. I'm just trying to watch out for you, and we don't need to do that up there."

"Dear God, brother, shut up," Jack whispered.

"Oh yes, and we all know how reasonable you can be, don't we, Joe Trainer. I'm going," Bailey said. "And you don't need to look out for me."

"Shit, shit, shit," Joe gritted out as she walked away.

"How the hell have I missed all this?" Luke said, shaking his head. He'd obviously been listening to the conversation too. "Seriously, I do a week of lates and suddenly all the good stuff happens."

"It's not good, believe me," Joe said, watching Bailey stalk away from him.

"Part of it must have been good, surely. Because I'm guessing the fireworks between you and sweet little Bailey Jones came to a head, then you sabotaged it like you usually do?"

"Shouldn't you be on my side?" Joe said. "And I don't deliberately sabotage relationships."

"Joe, Joe, Joe." Jack tsked. "I may love you like a brother, because you are, but you have the emotional maturity of a Twinkie."

"The hell you say," Joe said, walking to the tack room with his brothers flanking him.

"Okay, I have to go to the house and change out of my uniform," Luke said. "But before I do, here's two pieces of advice. And only use these if you really want to have a thing with Bailey."

"What's a thing?"

"Aww, son, have we not had the talk yet?" Luke punched him in the shoulder. "Beg for forgiveness, and grovel," he said before heading out the door.

"Fuck off," Joe growled.

He saddled Beccy, the horse Pip brought in for him, and rode out to join the others. Bailey, he noted, was mounted on Jack's horse, Sandy, back rigid. She had a cap pulled low, and wore a windbreaker tied around her waist. She threw him a cool look, then turned away.

"Buzz, let's go," Joe called to his dog. He then rode out of the stables. The others fell silently in behind.

Chapter 28

BAILEY WAS TIRED, she just hadn't wanted to say that to Joe when he'd been so intent on her not going on the search for Elijah Neil. Pride, it seemed, was something she had supply of after all. Her head could still not get around the fact that someone had tried to burn down the barn with her in it. But she was okay, and the water damage to the stables minimal, plus the animals were unhurt. That was all that mattered. That, and finding Elijah.

She'd never really been determined, but something had changed inside her since coming to Ryker. Something had grown... her resolve and strength, yes, but self-belief also. She could survive without her grandfather mapping the course of her life, she'd proven that now.

Ahead of her, Joe rode lead. Broad shoulders back, head turning from right to left. She'd kissed those shoulders, and a great deal more. Now, they were angry with each other again. She knew his worry had been driven by fear, and her anger by stubborn pride. It seemed they were destined to constantly bring out the worst in each other. This was such a depressing thought, she pushed it aside.

They'd been riding twenty minutes when they stopped in a part of Ryker Falls she had not visited since returning. It looked different now. A wooden log building with pitched roof was the Ranger station for the area. People were gathered out front on horseback. Beyond that, further up the hills, she saw the lodge she'd heard locals talking about.

It was owned by the wealthy Ted Hosking, who from what she'd gleaned had more money than any one person had a right to. He was also arrogant, according to Piper.

Fin walked out of the ranger station as they dismounted. He wore his khaki uniform, and his usual smile was nowhere to be seen.

"Nothing new come in?" Joe asked him.

"Nothing."

The group was worried, Bailey could feel it.

"Elijah has four children, three girls and a baby boy." Piper rode up beside Bailey. "He's a good man, and worships his family. I hope he's okay."

"I don't remember him," Bailey said. But then she hadn't been very social when she lived here. She gripped her friend's hand briefly, and then listened to Fin's briefing.

The Trainers asked questions, and she watched as they interacted, their familiarity with each other obvious. She loved her brother, but Beau was six years older than her, and he'd left the house at twenty to pursue his career, so she'd lived most of her life since then with just her grandfather at her side. Her mother was under his control too, and pretty much did what she was told, so Bailey had never had much of a relationship with her either.

Looking at Piper, Bailey thought it must be wonderful to have the support of the Trainer brothers.

"You can stay here and wait for us if you want, Bailey."

Joe wore sunglasses now, so she couldn't read his expression as he moved to her side.

"I'm coming."

He snapped his teeth together, Bailey guessed to stop more words from pouring out, and simply said, "You're with me then."

"I'll be okay, Joe. Really. I won't take risks, and I'll stay safe. You don't need to watch over me."

He didn't answer, just nodded, and she saw the worry sat hard on him. Worry, Bailey realized, for her, his siblings, and what was going on in their lives. Knowing his own father may want to harm them must be hard to accept.

She nudged her horse closer, and touched his hand. "Joe, I know you're scared for me and your siblings, but we're okay while we're all together."

He didn't answer, just closed his hand around hers briefly, and then urged his horse away. Buzz followed at a trot. They headed up past the lodge, which allowed her to study the huge building. It was impressive. Pitched roof, massive glass windows, and several floors high. It had wings left and right, and an equally impressive beige stone front entrance.

"You been there yet?"

Bailey shook her head at Piper's words.

"Worth the experience, even if the guy running it's a jerk."

"He's not a jerk, he just doesn't happen to think the sun rises and sets over you, like half the other males in this town," Jack drawled.

Piper poked out her tongue, then they fell silent again. What was waiting for them up in those hills? She hoped it was an injured Elijah Neil. The other option wasn't something she wanted to contemplate.

. . .

"I JUST WANTED to keep you safe, Bailey." Joe found his voice when they left the others to start searching their allocated area. He turned in his saddle to look at her over his shoulder. "I just wanted to—"

"I know, but I'm good, and I want to do this," Bailey said. "Sitting back there, thinking, waiting, with nothing to do would have been worse."

Not for me. He wanted her sitting in Maggie's house with the doors locked, where she couldn't be hurt, where nothing could touch her. No more ugliness, nothing. His need to protect this woman was as strong as ever.

"I also know you're worried about the others, Joe."

"Yes." He said the word slowly. He was worried. More than worried, he was plain shit-scared. Too many incidents had happened now, including whoever that man was at the bar last night with the knife. It had to stop, and to do that, they had to find whoever was responsible. "I don't want to lose anyone," he said. "And you're in that anyone, Bailey."

"I don't want anything to happen to any of you either."

He shot her another look. Tiredness was etched in her pale face, but she was here, and at least he could watch over her. Now wasn't the time or place for this conversation, he knew that. They needed to focus, but at least they each understood where the other was coming from right now.

"We're nearing the falls, Bailey. You don't leave my sight, not even for a second."

"I understood that the first and second time you told me, Joe."

Her voice was calm, and he wasn't sure how she managed that when inside he was a seething mass of emotions.

"Fine, then make sure you do as I say, and everything will go all right."

"Yes, sir."

"Did you just salute me?"

She threw him a cheeky smile that had him shaking his head. "You're gonna pay for that later."

"Okay."

One word, nothing erotic in it, or the way she said it. She didn't lick her lips or send him a sizzling look, and yet he was aroused in seconds. *Not a good move*, he thought, and made himself imagine a pile of steaming horse shit. That cooled him down some.

"Buzz, go on." He urged the dog ahead. Joe then nudged his mount off the path, and headed left to the trail that would take them down to the falls.

"It's steep. Lean back, and let Sandy do the work, Bailey, she knows the way."

"Will do."

He went first, having been down here many times before. It never failed to catch his breath. The sheer beauty of what was below them was amazing.

"Wow."

He managed a half smile at the awe in her voice. The falls were getting louder as they descended, and worry gnawed in his gut. Worry for Elijah, and the heavy weight he felt that something bad had happened to the man. Worry that someone wanted one of his people hurt... or all of them.

They reached the bottom seconds later, where huge jets of water shot out from the mountain and into the blue pool below. Surrounded by hills on all sides, this was the only way in.

"It's amazing. I only came here a few times when I was young, and I'd forgotten how wonderful it is."

It was, Joe thought. Even after seeing it constantly for most of his life.

"Hold up there for a second, Bailey, I want to check that cave." She nodded as he pointed to an opening in the mountain. "Elijah could be hurt and in there waiting for help. I'll check under the waterfall after. You stretch your legs, and take a drink."

"Okay."

He caught her as she swung her leg over the saddle, and lowered her down.

"Thanks."

"She's a big horse, I didn't want you to fall," Joe said, releasing her when what he wanted was to sink his hands into her hair and kiss her senseless, find all that passion and togetherness he'd felt this morning. But now wasn't the time for that; now was about finding Elijah. "I'll be back soon. Just drop Sandy's reins, she won't go anywhere."

"Okay."

It was more an opening than a cave. Shallow, but offering protection for anyone caught in the rain up here, or needing shelter. He and Buzz found no sign of Elijah. *Where the hell is he?* Elijah was a local, and one of the friendly ones. They needed to find him and bring him home to his family.

"Joe!"

He heard Bailey's scream, and started running. She wasn't where he'd left her, but in the water, swimming toward the waterfall.

"Bailey!" He roared for her to stop. She'd be drowned by the weight of the water. But she didn't stop, she kept swimming until he lost sight of her as she dived under the water.

Stripping off his boots and jeans, Joe threw off his hat beside Bailey's clothes. "Stay, Buzz!" Seconds later, he was in the water. Adrenaline had him at the falls in minutes; he dived under and came up the other side.

"Bailey!" His heart thudded as fear clawed at his throat. She surfaced before him.

"Jesus!" He grabbed her. "What the fuck are you doing?"

"I s-saw a shirt floating, and then a c-cap," she stuttered. "I thought it must be Elijah's so I dived in, but he's dead, Joe. He's d-down there, I saw him as I went under the falls. You have to get him!"

"Stay here!" Joe dived under, and swam down. He found Elijah on the bottom, wedged under a ledge. Needing air, he returned to the surface.

"It's him, isn't it! Elijah N-Neil?"

He caught her as she launched at him, and moved to the ledge where he could stand.

"He has a family, Joe, and he's dead."

"I know, baby. But we need to get him out of the water now. To do that I need you to get out, then go and use the radio in my pack to call Fin. Can you do that for me?"

She nodded, her damp hair brushing his cheek.

"Good girl. I'm gonna boost you up, and you run round and under the falls, okay?"

"But I should stay and help you, Joe?"

He eased her face out of his neck, and cupped a cheek.

"I'm stronger physically, Bailey, so I can bring him up. I need you to radio Fin for me now. It's important."

She nodded.

"H-he's dead, Joe."

"I know. But let's get him home now, Bailey. We owe him that, okay?"

She sucked in a deep breath, then nodded. He kissed her, just a soft brush, then turned and boosted her out of the water. She scrabbled onto the rocks, and then was up and running along the narrow path.

"Be careful!"

Joe watched her go, then drew in a couple of deep breaths himself, before diving back under the water to get Elijah.

Chapter 29

HE TRIED TWICE to get the body up, but it was on the third attempt he managed to get Elijah out from under the ledge and float him up to the surface. Bailey stood above him, looking scared, with Buzz. Her fingers were in his fur, and the dog stood silently at her side, watching him.

"Thank God, Joe, I was worried when you didn't surface!"

Joe hauled in several breaths before he could speak.

"Did you get hold of Fin?"

She nodded, keeping her eyes on him and not the body he held.

"Look away now," he warned Bailey. "Dead bodies that have been in the water for a while are not something you need to see."

"But you're looking."

"I've rescued a body before from here, I know what to expect. You don't."

"Let me help you, Joe."

"I got this, you go and put on my jacket and stay out in the sun, and I'll stay with him.

"I'll help you bring him up here, then go do that."

"Just do what I asked you, Bailey, please."

It was the please that had her turning away and running under the waterfall again.

"Okay now, boy, you need to back it up because we're coming out," he said to the dog, who was still watching him closely.

Joe used the last of his strength to get Elijah onto the ledge, then followed, and sat there sucking in air until his lungs filled, and his breathing returned to normal. Buzz sat at his side, leaning into him, and he wrapped an arm around him, enjoying the warmth.

"I have a blanket."

He should have known she'd disobey him. She hurried back to his side with her arms loaded. Joe watched her shake out the blanket and lay it over Elijah.

Dressed in her jeans and jacket, at least she didn't appear to be shivering now.

"You need to dress, Joe, before you get sick."

He didn't argue, because he was cold. Climbing to his feet, he stripped off his shorts, and pulled on his jeans, shirt, and lastly the jacket. He then leaned on the inside of the cave wall, because suddenly he was exhausted.

"Here." She handed him one of the two chocolate bars in her hand.

"You're not very good at obeying orders, Bailey Jones."

"I've been obeying them for years. I've decided now's the time to rebel."

He snorted, and then started on his bar.

"Was he a friend, Joe?"

"Elijah and I weren't close friends, but we always respected each other. Now, how about you let me hold you for a while, just until they reach us. We're both cold, and God knows you must be exhausted after the hell you've been through today. Where are you getting this energy?"

"Adrenaline."

"Makes sense. I feel like I've been run over by a large semi."

"The shock of what's been happening must be hitting you too, Joe."

All the fight went out of her as she rested against him, her face turned away from Elijah's body. They sat like that, in silence, until Buzz started barking and took off out of the cave. The others were arriving.

"Let's go now, Bailey." Lifting her to her feet, he followed her out to where the others waited, grim-faced.

THEY TOOK the body to the ranger station. From there the police would come and take Elijah to the morgue. Someone would notify his wife and children.

The Trainer siblings and Bailey made a silent, sad procession as they headed back to the stables. Joe had watched her, making sure she wasn't showing any signs of shock or exhaustion. But Bailey kept her back straight, eyes forward, and Sandy did the rest.

One thing he'd realized today was that she was a lot stronger than he, or she, believed. Bailey had an inner strength; he just doubted it had ever really been tested. Or more importantly, that anyone had let her test it over the last few years.

They rode into the stables, weary and tired. Joe dismounted and went to Bailey's side. She didn't say anything, just fell into his arms.

"You go on and sit down now, we'll deal with the horses."

Her spine stiffened, shoulders snapping back.

"No, I'll take care of Sandy. Everyone is tired, Joe. Not just me."

"No one expects you to, Bailey. Or will think any worse of you for not rubbing her down."

She didn't answer, just took the reins, and led Sandy into her stall. Joe answered his cell phone while he watched her walk away.

"Elijah was murdered, Joe," Fin said in his ear. "Bullet to the back of the head."

"Fuck," Joe said, running a hand through his hair. "Come over later, and we'll talk." He ended the call, then went to find his brothers. They were in the tack room.

"Elijah was murdered. There was a bullet hole in the back of his head."

"Hell!" Jack said.

"I know it, and add in the crap that's going down with us and it's a massive pile of shit."

"This shit is just pissing me off now," Luke said, looking worried.

"Be diligent," Joe said, then he went to rub his horse down. After, he found Bailey. She'd done what needed to be done, and was now hugging Sandy while she ate.

"Hey." Joe leaned on the half door.

"I love horses."

She didn't move. Just stood there with her eyes closed, resting.

"I think she loves you too."

"Every time I close my eyes, Elijah Neil is going to be there, isn't he, Joe?"

He let himself into the stable and put his arms around her where she still rested against the horse. Her hair was damp, and he could feel that even standing here was an effort. It was all done now, the adrenaline and courage. She was out on her feet.

"For a while you probably will. So maybe the doctor can help you with that. Something to help you sleep for a while."

"I don't take pills."

"Why?"

"My mother lives on them. They keep her sane, she says. But what she really means is they let her zone out instead of dealing with my grandfather."

"So she wasn't there for you?"

"She tried." Opening her eyes, she placed a soft kiss on Sandy's neck, then slid sideways out of his arms. "Just not very hard."

"I'm sorry."

The smile she gave him was sad.

"It's not your fault, just as it's not mine your father wasn't a good one. But it's moments like this that you really want a special someone in your life."

He'd been about to tell her he was here for her, when he heard Piper shriek.

"Mom!"

Joe watched his cousin sprint past him and into the arms of the woman standing in the stable doorway. Big like Piper, she had been the rock that the Trainer family had needed to tether themselves to. With long gray hair, usually piled on top of her head, Aunt Jess had a ruddy complexion, working-woman hands, and a belly laugh that made everyone join in. Before he realized he was even moving, Joe was heading her way.

BAILEY WATCHED the four Trainer children surround the woman. She'd heard about Piper's mother, Aunt Jess, and there was no doubt they all loved her very much. She felt a small tug of pathetic jealousy that there was no Aunt Jess in her life.

Her life had been a good one, but she was beginning to understand that if she'd stood up for herself, it may have been better. Standing up to her grandfather wouldn't have been easy, but Bailey knew she could do it now... and would one day soon to get back what was hers.

She had Maggs and Beau in her life now, too. Plus, there was Joe, but she wasn't sure what label to put on what was between them yet.

Deciding that her bed was what she needed before she simply fell onto the hay and gave in to exhaustion, Bailey moved quietly out of the barn, leaving the Trainer family to their reunion. Early evening was settling over Ryker Falls. The twins were blocking the lowering sun, and the air was cooler now. Maggie would be home, and she wanted to see her friend, and explain what had happened. She then needed a bath and food, in that order, and lastly sleep.

She saw him again, Elijah Neil and his wide-open eyes. He'd been pale and bloated, his hair floating off his head. She'd not known him in life, but in death he'd been a frightening image.

Pushing the memory aside, she concentrated on walking down the driveway. She couldn't remember a time in her life when she'd ever been this tired. But she'd been strong, Bailey thought. Strong enough to cope with what the day had brought.

The hum of an engine had her moving to the side of the road. But it slowed as it approached, and then pulled up beside her. It was an ATV, and Joe Trainer was riding it.

"What the hell are you doing?"

Bailey frowned at the ridiculous question.

"Walking home."

"Someone attempted to barbecue you today, then you saw your first dead body. Exhaustion is dogging your every step, and you're so pale I'm not entirely sure that you're not a ghost."

"And your point is?" Bailey yawned.

"For a person with your smarts, you're not using your head."

"Are you deliberately trying to insult me?"

"Just get on the back Bailey."

His hair was standing up off his head, and she saw the exhaustion in his face too.

"I'm tired, Joe, so I'm going home. See you." Lifting a hand, she started walking.

"Get on the ATV, Bailey. You're coming back to the main house for a meal, and then you're staying the night with me. You don't need to be alone."

Her stomach made a loud growling noise at the mention of food, but she didn't think he'd heard that. "No, but thanks. I'm good, Joe. I just need some time to process today, and to do that I need to be alone. Plus, Maggs will be there. You go on back to your aunt Jess, and spend time with her and your family."

She thought she'd won, because he said nothing else.

"Funny how I never noticed that stupid streak right off."

Bailey shrieked as he picked her up and dumped her on the back of the ATV.

"Stay!"

Stunned, she didn't move in time, and suddenly she was grabbing Joe's waist as he turned them around and headed back where he'd come from.

"You c-can't just do that!"

"Seems like I can."

"Take me home then."

"No."

He drove up the drive while Bailey argued with him, and then up to his house.

"Okay, we shower here, then go down to the main house for food."

"Do I get a say in this?" She tried to glare at him.

"Not so much."

Once inside, he nudged her up the stairs to his bedroom, then into the shower. While he turned on the water, she slumped onto the toilet. Her legs had finally given up working.

"Okay, in you get."

"Where is Buzz?"

"With Aunt Jess. She's one of his favorite people, because she feeds him constantly. Now strip."

"I'm just taking a minute here."

"Lost the use of your limbs?"

"Something like that."

"How about I help you?"

"I got it." Bailey attempted to rise, but he was there and simply lifted her to her feet. "I said I got it, Joe."

"I get that suddenly you have this newfound need to be in control of your own destiny... really, it's admirable," he said, reaching for the hem of the jacket she wore. "I'm all for strong women, but right now you need my help, so let me give it."

"You are not undressing me." She attempted to slap his hands aside as he reached for her clothes. Resistance, it seemed, was futile. "I'm sure I should be putting up more of a fight." As the words finished on a yawn, he snorted.

"Just give in gracefully, sweet cheeks."

"Sweet cheeks?" Bailey was now naked, and too tired to care.

"You are sweet, even dirty and tired."

Bailey found the mirror that was rapidly steaming up. Her face was pale and dirty, and her hair hung in a damp braid.

"Get in the shower, Bailey."

She did, because she wanted to. The spray made her moan.

"That good, huh?"

"And more. Sorry, Joe, I won't be long, I know you must be tired too."

"I have another shower in the house if I wanted to use it."

"Why don't...." Bailey's words trailed off as he stepped through the door.

"Got room in there for me?"

"I'll be out soon." Her mouth had gone dry.

"It's my duty to make sure you don't fall down the drain. So move that cute butt."

And suddenly the shower stall that had seemed big was now not. He moved in, all sleek muscles and big body.

"I've never showered with someone before."

"Let me educate you, then," he said, picking up the soap, and beginning to do just that.

Chapter 30

THEY PULLED up outside the main house thirty minutes later. Bailey was quiet as she got off the ATV. Joe followed, moving to stand behind her as she looked up at the house she'd lived thirteen years of her life in.

They'd showered together, and he'd washed every inch of her lovely body. He'd then taken her right there against the wall. It had been slow and wet, and he'd swallowed her moans, bracing her hands above her head while he kissed her. Joe wasn't sure he'd ever get enough of her.

He'd found her one of his old denim shirts to wear. It came to her knees, and the cuffs had to be rolled several times. Her hair was loose and damp, face bare, cheeks pink from the shower. On her feet were the peach sneakers. She looked innocent and sexy at the same time.

"You're rocking that look."

She didn't take her eyes from the house.

"Your family will know this is your shirt, Joe."

"Sure, and that we're sleeping together, so you probably just need to deal with that fact."

"I'm a private person."

"I'm not," he said, touching her shoulder. "And they're all good people who like you, Bailey."

"I like them too."

She hadn't taken her eyes off the house yet.

"That's good to know."

Her sigh came from the soles of her feet.

"I don't know if I'm ready for the memories that will hit me when I walk through that door, Joe."

"They weren't all bad surely?" He moved in behind Bailey, and wrapped his arms around her.

"No, not all of them."

"It's changed in there now, baby. Come and see."

She didn't speak, just let him lead her inside. Her eyes moved around the entrance that was now bigger than when she'd lived here.

"We knocked out a few walls, and opened it up. So things are going to look different."

Bailey touched the wood paneling as she walked. Her eyes went left to right as she took it all in silently. He walked her through the big lounge that had large, comfortable furnishings and an open fireplace. Piper was into plants, so there was plenty of greenery scattered about the place.

"We went for light colors inside, with a few feature walls. There were plenty of battles over what eventually went up, with so many strong-willed people involved, but we got there in the end."

She stopped by a window they'd put in recently, and looked out.

"Speak, woman." He didn't like her silence, or not knowing what she was thinking.

"It's a different place now. I still see touches of the house I lived in, like the paneling, of which there are forty boards, by the way. But I like it, and somehow it feels easier being in here because of the changes."

"You counted them?" He moved closer to touch her cheek.

"What?"

"The boards, how come you counted them?"

"When my mom called me down for dinner, I would count each one before I went to the dining room. It was like a nightly ritual, and a small rebellion on my part."

"How did you figure that?"

"Because I wasn't coming at once like she wanted."

"Such a tough girl."

She gave him a small smile.

"I'm glad you like the changes, Bailey."

"I really do. It's lovely, Joe. I like all that I've seen so far. I mean that. This place was like a show home when I lived here, but now I have a feeling it's a family home."

He'd known about her mother. How Bailey wasn't allowed to touch anything. Everything had to be in its place and spotlessly clean.

"I stayed here for a while, until my place was built. And I used to imagine you here. Where was your piano?"

She lifted a hand to the right. The room was now a small study off the main living area. "That was the music room when I lived here."

"Okay, I hadn't figured that. I thought you'd be in the living area."

"My mother didn't want sheet music all over the place."

Bitch. Joe kept that thought to himself, but he'd come to the conclusion long ago that Mrs. Jones wouldn't win any awards for child-rearing, just like his parents hadn't.

"So I don't know about you, but I'm starving. Want some food?"

Her stomach rumbled again.

"I'll take that as a yes."

The family was gathered in Joe's favorite room. The hub of the house, Aunt Jess called it. A big, open-plan kitchen and dining area, with tiled floors, a huge wood burner on one wall, and a long, solid dining table. The kitchen had a big cooking range, and spacious benchtops with plenty of cupboards and every appliance Aunt Jess wanted. An island separated the kitchen from the dining area. His family was all lounging in seats while Aunt Jess threw together food. She didn't like anyone else in the kitchen while she was.

"Something smells good," Joe said, walking in with Bailey. "Aunt Jess, this is Bailey Jones. Her family owned this house many years ago."

"Well, aren't you a pretty thing."

Her fingers eased their grip on his as his aunt smiled, and then Bailey was gathered into the arms that had held Joe and his siblings many times, over many years.

She accepted the hug, but wasn't exactly relaxed, and then Joe nudged her to the seat beside Luke. He took the one on her other side.

"I heard about how you saved my Jack, and put out that fire in the stable," Aunt Jess said.

"Oh well—"

"Now you take the praise I'm handing you, sweetie, because anyone who looks out for my kids deserves it."

Aunt Jess had always been someone who spoke her mind.

"You must be exhausted, Bailey, after the day you've had. First the fire, and then that horrible business with Elijah."

"I'm okay."

"You want a coffee?" Piper offered.

"Yes, please," she said.

They talked about Aunt Jess's trip, then moved on to what had been happening while she was away.

"And you think your father is responsible for everything?"

"We can't say for certain, but he did ask me for money, and then make those threats," Joe said. "I know this is upsetting for you, Aunt Jess."

"He's my brother, and yes, it's never easy to realize your blood is bad, but I reconciled myself with that long ago."

"I'm sorry you had to." Bailey surprised Joe by speaking. "You should be able to rely on your family."

Sliding his hand under her hair, Joe stroked the soft skin of her neck. She shivered, but didn't pull away.

"You should, but it's not always the case," his aunt said, looking at her. "Friends step in then. They're just as good if you don't have family. Of course, I have this lot, so I have plenty of support."

Bailey nodded. "Yes, friends are important."

"Chief Blake is looking for him, our father," Jack said.

"He is, but we need to be diligent also."

"You don't think he's involved in Elijah's murder, do you, Joe?" Piper asked.

"I don't know why he would be, or what the connection could be there, but we can't rule it out, to my way of thinking."

They discussed that in detail, as was their way. They gnawed on a subject until everyone was happy before moving on. Beside him, Bailey sat silently listening. She didn't add anything else to the conversation, but he knew she was taking it all in.

"You doing okay?" He stroked a finger under the collar of her shirt... which was actually his shirt.

"Yes, thank you."

"And there's my polite Miss Jones again."

She turned, her face now close to his.

"I'm trying to work out why your father would want to harm you. I understand that he's angry you didn't give him money, but to want you hurt or worse... would he really do that to his own children?"

"You know what he's about, Bailey. You remember," Joe said.

She nodded. "I remember him hurting you, and wanting to hurt him back because of it, but to kill? That's different again, don't you think?"

Joe shrugged. "He's an asshole. My take is he's just moved that up another notch, and has no regard for anyone or anything."

"You need to be careful, Joe."

He leaned in and kissed her. Around him, his family talked, but he knew they were taking it in.

"You worried about me, sweetheart?"

Her cheeks went pink, but she stood her ground.

"Of course, and me too, as I seem to be caught up in it."

He thought about the fire that seemed so long ago, and how he could have lost her.

"Yeah, you need to take care too, because I won't let anything to happen to you... ever."

"You can't protect me, Joe."

"Yes—" He kissed her again. "—I can."

"Evening, all." Mr. Goldhirsh walked in, and Joe dragged his eyes from Bailey's. The man had been coming and going from the house for years. This time he had a large bunch of colorful flowers in one hand.

"Aww, you bringing me flowers again, Mr. Goldhirsh?" Luke teased.

Mr. Goldhirsh ignored him and made for Aunt Jess.

"And there she is, the most beautiful woman in Ryker Falls."

His aunt blushed as she always did, and took the flowers, accepting the kiss he gave her.

Joe caught the shocked look on Bailey's face before she took another mouthful of coffee.

"They've had a thing for years."

"Really?"

"Really."

"That's very sweet."

"It is," Joe agreed. "It makes them both happy."

"How come you only get out of your running gear for Aunt Jess?" Jack asked.

"She's special," Mr. Goldhirsh said, pouring himself a coffee. He wore black trousers and a collared gray shirt. "You lot aren't."

This produced hoots of laughter.

Mr. Goldhirsh then made for Bailey. Placing a hand on her back, he leaned in and kissed the top of her head.

"I heard how brave you were today, girl. I'm proud of you."

"Thank you," Bailey said politely, and the smile she gave him was genuine.

"You need anything, you call."

"I will." She patted the hand he had on her shoulder.

Joe wondered if she knew how many people she was friends with in Ryker. How many people would be there if she needed them. The girl who'd been alone for so long, wasn't anymore.

The meal was laid on the table, and consisted of burgers, fries, and chocolate cake. Food for the gods, as far as the Trainer siblings were concerned, and Bailey didn't look unhappy either as she picked up a handful of fries and stuffed the lot in her mouth.

She raised a brow at his look. "What?"

"You're losing more of your prissiness."

She poked out her tongue, which made him laugh, and then placed more fries in her mouth.

"Oh my God, tell me that smell is homemade burgers, Aunt Jess?" Fin arrived, looking as tired as anyone else in the room, and probably more so considering he'd spent time calling people, and dealing with the local authorities.

"It is, and you come on here for a hug, then you can eat." Aunt Jess treated Fin like one of hers.

They ate, they talked some more, usually over each other, and Bailey observed, her eyes moving around the table, her face bemused. Joe wondered if she'd ever shared a meal like this with anyone, or eaten alone most of the time. The thought made him sad. He'd always had his siblings, even if he hadn't appreciated them.

When a knock sounded on the door, Mr. Goldhirsh went to answer it, and came back with Clark Munro on his heels, which turned an already shit day into an even bigger pile of crap.

"Clark, what you doing here?" Bailey got to her feet, and went to him. He reached for her, hugging her hard. Joe was pleased to note she patted his back, but didn't lean into the man like she did when Joe hugged her. She then stepped back out of reach.

Munro's eyes shot to the people all seated around the table, listening and showing no shame about it.

"Can we go somewhere quiet, Bailey?"

"Clark, I'm tired and hungry. If you want to talk, it will have to wait, because those burgers are probably the best I've ever tasted."

He hadn't expected that either. Joe noted the surprise on his face that Bailey hadn't complied with his wishes. *Believe it, buddy, this girl is changing.*

"I was in a store on the main street, and was told about the incident, and that you were involved. The fire, Bailey...." He seemed at a loss for words. "And then going up into those hills on a horse to look for the man. I don't understand what you were thinking, to behave in such an irrational manner. Is it true you dived into the water to retrieve the body?"

He looked confused and worried. Joe guessed he was used to the quiet, subdued version of Bailey.

"I didn't even know you could ride a horse before I came to Ryker."

"There's a great deal you don't know about me, Clark, or that I know about myself for that matter, but I'm enjoying finding it out... for the most part anyway."

Joe wondered if she was thinking about him or Elijah Neil. Looking at her in his shirt, hair loose, face scrubbed bare, Joe guessed she was a world away from the uptight, label-wearing pianist Clark Munro knew.

"We don't stand on ceremony here. I'm Aunt Jess, and Clark, is it?"

The man nodded as Joe's aunt got to her feet.

"It is, and please excuse my manners for not intro-ducing myself to you sooner."

He was slick, Joe would give him that, but nothing else. The man had been in Ryker too long as far as he was concerned, and the sooner he left—alone—the better.

"Wouldn't hurt you heathens to learn a few of his manners," Aunt Jess said, taking the hand Clark held out to her, and pumping it twice.

"Thanks for that, Clark," Jack drawled. "She'll spend the next two months making us dress for dinner and pull out her seat now."

"You ignore them now, Clark, and take a seat. Have you eaten?"

Looking trapped, he turned to Bailey, but she was already back in her seat, inhaling food.

"I haven't, no."

"Sit, then." Aunt Jess led him to the seat between Luke and Piper, then pressed him into it. Luke handed him a plate and waved to the food.

"Have at it, bud, before it's all gone."

Joe wanted to laugh as Clark looked around the table, clearly uncomfortable. His family was eating as if it was their last meal.

"You might want to remove that jacket, Clark. Wouldn't want a grease stain on it." Bailey waved a french fry at him. He quickly stood and removed it.

Everyone started talking again, except Clark and Bailey, who watched. She ate, he used the tongs supplied, as yet unused, and put some fries on his plate. He then attempted to get a burger. Piper made a noise, and picked one up and dumped it on his plate.

"I washed my hands yesterday, should be sweet."

His smile was tight, as was the thank-you.

Chapter 31

BAILEY FINALLY FILLED the gnawing ache in her stomach. She sat back and sipped her second cup of coffee, and watched Clark. She'd never loved him, and seeing him close to Joe, knew she never would. He was handsome, she conceded, but Bailey didn't get that small kick to the stomach when she looked at him. Like her, he was a product of the life they'd led, uptight and unemotional. Had they spent their life together, they would have learned to hate each other, she was sure, and probably one day would have separated.

"So, Clark, you're Bailey's manager, right?" Jack asked.

"I am, but I also have other clients."

He spoke in a polite, well-modulated tone that suggested he'd been raised on vacations in the Hamptons, and private schools. Which he may have, but strangely, Bailey actually didn't know anything about his family life or where he'd been born and raised, which was sad considering they'd once been engaged.

"Anyone famous?"

Clark looked at Bailey, his smile small.

"She's the most famous."

"Really?" Luke whistled, then nudged Bailey with his shoulder.

"She's played for royalty, and with some of the best musicians in the world. Bailey is very talented."

"Thank you, Clark." Bailey knew she was good; you didn't receive the praise she had, and not be.

"So what, you're ridiculously rich as well?" Luke asked.

Bailey leaned in and nudged Luke back, a gesture that a few weeks ago she'd never have done, but felt right now.

"I did okay." *Not that I can spend any of it.*

"Do," Clark corrected.

"Joe saw you play."

"What?" Bailey looked from Piper to Joe. He shrugged, and the look he threw at his cousin told her he wasn't pleased to have the subject raised. "You came to watch me play, and never tried to see me?"

"It was five years ago, Bailey. We hadn't spoken in a long time. What did you want me to say?"

"Hi, Bailey. Remember me?" She felt an uncomfortable swell of heat fill her body. Why did Joe's actions hurt so much? Maybe because she'd longed to see him for so many years. Long, lonely years. How hard would it have been for him to at least try and make contact? She'd written endless letters to him, and he'd never replied... not even once. It wasn't rational, this anger she was feeling, Bailey knew that, but the adult Joe should have at least made the effort.

"Too much time had passed," he said, holding her eyes. "Besides, I'm not entirely sure anyone would have let me get near you."

Bailey made herself shrug. "We'll never know."

"But surely you weren't friends before you left Ryker Falls?" Clark asked.

"We were, actually." Joe was still looking at her. "Bailey was my best friend."

She hadn't expected him to admit to that.

"How is that possible?" Clark frowned. "You were what... three or four years older than her, and she left Ryker Falls at thirteen?"

"He's right," Bailey spoke. "We were friends for two years."

Everyone fell silent as the people at the table who didn't already know about the relationship she and Joe had shared, grappled with the knowledge that a young, rebellious teenager, raised in hell, could form a bond with a child raised the exact opposite.

"You wrote the letter." Aunt Jess spoke the words softly, but Bailey and Joe heard. "It adds up," she added. "Joe's handwriting is not that neat, nor legible. Plus the words you used, and tone, weren't his." She threw Joe a smile. "Sorry, nephew, but your teachers told me you struggled with reading and writing back then."

He looked at Bailey, and shrugged, which told her it was up to her whether she acknowledged it or not.

"I did help write it." She remembered that day as if it was yesterday. Joe had arrived at their meeting place in a rage, his clothes torn, face bruised, and all she could do was sit and listen as he'd ranted about his father. When he'd calmed down, she told him he should write to his father's sister. Joe and his brothers had spent one summer with Aunt Jess, and he'd told her that she'd been a nice woman.

"Thank you." Joe's aunt reached across the table and grabbed Bailey's hands, squeezing them hard. "I'd never have known how bad things were if not for that letter."

"You got Aunt Jess to come here?" Jack looked shocked, as did Luke.

"She did," Joe said.

"Well, I think it's fair to say you're the Trainer guardian angel then. Getting Aunt Jess here, being there for Joe, and then saving Jack and the stables."

"Oh—" Before Bailey could finish the sentence, Luke leaned in and kissed her cheek, and Jack got to his feet, and took the other. Piper blew her a kiss from across the table.

Bailey found Clark's eyes on her. He looked confused, and who could blame him. The Bailey he knew had been closed off emotionally, and rarely got involved with people.

"So you're the Trainer family guardian angel now, how do you feel about that?" Joe whispered in her ear. Bailey didn't know how to answer that, or look at him yet, so she simply nodded. Thankfully, the topic of conversation moved on then, and to say she was pleased was an understatement. Bailey had spent years of her life avoiding emotions, and since being in Ryker she'd been hit from all sides with them. Today she'd had the fire, finding that body in the falls, and the knowledge that Joe had come to her concert and not seen her. Strange, how that last one had really rocked her back on her heels.

"Can I give you a ride home, Bailey?"

"Sure, thanks, Clark." Bailey was relieved to get to her feet. She needed the sanctuary of her bed, and some alone time.

Bailey knew Joe had wanted her to stay the night with him, but she needed some time to process what was going on inside her head. In her current mood she wasn't entirely sure she wouldn't say something to him. Something irrational, and that wasn't like her.

"If you need me, call." Joe followed her to the front door.

"I won't, but thank you."

He grabbed her arm as she went to follow Clark outside.

"I'm sorry."

"For what?"

"Everything." He ran a hand through his hair. "Not writing those letters. Not coming to see you after the concert."

She eased her hand free.

"Sure, I get that you had other stuff going on. I guess I just thought if ever there came a time you and I were near each other again, we would make the effort to connect."

"Ten years, Bailey. How did I even know if you'd still remember me?"

"Did you forget me?"

He blew out a breath, which was answer enough.

"I was wrong, all right. I'm sorry."

He looked confused and angry. Good, she was feeling some of those herself right now.

"Leave it alone now, Joe. We're tired, and I'm feeling a bit raw from today. I need to get some sleep."

"I don't want you to go."

"But I want to."

"At least promise you'll call if you wake upset—at any time. Better yet, tell Clod to go, and come home with me. I want to get my shirt back."

She nearly gave in. The urge to feel his hands on her again was huge, but she had to be strong. She couldn't allow herself to need him, not when she had no idea where she was going to end up. Now was the time, Bailey realized, to back away, and find out what her next step could be. Joe Trainer, Bailey knew, could really hurt her if she let him.

"I have to go, Joe. Clark is waiting."

He pulled her close as she turned to leave, then kissed her. It was brief, but still... the man could kiss.

"I-I need to go."

His sigh was loud.

"I hate the feeling that you're leaving angry with me, which is pretty pathetic after what you've been through today, and the fact that Elijah's family are mourning him right now. But I don't feel rational around you, Bailey."

"Joe—"

"You're important to me, dammit!"

She didn't know what to say to that.

"Do you understand that? Understand that you matter to me?" His face was serious, eyes focused on her.

"I can't deal with this now, Joe. It's all too much. I need to go."

"Running never solved anything, Bailey. And it won't solve this... what's between us. Plus, there's the fact that if you run, I will follow."

"What?" Bailey had been in the process of turning away from him, but his words had her facing him again. His big body was tense, T-shirt stretched across his shoulders. The man had no right to be that hot.

"You heard me. I'm not letting you walk away from this, Bailey."

"I-I don't know what this is, Joe. We seem to either hurt or lo—like each other. Everything about us is volatile."

"Because we need to spend time getting to know each other again. I don't know what this is either, but I want to find out."

"I have to g-go." Bailey turned and ran down the steps. Exhaling as she reached the bottom. Clark was waiting in the car, engine running.

They drove in silence out of the drive while Bailey grappled with what Joe had just said.

"Are you all right?"

"Tired. It's been a long day," Bailey said. "Have you decided when you're leaving, Clark?"

"Soon. I need to get back, but like I said, I'm enjoying the break."

"It's nice here." Nice. Bailey nearly laughed at the word. What she felt about Ryker—or more importantly, Joe Trainer—was so far beyond nice.

"And is what's between you and the eldest Trainer nice, Bailey? And don't insult my intelligence by denying it."

"No, I won't deny it, but I'm not sure where it's going."

"Do you want it to go somewhere?"

"I don't know... maybe. It's complicated, and I don't want to be hurt again." She hadn't meant to say the words, especially not to him. She and Clark didn't discuss personal issues.

"Again?"

She looked out the window at the rapidly darkening sky. Even the stars were different here. Everything was so much clearer, the air fresher.

"Has there ever been anyone in your life, Clark, that you just can't forget? Someone who makes you feel different from every other person?"

"Once," he said quietly.

"Who?"

"A woman I used to know. She died, and I remember thinking the day she left me that I wouldn't recover. Maybe a part of me never did."

Bailey touched the hand he had on the steering wheel.

"I'm sorry, Clark. Sorry for your loss, and sorry we never talked before about things like this."

"Things?" He threw her a smile.

"Personal things."

He shuddered. "I've pretty much shut myself off from

personal things since Alison's death, and I don't think I ever want to go back there."

"I thought that," Bailey said. "Believed it was for the best."

"But now you don't?"

"I don't honestly know. Personal stuff comes with messy emotions and feelings, and I'm not sure I like that."

"Sure you do. And you feel messy emotions for Joe Trainer, don't you?"

"Clark Munro, I do believe that is a personal question," Bailey tried to lighten the mood.

"It is, but then things have changed between us too, since coming here, haven't they?"

"I guess they have. I like to think we're real friends now," Bailey said.

"Sure, I like that we are." He threw her another smile. "I never thought I'd see the day you rode horses, mucked out stables, and went on search and rescue missions. Jesus, Bailey, I still can't believe you were in that stable when it was burning."

"It was not burning, a bunch of cloths were."

"You know what I mean. It's dangerous here for you. I heard about the shots fired when you and Jack Trainer were out riding, and now this stuff today. Maybe you should think about leaving with me?"

Should she? Would it be better to go now and decide what she wanted to do? Joe had said he'd come after her, but did she believe him? Maybe, but the thought of leaving Ryker was not a happy one. She felt like this was home now, but then what if Joe and she didn't work out, and she had to see him with other women? Also, she couldn't spend the rest of her life working in the stable or playing in Apple Sours occasionally. She needed a plan, a career path.

"I'm not going back to Boston, Clark. You need to understand that."

"You're really giving it all up?"

She nodded. "I am, and when I get my money back I'm going to find out what I really want to do."

"What do you mean, get your money back?"

"My grandfather originally started my bank accounts, and I never changed that. I have one of my own, which he put money into, but he won't let me have any more until I go back and do what he wants."

"You are shitting me!"

"Clark!" Bailey's mouth dropped open. "What has gotten into you, speaking like that?"

He slashed a hand through the air, then returned it to the wheel. "That bastard is actually withholding your money? Money you earned? I can't believe you let him control everything like that."

"Yes, you can. He controlled you too, and it was just easier that way."

"I'm sorry, Bailey. I'll speak with him and make him see reason," Clark said as he pulled into Maggie's driveway.

"This is my battle, not yours. Now, I'm going inside before I fall asleep in your car."

She watched him drive off, then went in to tell Maggie about her day. It was another hour before she stumbled to bed. She was asleep before her head hit the pillow.

Chapter 32

JOE HADN'T SEEN Bailey for two days. He knew he needed to talk to her again, because she was pissed he'd not at least tried to see her after that concert. Which made no sense to him, as they were strangers then, but he'd never really understood women. He was also no closer to understanding why he'd avoided her. She'd just seemed so far away from him as he'd sat in that audience and watched her perform. Bailey had been in a long blue dress. It had sparkly stuff over it, and her hair had been on top of her head in some elaborate thing, and he'd remembered thinking she looked a million miles from his Bailey. The girl he'd once loved deeply. He'd sat there in awe of her, and clapped with the others in the audience, then when she'd walked off the stage he'd left the concert hall and walked for hours. Seeing her had brought it all back. The ugliness of his life when she'd been in it, and the solace he'd found in Bailey Jones's company.

Was that the reason he hadn't gone to see her? Had the memories been too painful?

Pushing the thoughts aside for now, he vowed to see

her today, even if he had to lock her in somewhere so she would talk to him.

He'd woken early after a long sleep, and gone into town to talk with Chief Blake. They'd discussed his concerns regarding his father, and the fire. Plus, Elijah's death. The chief had promised to keep him in the loop if he heard anything new. He'd come away frustrated with the inaction, even though he knew Chief Blake was doing what he could to get results.

Joe was now in the bar checking supplies, while he tried not to think about Bailey. He heard the knock on the back door, and when he opened it, Clark Munro was standing there.

"Munro."

"Trainer, can I have a word before I leave town?"

"You're leaving? Now that is bad news," Joe drawled. He should be a bigger man... should be able to shake the man's hand and send him on his way, but the simple fact was, he wasn't. Not when it had anything to do with Bailey, anyway.

"I know you and she have something, and while I wish she would come back with me to Boston, she is refusing. All I'm asking is that you give some thought to what is best for her."

"And you think you're best for her?"

The man shook his head. "No. I realize now that what I felt for Bailey was friendship. We would never have worked, and probably would have ended up hating each other."

"Bailey knows her own mind, she won't make decisions based on me. Maybe you should put some of your efforts into getting that asshole grandfather to release her money, then she'd be free to do whatever the hell she wanted."

"You know about that?"

"I do, and a lot more."

Clark studied him. "What's the deal with you two?"

"I believe that was covered the other night. We were friends when we both needed one."

"Yes, I heard, but there's more to this. She's hung up over you, and I'm not sure that's a good thing."

He liked the thought of Bailey being hung up over him.

"If you don't want to be with her, and I do, then her being hung up over me is a good thing from where I'm standing, Munro."

"She thinks you could hurt her."

"I won't, and I'm pretty sure you're talking out of school there, bud."

"Probably, but I just want what's best for her."

"As do I," Joe added.

"She told me once about this person in her past. It was probably the only personal conversation we ever had."

"And that's weird, considering you were engaged."

"Not all people are like the Trainer family, Joseph. Some of us don't share every detail of their life."

"Just Joe, and we spent years living with an asshole who pretty much kept us in check with threats. Once that threat is lifted, it tends to change you."

"I'm sorry, I didn't know."

"I didn't tell you for sympathy, just stating facts. I like the way my family is now. Being open is better for your digestion."

"Yes, well, Bailey and I were brought up differently."

"Uptight," Joe added.

"Why don't you just hit me, and we can leave the innuendoes out of the conversation then, because it'll be out of your system."

Joe pushed off the doorframe. "Shit, why did you have to go act all manly just when I had you pegged as a wimp."

Clark snorted. "I may appear polished, with a side serving of manners, Trainer, but it wasn't always the way."

"I had you down as a trust-fund baby." He battled it, but Joe felt a begrudging admiration for the man who stood before him. He was standing his ground, and you had to respect that. Plus, there was that "hit me" comment, which was something he would have said.

"No. It couldn't be further from it, actually."

"Okay, I'm done poking at you, so let's have the rest of the story."

"Bailey had just had the third operation on her wrist and was still out of it on drugs. I came in to see her and asked if there was anything she wanted."

It was telling to Joe, that he didn't like thinking of her anywhere in pain without him.

"She said that just once, she wanted to go back and see him. See if he was doing okay. I asked who she was talking about, and Bailey told me that it was someone who had once been her best friend. She fell asleep shortly after, so the conversation finished. I forgot her words until now."

She'd asked for him, even all these years later. She'd never forgotten what they had, just like he hadn't. There had always been a link between him and Bailey Jones, and he also knew it was growing stronger every time he saw her. He should have gone to visit her after that concert. She'd deserved that much from him.

"That was you, wasn't it, Joe?"

He managed to nod.

"Well, here's a bit of advice."

"Shoot" was all he could manage, because his throat felt tight.

"First. If you love her, as I suspect you do, then make

sure she knows it, because she's not had many people tell her that, me included. Second. Don't hurt her."

"I would sooner hurt myself. Now tell me, why did she let him bully her?"

"Him, being her grandfather?"

Joe nodded.

"He's smooth, and can pretty much talk anyone round to his way of thinking, and I think deep inside him, he loves Bailey. The problem is, she allowed him to take control of her life from day one is my observation, and that never changed. So when she rebelled, it shocked him, and he reacted by cutting off her money. Hell!"

"What?" Joe looked at Clark.

"I just remembered that today is Bailey's birthday. Damn!" Clark shook his head. "I usually remember things like that."

"I'll take care of it," Joe said. He'd make some calls, and ensure this was a birthday Bailey never forgot.

"Just so you know, Leonard Southby is a strong man who believes he has always had his granddaughter's best interests front and center in his life."

"Not so much, is my guess."

"No, and again I should have seen that, but Bailey never raised any red flags with me, she just did what he asked of her, and showed no emotion doing it. I thought she was incapable of it, until I came here and saw different."

Joe found a smile. "She's amazing."

"She is."

Joe stuck out his hand, and Clark shook it.

"Take care of her, Joe, and I'll see if I can sort out this business with her grandfather."

"I will, and come back in a couple of years."

Clark laughed, and Joe walked with him around the

front to the main street, where his car was parked. They were standing at the curb when Clark squinted down the street.

"Don't tell me that's who I think it is?"

"Who do you think it is?" Joe followed Clark's gaze and saw a long black sedan coming down the main street.

"The only man I know who drives around in a chauffeur driven car just like that is Bailey's grandfather."

"We have celebrities here in Ryker." Joe kept his eyes on the black sedan.

"Let's hope it's one of them then."

"Shit," Clark whispered. "I recognize the driver."

"Fuck," Joe added as no other word fit the moment. "We've got her back here, Clark. Remember that for me, will you, and don't let this asshole make her life hell."

"Yes, we do, and she'll need it, Joe. He's one intimidating man."

"Don't you go all chicken on me now."

"No." Clark's mouth thinned. "I'm done dancing to his tune."

"You too?"

"There must be something in the water here."

Joe snorted, his eyes once again on the car that was pulling up beside them. The rear tinted window rolled down and there he was. Bailey's grandfather.

"Leonard." Clark moved forward. "What are you doing in Ryker Falls?"

He couldn't see all of Bailey's grandfather, but what he saw was impressive enough. Silver hair was parted on the side and swept back to settle in a way that suggested to Joe he'd used some kind of product to keep it there. His moustache and beard were also gray, and neatly trimmed, eyebrows the same. Face long and lean, and to Joe's mind he'd be the perfect King Arthur in the next film—or maybe his grandfather.

The door opened, and a black polished shoe came out. The leg that followed was in a tailored trouser, and on top he wore a pale blue shirt, silver-and-blue-striped tie, and waistcoat that told Joe somewhere in the depths of that car was a suit jacket hanging from something.

"I've come to take my granddaughter home, as you have yet to achieve my wishes, Clark."

He was tall, only an inch or two shorter than Joe. Lean, and fit, was his guess, even considering his years were considerably more advanced than both the men before him.

"She doesn't want to come back to Boston, and is happy here in Ryker Falls."

At least Clark had now come round to the fact she wasn't going back.

Leonard Southby's mouth thinned. "She has no idea what she wants, foolish girl. I will take control as I always have. Bailey is not fit to make her own decisions. I will talk to her, and we will leave shortly thereafter."

"Not going to happen." Joe drew the man's eyes with his words. "Bailey is a friend, and I know the influence you've had on her, her entire life, Southby, and it's stopping right now. You may want to look at releasing her money too, before we get lawyers involved."

For a brief moment the cool, arrogant facade slipped, and in its place was shock. He scrambled, and soon it was back in place, but Joe enjoyed the moment of weakness.

"And who are you to speak to me this way?"

"Joe Trainer. Friend... really good friend." He saw the man had read between the lines.

"My granddaughter has a fiancé, and he is standing here. Perhaps he has something to say about that."

"Bailey and I broke our engagement, and it was the right thing, Leonard. Neither of us loved each other, and we're better friends."

"Love!" The man scoffed, and Joe felt his dislike for him notch upward. "She needs someone like you, Clark. My granddaughter does not need the complication of love."

"Oh hell no," Joe said softly. "You did not just say loving Bailey would be a complication. She's funny, intelligent, and so goddamn beautiful it hurts just looking at her," he snarled. "She deserves better than the cold, lifeless world you created for her, and she's going to get it."

"Grandfather?"

Joe looked over his shoulder and saw Bailey. She'd obviously just come from the stables. Her hair was in a single braid, wisps everywhere. A streak of mud ran along her chin, and she wore an old black T-shirt that he thought may have belonged to Maggie, as it had the words Art is for Life on it. Her long legs were in designer jeans that now had a rip midthigh. On her feet were her now-grubby peach sneakers.

"It seems I have timed my arrival perfectly, if this is the state you are walking about in public in. You are a disgrace, Granddaughter. Get in my car at once."

She'd inherited something from her grandfather. Her expression. Not by a flicker did she betray what she felt, but Joe knew her well. She was shocked, and her grandfather's words had hurt her. The old bastard hadn't even hugged her.

"And there was me thinking she looked hot." Joe moved to her side, and wrapped an arm around her shoulders. "How you doing, sweet cheeks?"

Chapter 33

BAILEY COULDN'T BREATHE. She felt it again, the tight band of tension inside her. Leaving her grandfather had made her realize just how much he controlled her, and how much being near him had made her feel small and uncomfortable.

"It's all right, Bailey."

Joe leaned in and placed a kiss on her head. She loved him right then. Admitted that what she felt was a total and unconditional love for the man at her side. As a child it had been a sweet, painful thing, but now it was another level. Suddenly, all the arguments and disagreements they'd had seemed silly.

But she couldn't think about that now; she had to deal with the man standing before her. Later, she'd talk to Joe.

"Why are you here, Grandfather?"

His eyes narrowed at her tone. Bailey had never questioned her grandfather. Never made waves, always complied with his wishes.

Silly, weak-kneed fool that I was.

"To bring you home. It is time for you to start playing again. I have had requests, and people are starting to talk."

"She's not coming back, Leonard, I told you." Clark followed these words up by moving to her other side. Suddenly she was supported on both sides. Her grandfather did not like it.

"You're fired, Munro!"

"I don't work for you, Leonard, I never did, and now Bailey is no longer performing I will have no further contact with you, which pleases me greatly.

"He's powerful, Clark," she said, looking up at her friend. "Don't upset him.

"It'll be okay, Bailey." He patted her hand. "I'm growing a pair, like you."

"Pair of what?"

Joe snorted, and Clark smiled.

"I'll explain later."

"Your hand is healed, what is stopping you from performing? Nothing." Her grandfather often did that, answered his own questions.

"This is not the place for this discussion, Grandfather." She moved out of Joe's embrace, and missed him instantly. "I will ride with you to the lodge, where you can stay for the night, then you will leave in the morning."

"I do not take orders from you, Granddaughter!"

"And yet I must take them from you?"

She'd shocked him again, but she knew this discussion was far from over. However, he was a man to whom appearances were everything, so he gave her a final look before getting back inside the car. He would not lower himself to argue on a main street where anyone could see them.

"I don't want you going with him alone, Bailey." Joe held her arm as she went to follow.

"I know, but I'm stronger now, and he won't kidnap me. For all he's a stern, autocratic man, he's still my grandfather. I need to do this, Joe, for me. I need to stand up to him, or I never will. This has to be resolved."

He wasn't happy about it, but he nodded. "All right, but if you need me, call."

"On what?" She tried to lighten the mood. He scowled.

"I'm getting you a phone."

"I'll come with you then."

"No, Clark, I have to do this alone."

Bailey kissed Joe's cheek, then did the same to Clark. She then made herself walk the steps to her grandfather's car. They were some of the hardest of her life. Sliding inside, she closed the door, and the car pulled away from the curb.

"Take a left at the end of the street," she told the driver.

"We will pack your things and leave in the morning."

"I'm not coming with you, Grandfather. I like it here for now. I am working in the stables, and playing honky-tonk in a bar. It suits me, and for the first time in many years, I am happy."

"Honky-tonk! Mucking out stables! I did not pay for you to have the best tutors and education for that."

"I have made you enough money to reimburse those costs, Grandfather. Plus, if you remember I received a scholarship on my own merits for Juilliard."

"I do not like your tone, Bailey."

She would have once been cowed, and apologized, but not now. Looking at the man who had been the main influence on her life for many years, she realized that he was just that... a man. He couldn't hurt her if she didn't allow it.

"I allowed you control over me and my life, and for that I am sorry. I know you believed you were doing what was right, and for a while it probably was, but I am no longer the girl you can control, Grandfather. I want to make my own decisions and live my own life. If mistakes are to be made, I want to be the one to make them. I no longer want to be your performing puppet."

The shock on his face was real.

"And is that man part of this rebellion?"

"No, I was rebelling by leaving Boston, and my courage grew with every mile I distanced myself from you."

"I have devoted my life to you, Granddaughter."

"And I am grateful to you for that. I understand the sacrifices you have made." Because she did, and knew to his mind he had done everything he believed was right for her and her career. "But I no longer wish to live in that cage," she said softly.

"Cage," he scoffed. "Expensive hotels and clothes— you never went without anything. Adoration, and being showered in flowers. Yes, your life must have been horrible."

"I did not say it was horrible, Grandfather. But when you reach the age of twenty-seven and you have no cell phone or laptop, you don't know how to use a washing machine, or fend for yourself in the world without help, it is not good. I allowed that to happen," she added before he could speak. "Allowed it, and enjoyed it for a while, but now...." Bailey sighed. "Now I no longer want that world."

He talked at her on the way to the lodge. Then all the way inside. Angie greeted them at reception.

"Hi there, Bailey."

"Hi, Angie. This is my grandfather, and he would like a room for one night, please."

"Two, possibly three," he corrected, much to her horror.

"Why would you want to stay longer?"

"I'm taking you back with me, but I see now that will take time to achieve. But I will achieve it, Granddaughter, believe me."

"It's the influence of that no good Joe Trainer!"

Bailey and her grandfather turned, and behind them stood Mary Howard. Excellent, that was all she needed.

"And you are?" her grandfather said with a raised brow.

"Mary Howard, and my family are important people in this town, whereas those Trainers are troublemaking scum."

The woman's chins quivered as she stood there glaring at Bailey.

"I believe I told you last time we talked, Mrs. Howard, that I don't like hearing you speak about Joe or his siblings in that way," Bailey said, trying to hold onto her temper. "You have no grounds for this vendetta you are carrying out against him. The truth is your son was sent away because of his own actions, not Joe's. If he hasn't returned maybe you should ask him why and stop blaming Joe!"

"How dare you speak about my boy that way! He was twice the man of Joe Trainer!"

Bailey stepped closer to the woman, her patience now well and truly gone. "Leave him alone, Mrs. Howard, because I'm telling you now, if I hear you've been rude to Joe again, I'm coming to find you and it won't be pretty."

"Bailey, apologize at once for speaking to this woman in such an insulting way!" her grandfather said sounding shocked.

"This does not concern you, Grandfather."

"I can see I have arrived just in time, if this is the way you are now behaving. We shall leave instantly."

"No, we won't," Bailey scowled at Mary Howard again, and then her grandfather. "So the sooner you come to that realization, the better it will be for the both of us. Now I am leaving, before I get angrier. I shall see you tomorrow... before you leave. Bye, Angie."

"Bye, Bailey."

"Bailey!"

Ignoring her grandfather's roar, and surprised that he had done so in such a public setting, as appearances were everything to Leonard Southby, she kept walking out the door.

"Hi, Bailey."

"Mr. Goldhirsh." She nodded and attempted a smile. He didn't buy it.

"Problems?"

"My grandfather has arrived in Ryker Falls, and I just went at it with Mary Howard again. That woman's full of nasty."

He fell in beside her as she began to walk out the lodge gates.

"Forget Mary Howard, she's not worth your anger."

"I'll try."

"Your grandfather's visit is obviously not a good thing, is my guess?" As usual he was in his exercise clothes, although this time he also wore a small backpack.

"Not so much. Do you ever not exercise?"

"It keeps me fit and feeling young, Bailey. It is now something my body craves, almost an addiction."

"I could never be addicted to exercise."

"It's not for everyone. However, we could walk a bit together and you can explain what is troubling you, and I shall give you wonderful and insightful advice."

That surprised a laugh from her. "I could do with that, if you're free?" she said, further surprising herself.

"Indeed I am. I just need to make a call, then I am at your service."

He walked away while Bailey took several deep breaths. Dear Christ, her grandfather was here in Ryker Falls. Just the thought made her stomach twist into knots.

"Right, we shall go back up past the lodge and cut through the trail that leads back down the mountain to Trainer land."

"I may not keep up, and am probably not dressed for hiking."

"We'll take it easy."

He kept his pace slow, and she enjoyed the distance that grew between herself and her grandfather. Roxy and Phil stood over them, and the sun was nice on Bailey's bare head. She looked around at the nature on display, and slowly began to relax.

"So tell me about this grandfather." Mr. Goldhirsh had taken the lead, and threw the words over his shoulder.

"It's complex."

"Most good stories are, and as it is just us up here, and I am of course the soul of discretion, whatever you say will not be passed on."

Why not? She'd changed so much since coming here, what would it hurt to talk to Mr. Goldhirsh? His advice may even be helpful.

"My mother has always been under his control, which is part of the reason why my father left, so when we moved to live with him in Boston, he just carried on controlling her, and me. I finally rebelled, and he doesn't like it, so he's come here to collect me and take me back to Boston."

"And you let him control you?"

"To my shame, yes I did."

285

"What changed?"

She thought about that as they moved deeper into the trees. They formed a roof overhead for them to walk under, and the dappled sunlight was pretty.

"I enjoyed parts of the life for a while. I handled the performing, but I did get terrible nerves beforehand. But it was mainly the rest of it that I didn't enjoy. The press, the hotels, the parties and insincere people."

"They can't have all been insincere."

"No, there were a few good ones. Clark was good, but he was controlled too, by Grandfather."

"What was the catalyst for change then, Bailey?"

"I had an accident, and suddenly felt the need to break free, and so I did. I told Grandfather I was leaving, and got in my car and drove away."

"That can't have been easy."

"No, for many reasons, but the point is I like being in control now. I like working in the stables, because I do so by choice. He can't accept that."

"Then you need to make him accept that."

Bailey grabbed a tree as they passed and stripped a few leaves. Crushing them, she inhaled the lovely earthy scent.

"I tried just then. He's staying in Ryker until I'm ready to see reason."

"He can't kidnap you, Bailey. You don't want to go, you don't go."

"You make it sound simple."

"No, it's not simple, but you need to find the strength that helped you walk away, to make him believe you when you say no."

"I know it sounds weak when compared to what you have suffered. What so many have suffered, but at the time I just couldn't seem to find a way out of my life." Which pretty much summed up the person Bailey had been.

"Not weak, no. You could never be that, Bailey. You saved Jack, and helped Joe bring in Elijah, and then there's this business with the fire in the stable."

"Have you heard any word, Mr. Goldhirsh?"

"Chief Blake said they are trying to find Joe's father, because they believe he may be involved. He could not say much, but suspects both incidents on the Trainer land are connected and could be related to him. As for Elijah, they are unsure, but it's a terrible time for his wife and children. The community will fully support them of course, but their suffering will be great, I fear."

They walked in silence for a while, just the sound of their footsteps and nature around them. Bailey let thoughts come as she followed Mr. Goldhirsh. She wanted to stay in Ryker, and she loved Joe. How did he feel about her? They had so much to talk about before either of them could move forward. For now, she had to deal with her grandfather. Once that was done, she could deal with Joe.

They walked for a while, and then Mr. Goldhirsh declared it was time to sit and eat. They found a spot that offered a wonderful view of the twins.

"So, you and Aunt Jess," Bailey said as she took the cookie he handed her.

"She's a wonderful woman, Bailey. We both love poetry, and many other things."

"Is she an exercise fanatic too?"

"No, in that we differ, but that is a good thing also."

She wasn't sure how long they sat there talking, but had to admit she enjoyed the solitude and company. They discussed music, and books, and then started on politics—on which they agreed to disagree.

"Well, my dear, we have been gone some time now. Are you ready to go back?"

"I am, and thank you, Mr. Goldhirsh. My head feels a great deal clearer for the talk, and exercise."

"Anytime. Sometimes a few hours away offers clarity."

They cut down through Joe's land, and as they reached the main house, Bailey noticed a lot of cars.

"I wonder what's going on in there."

"I'm not sure. Shall we go and investigate, Bailey?"

"Oh... well I don't think so, as we're not invited."

"They may have news, Bailey. We should really go and see."

She followed him as he headed up the front steps. Was Joe there? Her heart beat a little faster at the prospect of seeing him again.

Chapter 34

JOE HADN'T WANTED Bailey to deal with her grandfather on her own, and neither had Clark, who surprisingly
had turned out to be all right. But he hadn't been able to
stop her, and understood she had to deal with this her own
way. But it was a hell of worry knowing she was with that
old bastard.

Joe had hit on the party to keep his mind occupied,
and he'd rung his family and friends, told them it was
Bailey's birthday, and everyone had got busy. It was Mr.
Goldhirsh who'd saved the day by calling and telling Joe he
was taking her hiking. They'd had three hours to put a
party together.

They had cake, balloons, and presents, because Piper
had told him Bailey had never had a proper party, which to
Joe's mind was just another reason to go to the lodge and
give that asshole grandfather of hers a piece of his mind.

"Just got a call from Lenny up the lodge," Luke said
tying off the end of a balloon. "Said Bailey went at it with
Mary Howard again, told her, in his words, that she'd
better keep her mouth shut or Bailey would make her

sorry. He then said if you didn't want her, he'd be keen to step in."

"I told her to stay away from that woman."

"Seems she's defending you, brother, maybe you should let her."

Maybe he should, Joe thought getting that warm feeling all over again. If she was defending him did that mean she cared for him like he cared for her?

"Tell Lenny, I'll break both his legs if he goes near her."

"She's coming!" Maggie came back into the room at a sprint. She'd been lookout.

Shelving his thoughts for now, Joe moved to stand beside the door.

They all listened as Mr. Goldhirsh told Bailey that everyone must be out back. He then entered the room, with Bailey on his heels.

"Surprise!"

Her mouth fell open, and she looked stunned, her eyes moving around the room fast. They settled on Joe, who was closest. At his side sat Buzz, with a big red bow around his neck.

"I d-don't understand."

"It's your birthday party, Bailey. We're celebrating."

She bit her lip, then sniffed, and he knew tears were next.

"Clark has a big mouth," Joe said, moving to stand before her. He took her into his arms and held her close.

"Happy birthday, baby."

"I don't know what to say." Her fingers went to Buzz's head. The dog moved closer and rested against her legs.

The animal always had the knack of knowing when a person needed his support; it was one of the things Joe loved most about him.

"Go with thank you, that usually works."

She let him hold her while she sniffed and cried. When she lifted her head off his chest, she was smiling.

"I'm having a birthday party?" Her hair was coming down, and her face still had a smudge of dirt, but she looked pretty damn good from where he was standing.

"Yup, and you have presents to open, so get to it." He nudged her forward. She was then hugged and kissed, and the smile grew wider as she saw the balloons and cake.

"It's a Mickey cake!" Bailey hurried to the table. "How did you get that so quickly?"

"Piper went to Tait's bakery, and they had that cake in the window. It was for someone else, so she bribed Mr. Tait, and he caved. So some six-year-old is going without, but don't feel bad," Joe said.

"My chest hurts," Luke said softly to Joe. "I'm thinking we need to pay her granddaddy a call and mess him up a bit, if this is the first special birthday cake she's had in her lifetime."

"He's old, unfortunately, but we can serve him up a few nice words," Joe said, feeling the same pain in his chest as he watched Bailey inspect the cake and balloons.

"Thank you," she said, still smiling. "It's really lovely of you all to do this for me, and I know Maggs and Piper heard my drunk ramblings about Mickey cakes, and balloons, so thanks to them also. Twenty-eight is possibly too old for this."

Everyone said no, it wasn't.

"Now open the presents." Jack nudged her to a pile on the end of the table.

"Has she really never had a birthday party?"

Joe shook his head at Aunt Jess's words.

"Some parents don't deserve kids."

"To be fair, we didn't have parties until you came along, and by then we were teenagers."

"But we made up for lost time, didn't we, Joe?"

He kissed her cheek. "We sure did."

She'd seen to it the Trainer boys were spoiled every birthday and Christmas from the day she entered their lives, even if they were living away from home.

"Clark bought me a cell phone!" Bailey held up a box.

Joe didn't get the usual bite of jealousy as she climbed to her toes and kissed the man's cheek.

"I'm putting my hand up not to be the one to teach her," Joe drawled. "If she is only just mastering technology now, it'll need to be someone patient, and seeing as you bought it for her, Munro, you're it."

They shared a look, and the man nodded. Understanding, Joe thought. They each knew where the other stood now, and that they were united in making sure Bailey never got hurt again.

She got artwork from Maggs, and a shirt from Pip. His brothers bought her smelly stuff that there was no way in hell they'd picked, but Bailey didn't need to know that.

"I'm going to show you my present before we eat." Joe took Bailey's hand and led her from the house.

"Where is it?"

"You'll see."

"I'm not sure how it came out that it was my birthday, or why I got a party, but thank you." She was still smiling.

"You needed cheering up."

She sighed, and Joe wished he'd kept the words to himself. "I went for a walk with Mr. Goldhirsh, and that helped sort things in my head. He was at the lodge when I left grandfather there."

"Hmm," Joe said, heading toward the stables.

"Wait." She stopped. "He was part of the setup, wasn't

he. That call... it was to you?"

"Smart girl."

"Ha" was all she said as they resumed walking.

The stables were cool as he led them down the middle between the stalls. Reaching the last on the right, he opened it and walked in.

"Happy birthday, Bailey."

She was silver, and one of the prettiest mares Joe had ever seen, with long eyelashes, and a white stripe down her forehead.

"I-I don't understand?" Bailey looked at him.

"This is your birthday present from me."

She looked at him, then the horse, then back to him.

"You c-can't buy me a horse."

"I didn't. It's a friend's. His wife can't ride her anymore, and he needs someone who can. He gave her to me, and I'm giving it to you."

She turned to look at the mare, who wanted attention and moved to where Bailey stood, still as a statue. Nudging her in the belly, she pushed her back several steps.

"She's demanding, and will need plenty of attention, but I think you've got the time to see she gets it."

"B-but what if I leave?" The words were whispered.

"She can come with you, or be delivered there when you're settled." Joe didn't want to think about her leaving. In fact, now he gave it some thought, he was going to make sure she didn't.

The horse moved forward again, and breathed into Bailey's hair.

"She likes you."

"Joe...."

"She's yours, Bailey. I want you to have her."

Her arms came around the silver neck, and she buried her head in the mare's neck and held on.

"You crying again? Because that's getting old."

She shook her head. "What's her name?"

"Lucille." He moved in behind her.

"No way."

"Truth. But I'm sure she won't mind if you change it."

"No, but maybe we can abbreviate it to Lucy."

"Nice."

"You're not lying to me are you, Joe? I mean about her being given to you?"

"No." He fought back the guilt. This was the right thing to do, and he'd come across the mare two weeks ago in the next town over. He'd thought she should be Bailey's, and today he'd made it happen. Luke had gone and got her while Joe had collected the rest of the stuff they needed. "There's a whole heap of tack with her too. Saddle, bridle, and stuff."

"No way, really? It sounds almost too good to be true."

He prayed she didn't find out the truth until she was ready to hear it. It was just money to Joe, but he knew Bailey wouldn't see it that way.

"No money changed hands?"

"Why? You think I'm going to demand sex or something?"

"I just don't understand why someone would give you a horse, Joe. Not one like her."

"I knew about her a few weeks ago, and always thought she'd be perfect for you." At least that wasn't a lie.

"She's so beautiful, Joe."

He stepped closer to her, crowding her body.

"You're beautiful. Do you forgive me yet?"

"For what?"

"Everything. The not writing, not coming to see you after the concert."

She rested on his chest. Her head turned to look at the

mare. "Yes, and it all seems pathetic now, doesn't it? Our arguments, the recriminations about the past, especially with what's happening around us."

"It does." Joe kissed the top of her head.

"Is she really mine, Joe?"

"She's a gift, Bailey. Pure and simple, no strings attached. A gift for everything you were to me, and still are. Don't complicate it, accept it for what it is."

"She's the most beautiful present I have ever had, Joe. Thank you."

She lifted her head and kissed him, and he felt it again, the total capitulation. He loved this woman, madly, deeply. It was simply stronger and deeper, this love they'd always had. At that moment he gave in completely. She was a part of him, and always would be.

She looked up at him. "I wish I could go riding with you now, Joe."

His eyes crossed.

"Not that kind of riding—although…." She gave him a cheeky smile. A smile that a few weeks ago would never have been in her arsenal.

"Later. Right now, Aunt Jess will be serving up food, and if we don't hurry, Luke, Fin, and Jack will eat it all."

She kissed him again, and then the mare. "Thank you."

BAILEY WAS PRETTY sure she'd never had a better day than this one. She'd eaten her Mickey cake, which granted was silly, but she'd loved it. She sat with her friends, people who not long ago she had not even known, and laughed, sang, and when Maggie told Luke he was dancing with her, she did that too. Buzz ate cake, and anything that fell on the floor, and wore his red bow all day.

She had a horse. Looking to where Joe was dancing his aunt around, she wondered if he realized just how much he now meant to her. Sure he always had, but this... this was so much more. She'd put the past aside today, and walked into the future, and she hoped that was with him... wanted it desperately to be so.

"Bailey." She turned as Clark called her name, and behind him was her grandfather. "I'm sorry, I went to answer the door and he was there. Apparently someone directed him here."

"You must be Leonard Southby?" Mr. Goldhirsh came forward before Bailey could react. He stuck out his hand, and her grandfather took it. He was nothing if not polite.

"I am. Bailey's grandfather." His eyes went to her. "I'm here to take her home."

"She's not going home."

"I beg your pardon?" He dragged his eyes from her and looked down at Mr. Goldhirsh.

"She has no wish to go with you, and likes it here. Perhaps it's time you came to that realization, and actually paid attention to her wishes instead of your own."

Her grandfather's eyebrows drew together in a fierce frown. Usually this was a warning sign to back off; not for Mr. Goldhirsh, however. Bailey should really intervene.

"You have no business telling me what is best for my granddaughter, sir. Nor will I conduct such a private conversation in a public setting."

"Seems to me you didn't listen when she tried to discuss matters in a private setting, so I'm taking it public. You have no business not listening to her wishes, Mr. Southby."

She felt Joe's hand on her shoulder as she went to move. Holding her in place. How she knew it was his hand was a mystery—or maybe it was the tingle of awareness.

"Why is it so hard for you to let her live the life she chooses?"

"She is living her life as she chooses."

"No." Bailey patted Joe's hand, then moved away. "I'm not."

She saw it then, the realization that maybe he may not win an argument for the first time in his life.

"But this is important to you... to us."

"It was," she said gently, "but not anymore, Grandfather, and I wish you would respect my wishes in this matter."

As if realizing that he'd intruded on something private, he looked around the room.

"It's your granddaughter's birthday, Mr. Southby. Perhaps if you'd been more aware of her needs, you may have realized that."

He looked shocked, his eyes going from Mr. Goldhirsh to Bailey.

"I didn't realize."

"That's all right. Would you like a piece of cake?" She took his arm, and led him forward. Aunt Jess and Mr. Goldhirsh then took over, and Bailey watched as they poured him tea, and cut him cake. He looked bemused, and yes, a little lost. Leonard Southby liked control and suddenly he was losing it.

"Small steps," Joe said, coming to her side. "And if that doesn't work, we'll just unleash Mr. Goldhirsh on him again."

"I feel different, Joe."

"Different, good?"

"Yes, as if suddenly my life is about to begin again."

"Definitely good then, especially as I'm going to be in the rebuild."

Chapter 35

"I HAVE TO GO NOW, baby. I'm due at the bar. We need to do stock take this morning."

Bailey stretched in Joe's big bed as he got out and walked naked to the bathroom. She'd stayed the night with him, as she had for the two since her birthday.

Reaching for her cell phone that Clark had spent two painful hours yesterday teaching her how to use, she knocked Joe's ring off the nightstand, the thick silver band he always wore on his middle finger. Swinging her legs out of bed, she picked it up. Her fingers encountered a ridge on the inside. She turned it, and the breath lodged inside her throat.

"You can stay in my bed as long as you like," Joe said, returning after his shower minutes later. "In fact, if you're there when I.... Bailey, what's wrong?" He was at her side in seconds, dropping to his knees before her.

"Y-you kept it." She held out the ring so they could both see the small round silver disc attached to the inside.

His eyes were level with hers, the green dark with emotion as he looked at her.

"I felt close to you when it was near; this was the only way I could think to keep it that way."

"Hold out your hands," Bailey said reaching for her locket. Opening it, she let the matching silver disc fall into them.

"I wondered if you still had it." He ran his thumb over the surface. "I remember the day I made them at school. I just wanted us to have something that held both our names. Wanted something to remind me of you in case we were separated." His voice was thick with emotion.

"I felt close to you when I had it near too, Joe. I took it out and just stared at it so many times when I missed you."

His face was inches from hers now, so close that she just had to lean in to touch her lips to his.

"I love you, Joe." She let go and bared it all. He was silent for long, agonizing seconds, and then made a sound deep in his throat.

"God, I love you, Bailey. It terrifies me how much you mean to me. It was strong before, when you were young, but now it's fierce."

She cupped his face. "It's no different for me, even though I may not be good at showing it."

"You do okay." He smiled.

"I don't want to leave here, Joe. Don't want to ever lose you again."

"You'll never lose me, sweetheart, we just needed fifteen years to find each other again."

"If I hadn't come back—"

"Maybe I would have eventually plucked up the courage to find my way to you. Because while I was a coward that day five years ago, Bailey, you need to know that I never forgot you. You were always there inside my head, making me a better person."

"Promise me you will always be honest with me, Joe.

Promise that from now on we only have the truth between us. No more secrets. If you feel something, I want to know what it is."

"Promise." He kissed her then, taking her back with him onto the bed. "I want to be the best man I can be for you, baby." He used her words again, and the fact he remembered them made her warm all over.

Their kiss was deep and intense and had them both breathing hard in seconds. He stripped the shirt off her body, and she opened his jeans, and then he sheathed himself in a condom and was soon seated deep inside her.

"Every time," he rasped. "Every time, I feel more when I'm inside you."

Bailey grabbed a handful of his hair and tugged him down as he drove inside her again and again. It was fast and intense, and when it was over, she lay breathless in his arms.

"I love you," he whispered into her hair.

"I love you too," Bailey said, nudging him out of bed. "Now go, because I know you have to get to work... but I get to lie here for a bit longer."

"Witch." He braced his hands beside her head and kissed her softly, before reaching for his jeans.

Bailey enjoyed the view, admiring the muscles of his body as he moved.

"Are you checking me out?"

"Totally."

"Totally," he mimicked. Minutes later, after another kiss, he was gone.

Bailey showered and dressed after Joe left, and wandered downstairs still smiling. He loved her, and she loved him, the rest they could work out, and for the first time in a long while, Bailey felt hope. Her life was about to take another turn for the better.

She passed Joe's office, and saw two cups on his desk. Looking inside made her shudder. Lord knew how many days they'd been there.

Lifting the cups, she discovered one was stuck to the folder beneath, and papers flew everywhere. As she picked them up, she glanced at one and froze. Minutes later she'd read all the correspondence in that folder.

Walking into his bar twenty minutes later, she had herself under control. She was halfway up the stairs to his office when she heard the male voices. Joe's, and her grandfather's raised in anger.

"What's it going to take for you to understand she's not leaving, Mr. Southby?"

Bailey made herself stop outside the door and listen.

"My granddaughter is meant for more than you, Mr. Trainer."

"You have no clue what your granddaughter is meant for, because you've never asked her. And I'm telling you right now, I love her and we are going to marry and she is staying here with me."

Bailey clenched her teeth to stop the smile she felt at his words. He loved her, and wanted to marry her; that felt good. But he still had no right to tell her grandfather they were going to marry when he hadn't asked her yet.

"She will never marry you, and I'll fight you every step of the way if you try—"

"That's enough, Grandfather." Bailey walked into the room. Joe stood on his side of the desk, and her grandfather across from him. "I want you to leave now, please. Go back to the lodge and pack your things. You need to go back to Boston."

"Bailey—"

"No more, Grandfather. We're done, and I will not be returning with you, so you need to understand that. We have things to discuss, so I will follow you to the lodge soon, but then you must leave Ryker Falls."

He gave her one final look, then walked out the door, closing it softly behind him.

"He'll be all right, Bailey," Joe said. "But I think he finally understands you're not going back with him."

She looked at him, with his hands braced on his desk, pose as intimidating as he could make it, and felt that little kick again inside her chest.

"I doubt that, Joe, but you had no right to tell my grandfather we were going to marry."

"We are." He said the words calmly, as if she'd just accept them.

"You never asked me, and I had a right to that at least, before you told him."

He shrugged, brushing her words away. "You will marry me."

"I won't be controlled again, Joe."

"How is this me controlling you?"

"You told him we were going to marry!"

"We are."

"I haven't agreed."

He stood and folded his arms. "But you will, because you love me."

"I do, yes, but I have to have a say in things, Joe. Surely you can see that after what I went through with my grandfather?"

"I'm not getting why this upsets you so much, Bailey. I'm nothing like him."

She left that alone for now; there would be plenty of time in their lives to make him understand where she was coming from. "We'll come back to that. You misled me, Joe."

"About what?"

She paced around his office now, trying to get her words right, because she was hopeless at confrontation. "Lucy. You paid six thousand dollars for her and all that gear."

"I did, and lied about it because I knew you wouldn't accept the gift otherwise."

He was totally unrepentant. His defiance made her want to laugh, but she managed to keep her face serious.

"You know how I feel about manipulation."

"It's not manipulation if it's well-intended, Bailey. I did it because you're important to me, and you deserve to be spoiled."

"Joe." Bailey sighed, looking at him. "You paid six thousand dollars for my birthday present. It's too much money, especially as when you purchased her you had no idea I loved you or that we were going to have a relationship."

"Marry me then, and she'll just be part of our family. Then we can own her together."

Bailey put her hands in her hair and pulled.

"Feel better?"

"Control and honesty are important to me. I know you bought the horse with good intentions, just as I'm sure you told my grandfather we were getting married for the same reasons."

"Because I love you."

"It was thousands of dollars, Joe. I can't let someone pay that much for a birthday gift."

"I'm not someone!" His anger was climbing. Hands once again braced on his desk, he glared at her. "I'm the man you supposedly love."

"You think I'd lie about that?"

"No, and I didn't lie to you about the horse, I just didn't tell you the truth... yet."

"That's lying, and I'm paying you back."

"No," he gritted out. "You are not."

"I am. I can't allow that, it's not right."

"I'll be really pissed off if you do, Bailey. It was a gift for the woman I love. The woman who means more to me than any other ever has. If you won't accept it as a birthday present, then add wedding present to the list."

"This is not funny!"

"I'm not laughing."

He held her eyes, and she didn't look away. She needed to be strong with this man, or he'd walk all over her.

"I can't let you do this, Joe. It takes away my independence."

"What? How the hell do you figure that?"

"You paying all that money, it's wrong. I need to pay you back, or I'll feel—"

"If the next word to come out of your mouth is beholden, I'll be really fucking angry!"

"We'll talk about this later. Right now I have to go."

"What? Where are you going?"

"I have to talk to my grandfather, in case you're right and he is leaving. I need to tell him we are not getting married—"

"We are!" Joe cut her off before she could say "yet." "Don't you run away from me, Bailey!"

"I love you, Joe, but I need to go and talk to him. I need to get him to release my money."

"You are not paying me back!"

She leaned across the desk and kissed the angry line of his mouth. Stepping back before he could grab her, Bailey headed for the door.

"I love you."

"Bailey!" he roared as she ran out the door and down

the stairs. Once in the street, she got in her car and headed to the lodge.

Angie was at reception.

"Hi, Bailey."

"Hi. Do you know where my grandfather is, Angie?"

"He's in the sunroom."

"Thanks."

She found him drinking tea with Mr. Goldhirsh, and not packing like she'd hoped.

"I need to talk to you, Grandfather."

"If you have come to discuss marriage to that Joseph Trainer, then I have nothing to say on the matter."

"Joe is a good man, Leonard. Bailey would do well married to him," Mr. Goldhirsh said.

When had her grandfather become Leonard?

"But then she would stay here."

"Where she wishes to stay," Bailey interrupted. "I also want you to release my money."

He waved a hand. "I had planned to do that, and I apologize for keeping it from you, Bailey. I had no right to do so. But I was angry that you appeared to be happy to throw aside everything you worked so hard for."

"I no longer wish to perform."

He looked sad.

"Why were you in Joe's office, Grandfather?"

"To discuss you. I had seen how close you were to him, and after the conversation I had with Mary Howard—"

"You don't want to listen to that woman, Leonard. Nothing she has to say makes a lick of sense," Mr. Goldhirsh said calmly.

"Will you have dinner with me tonight, Bailey? So I can understand about this life you have chosen over the one you led with me?"

She nodded, because it was a start that at least he was

acknowledging her wishes. "I will, but I have to get back to the stables now. I'm starting work soon."

"You really are working in the stables?"

"It's honest, hard work that I enjoy, Grandfather."

"All right. We shall discuss this more tonight then. Frederick and I are about to play chess."

Frederick?

Bailey wasn't sure what to make of that, but she didn't have time to think about it now.

"Run along now, Bailey."

That was more like her grandfather, Bailey thought, watching as he waved his long fingers to dismiss her.

Lifting a hand, she waved, and then left. She drove to Maggie's, and parked her car. Walking to the stables would give her time to think.

She thought about Joe, and the fact that he would always be a man who liked control. Could she live with such a man?

Yes, because she never wanted to live without him again.

Bailey moved off the road as a car approached, but it slowed.

"Hello, Bailey."

"Hi, Angie."

"I'm heading to the ranch, do you want a lift?"

"Sure, thanks." She got in because Angie was being nice, and if Bailey was going to live in Ryker Falls, she wanted them to be friends. She closed the door.

"And now we're going for a drive."

She turned at Angie's words, and saw the gun she held. It was pointed straight at her.

"Angie, what are you doing?"

"I've just told you, Bailey, pay attention. We're going for a drive."

"What's going on? Put down the gun." She reached for the door, but Angie put her foot down on the gas, and the car shot forward.

"I've locked the doors, so there's no way you can escape."

"Why are you doing this?" Bailey looked at the woman.

"Because Joe was mine until you came along and stole him from me. I'm removing you so things will go back to the way they should be."

"B-but it was never serious between you."

"It would have been! I was taking it slow not wanting to scare him off. Joe's nervous about committing, one of his old girl-friends told me that, so I was easing him into the idea of a relationship with me. I wanted to marry him and live at the ranch. I wanted that bar and the money he could give me. I wanted the lifestyle I would have as Mrs. Trainer. You took that from me!"

"But you slept with Ted from the lodge." Bailey looked at the gun, hoping Angie wouldn't shoot her while she was driving.

"Sleeping with the boss made my life easier, but it was always Joe I wanted. Everything was going well until you came back to Ryker." She shot Bailey a hate-fueled look. "You managed to get under his guard, and then he no longer wanted me."it was always Joe I wanted. Everything was going well until you came back to Ryker." She shot Bailey a hate-fueled look. "You managed to get under his guard, and then he no longer wanted me."

"Tell me it wasn't you who lit that fire, and shot Jack?"

"Of course it was," Angie said calmly. "I saw you that day lying on top of Joe. I knew you were a threat to me so you had to be removed. But I missed and got Jack."

"You're insane," Bailey said.

"No, I'm perfectly sane, and know what I want. If that

fool Elijah hadn't overheard me offering to pay Tim Trainer to kill you, then he wouldn't have had to die, but he did."

"You killed Elijah?" Bailey was suddenly aware of just what she was dealing with, a maniac who had already killed, and would not hesitate to do so again.

"We killed him. Me and that fool Tim Trainer. He nearly had you at the bar, which was coincidence, by the way. He was out there waiting for one of his sons."

"H-he was going to harm one of his own children?"

Angie nodded. "I wanted you and one of Joe's brothers dead. He would need me then."

Bailey felt sick that this woman was willing to kill innocent people to get to Joe.

"Joe doesn't love you, Angie. He loves me, and he'll never want another woman, even if you kill me."

"Shut up!"

Angie sounded crazed now, so Bailey did as she was told... for now. She had to escape, had to find a way to get away from Angie and back to Joe. No way in hell did she want this woman anywhere near him again.

They'd only been driving a few minutes when Angie pulled off the road and down the Nook, a narrow track where local teenagers hung out.

"This leads to the river. I thought it would be a good place to drown you."

The words were spoken calmly, and sent a shiver down Bailey's spine. How the hell had Angie hid the madness for so long? She'd fooled all of them.

"With luck, your body will end up on Joe's land, then he'll know for sure you're gone."

"This will never work, Angie. Stop now, before it's too late."

"It's already too late."

The track was narrow and rutted, both sides lined with trees, and Bailey held the seat as Angie sped up it. Stopping the car, she waved the gun at Bailey.

"I'm getting out. You follow out my door."

Bailey had no choice but to do as Angie asked.

"Now we walk, because while I'd be happy to shoot you here, you're too heavy for me to carry you far, so drowning you will be much tidier after I knock you out. But if you try and run, I will shoot you, Bailey, and make up a story everyone will believe."

"You're insane, Angie, to think you'll get away with this."

"Oh I will, because people in this town like me. Joe will need someone to comfort him while he mourns your loss, and I'll be there for him."

"You can't be serious?"

"I am. Now move." She shoved Bailey forward, and they began walking. Every few feet, Angie prodded Bailey in the back with her gun. She didn't want to die today... or any day soon. Bailey had her life to live, and she wanted to live it with Joe at her side. The thought of him at the mercy of Angie had her determined to escape; she just had to find the right moment. She was strong now, she could do this. She concentrated on him then, focused on Joe.

I love you, Joe, please find me.

Chapter 36

JOE TRIED to work through the next hour. He also tried to call Bailey several times, but she didn't answer, which meant A. Her phone battery needed charging again, or B. She didn't want to talk to him.

He tried to focus, but something other than Bailey was making him anxious, and he couldn't put his finger on it. She'd said she loved him, and because of that, he knew things would be okay with them. Sure, he probably did need to start thinking about her when he made decisions—even, apparently, if they were in her best interest. In hindsight, six thousand dollars was a lot to spend on a birthday present. But she was worth that and so much more to him. Money meant nothing when compared to Bailey.

Okay, so maybe he should have asked her to marry him before he told the grandfather, Joe conceded.

He shrugged, as if to shake off something. His body felt tense, and the tension inside him had been climbing steadily since she'd left.

"What the hell is that scowl for?" Fin walked in.

"I don't know. Bailey and I went a few rounds, but it's not that."

"If you mentioned it, it probably is. So go make it up to her."

"How do you know she's in the right?"

"Is she?"

"No... yes. Maybe."

"Articulate."

"I bought her the horse. She didn't know and thought it was given to the stables, and got all bent out of shape when she found the invoices."

Fin winced.

"She's all about independence and taking control now, and apparently I wrested it from her."

"By buying her an expensive horse?"

"There's more."

Fin waved for him to continue.

"I may have told her asshole grandfather that we were getting married, and she overheard."

"Did you propose to her first?"

Joe shook his head.

"No way are you that dumb."

Joe sighed. "Apparently I am where she's concerned. Control and honesty are important to her and I broke both commandments."

"She's totally got you tied in knots, Trainer. I love it."

"Yeah, thanks for that."

"I guess after being under her grandfather's control, she doesn't want to go there again," Fin said. "Which makes sense."

"No, I get it actually. But you know me, Fin. I like control too."

"Sure, because of the life you were forced to lead. The

trick is communication, Joe. You can have both if you keep those channels open."

"You being such a good communicator and all."

Fin smiled. "Do as I say, grasshopper, not as I do."

"I love her way too much."

"I know you do, bud. So that means you need her to be happy, just as I'm guessing she needs you to be happy too. So make it work."

Joe nodded. "But we're good, because she told me she loved me before leaving."

"That's a positive then. So what else is bugging you?"

Joe frowned. "I'm not sure, it's just a feeling. I've called Bailey several times, but she's not answering."

They heard footsteps, and both turned to see who was coming up the stairs. It wasn't Bailey, much to his disappointment. The steps were too heavy.

"Chief Blake. What brings you up here?" Joe said, getting to his feet to shake the man's hand.

"Found your father on his way out of town. Have him in custody now, Joe. He's saying he has lots to confess about the fire in your stable and who shot at Jack and Bailey, but won't speak until you're there."

"Let's go," Joe said, stuffing his phone into his back pocket.

"I'm coming," Fin said, getting to his feet as Joe passed.

He didn't answer, just followed Chief Blake from Apple Sours, his stomach twisted into knots.

JOE HID everything he felt as he walked down the hall leading to where his father was being held. Every shred of anger, and hurt, he locked away, because he needed his father to know that nothing he had done to him had impacted on his life. That he'd risen above being the son of a violent, unloving scumbag like Tim Trainer.

He didn't inhale, nor clench his fists; he schooled his features and followed Chief Blake. Fin gripped his shoulder briefly, and he took strength from the contact. He wasn't alone anymore, he had people at his back. People he loved, who loved him right back.

"Well, well, well, if it isn't my eldest son. Joe, glad you came to bail me out."

He hadn't seen his father in years, and the first shock was that he'd shrunk, and his face was showing signs of the hard life he'd obviously lived. Lined, weathered, and with his two front teeth missing, he didn't look like the intimidating man he'd once been. The man who had put the fear of God into Joe and his brothers using violence.

"I knew you'd come, son. Knew you'd see reason and bail your dad out. Blood is important, boy, like I always told you. Just need you to post it, son, I'll see you get it back. I've had a few problems, but with a good lawyer I'll get off."

It wasn't anger that had him stepping up to the bars, it was retribution. Just once he wanted this man to know what he and his brothers had experienced. Dear old dad didn't see it coming. He leaned in as Joe drew near, with a look on his face that said he thought he'd win this round too.

Joe shot his fist through the bars and sent Tim Trainer reeling backward.

"Well hell, Joe," the police chief said. "I'm sure there's a few laws you just broke, but damned if I can remember which ones."

"You bastard!" Tim Trainer came up spitting. "I'll fucking kill you!"

"Open the door, Chief. Let him try."

The chief played along and moved forward, jangling his keys about. Tim Trainer's eyes widened as he looked at the fire in his son's eyes, and he stepped back.

"No! Don't let him in here!"

"Scared? Worried now I'm bigger than you, and you can't defend yourself?"

"You can't speak to me like that!"

"I can speak to you how the hell I like. I haven't seen you in years, and we've shared a total of two phone calls, both with you begging for money. Do you honestly think I would do anything for you, the man who made our lives hell as children?"

"I taught you respect!" Tim Trainer stayed away from the bars.

"You taught us fear and nothing more. Now you know how that feels, you piece of shit!"

"And now the family reunion is over, you can tell us what we need to hear." Fin stepped up to the bars. "Or I'll personally make sure he can get at you."

"Well now, Fin, you do have the spare set of keys," Chief Blake said.

He knew what Tim Trainer had done to his sons, and was pretty pissed about it, like a few of the other residents in Ryker Falls.

"I ain't talking without benefit."

"I'll give you a thousand to clear out of town and never come back. But I want it written and signed by you that if you return, Chief Blake will be within his rights to put you in a cell."

"He's going there anyway, Joe, and for a long time, so don't waste your money."

Joe shot the policeman a look. "Why?"

"He lit the fire in the barn."

"You didn't tell me that!"

"I didn't want you losing control outside the cells. Not good for you, or for anyone to see one of their town councilors with bloodlust in his eyes."

When Joe looked back, Tim Trainer was as far away from him as he could get.

"You tried to kill my brother and woman!" He grabbed the bars and shook them.

"You'll just tire yourself out doing that, Joe. Step away now." Fin grabbed his arms. "They make those bars pretty impenetrable, is my guess."

The look Joe sent the man behind those bars made him move back another step. He then walked away from everyone while he tried to rein in his rage.

"What else has he got to say?" Joe heard Fin ask.

"Tell them."

"I told you it was her. She paid me to do it. She did Elijah, shot him in the back of the head, then made me throw him in the falls, because he heard us talking about it."

"Who?" Joe moved back to the bars. "Who is she?" He looked at Chief Blake.

"Well, that's what I've been trying to get out of him, but he said he wouldn't speak until you came in here."

"She paid me to get rid of her because she wanted you for herself, but I couldn't do the job both times, so she decided to do it on her own."

"Carry on, or I'm coming in there!" Joe snarled.

"The fire, it was to kill the girl, the one you're with, Bailey Jones."

Joe's blood ran cold as his father nodded his way.

"I was desperate when I grabbed her that night outside the bar. She was getting angry, refusing to pay me. She wanted her dead, and then one of your brothers, so it made you weak. She was going to step in and look after you."

"Who?" Fin growled.

"Angela Pedderson."

Joe ran then, out the doors, with Fin and the chief on his heels. He pulled out his cell phone and called Bailey again, she didn't answer.

"I just called the lodge. They said Angie's not there. She was, but left, supposedly sick," Fin said, running at his side. "Bailey was there earlier, but left after talking to Mr. Goldhirsh and her grandfather."

Angie and Bailey both missing. She was in danger, he could feel it, knew that if he didn't get to her he'd never find her alive again. This was the tension that had been building inside him. He called Jack, who was with Luke. Neither of them had seen her. He filled them in on Angie, and that he needed to find her fast. He was sprinting now, heading to his pickup. Beside him, Fin called Maggie and Piper. Neither of them had seen Bailey or Angie.

"I can't lose her, Fin."

"You won't."

"Jesus, could it really be Angie?"

"She had us all fooled if it is, bud."

He jumped behind the wheel, and was driving seconds later. Where the hell he was driving to, he had no idea, but he had to be on the move.

His phone rang, and he shoved it at Fin, who put it on speaker. "Hello?" Fin answered. The call was from Luke, who had asked his firefighting buddies if any of them had seen Angie.

"Her car was seen driving down the Nook, Joe. We'll meet you there!"

Joe put his foot on the gas and sped out of town.

Was she in danger? He had to find her. Had to get to

her before Angie hurt her. Fin took the turn into the Nook so fast that Fin swore loudly.

"Your brothers are on our tail."

Joe braked, and was out while his pickup still rocked. He saw Angie's car tucked under some trees.

"Gun!" He walked to Jack's car. "Now!"

"What the fuck I can't believe this is happening?" Jack got out and went to the trunk. Opening it, he started handing out rifles. Joe just took the rifle and started running.

"Jesus, will you wait!" He felt his brothers and Fin arrive, but didn't stop. His heart was pounding, blood coursing through his body, and suddenly he was focused. She would stay safe until he got to her, he had to believe that. Right now she needed him to be the best and strongest person he could be.

The sun caught something on the path up ahead. Dropping to a knee, Joe picked up Bailey's necklace and wrapped it around his fist. She'd left this for him to find, he was sure of it.

"It's her necklace... Bailey's."

"You think she left it for us?" Jack asked.

"That's my take."

"The tracks head down to the river," Fin said.

Joe started following, running again, as fast as he could through the dense bush.

I'm coming, Bailey, stay safe until I can reach you.

Chapter 37

BAILEY WALKED where Angie told her to, and when she heard the river, she knew it was time to act. Once they reached it, Angie would kill her.

"Ouch!"

"What?" Angie nudged her in the back with the gun when she stopped.

"I have something in my shoe."

"That's the least of your problems. Anyway, you'll be dead soon."

Bailey started to limp.

"Just walk, and hurry up. I want this done before anyone notices you're missing."

"Joe will notice. He loves me."

"No! He's going to love me!"

"That's not true, Angie. He thinks you're his friend, but he doesn't love you."

The gun nudged her again, harder. "Shut up!"

"He'll never forgive you for killing me."

"Shut up!" Angie pushed Bailey, hard this time, and she made herself stumble forward. Just below them was the water; she pretended to trip.

"Stop!"

She felt Angie's hands reach for her, but it was too late. Bailey hit the ground, rolled over the edge, and down the side of the hill. She heard the gun fire, the bullet digging into the bank beside her. The next one struck her leg, the pain tearing through Bailey's thigh.

"I'm going to kill you!"

She heard Angie's scream, and knew she'd be coming down the bank. Seconds later Bailey rolled into the water. She dived under and let it carry her downstream.

The current was strong, and her thigh was on fire, but the cold water would slow the bleeding. She couldn't allow herself to stop, she had to keep moving or Angie would catch her. Coming up for air, she heard a shot whistle over her head, and dived under again. Lifting her head when her lungs felt like they were about to burst, she searched for Angie. She was some distance behind her now.

Kicking with her good leg, she used the last of her strength and dived under again. The next time she came up, she couldn't see Angie at all. Struggling to the bank, she dragged herself out. Looking up, she saw the cave. If she could reach that, she'd be safe... she had to be.

THEY HAD BEEN SEARCHING along the river, where the tracks stopped. Someone had rolled down that hill. They'd found blood at the bottom. *Please don't let it be Bailey's blood.* Every minute that passed without him finding her, his fear for her grew.

"Stop!" Fin was in front of him, and it was he who raised his hand. "Someone is up ahead."

Lifting his rifle, Joe moved closer, and together he and

Fin walked slowly until they could see who it was. Jack and Luke followed.

"Angie," Fin whispered.

She was standing at the base of the hill that led up to Trainer land. Feet braced, arms raised, and in her hands was a handgun. As he watched, she fired off a shot. Raising his gun, he fired, the bullet lodging in the ground at her feet.

"Drop the gun, Angie!"

She turned, eyes wide, gun still clasped in her hands, now pointed his way.

"Joe!" She screamed his name. "It's Bailey, Joe! She's gone crazy and tried to shoot me! I-I wrestled the gun off her."

"Drop the gun or one of us will shoot you, Angie. Even if you get off a shot, there are four guns here. The numbers are not in your favor."

"I-I don't understand." She dropped the gun. "I just told you, it was Bailey, she's gone crazy."

"No more lies now, Angie. We all know what you've done. Now tell me where Bailey is."

"No, it's me you want, not her!"

"Tell me where she is," he said as calmly as he could manage.

While Fin moved in and grabbed the gun, and Jack her, he watched Angie's eyes go to the top of the hill, and knew then where Bailey had run to hide.

"Take her back, and hand her over to Chief Blake," he told Fin.

Angie screamed his name as Jack and Fin took her away.

"It's a big area, Joe. How the hell will we find her?" Luke came to his side.

"I know where she is."

"Where?"

He didn't answer, just started climbing until he reached their special place. She'd climbed down here all those years ago, using a rope, and he'd climbed up it many times to meet her.

"Bailey?" He called her name as he climbed, but it was as he reached the top he heard her voice.

"Joe!"

He hurried inside and found her sitting at the back, and the relief was acute. She'd torn her shirt into strips and tied them around her thigh. Blood colored the bandage red.

"Bailey," he rasped, dropping to his knees before her. "Jesus, your leg."

"It's Angie, Joe. Sh-sh—"

"Shhh, we know, love." He cupped her face. "I love you."

She held on to him, her fingers grabbing the front of his shirt. He could feel the thud of her heartbeat pressed to his chest.

"Angie killed Elijah, Joe."

"We know, love. Let me get you out of here now." She'd lost a lot of blood, and he needed to get her to a doctor fast. He lifted her into his arms, gently holding her close so he didn't hurt her. "It's all right now, I have you."

"Sh-she wanted you."

"I know. Don't talk now, baby."

She nodded, her hands gripping his shirt as she held him close.

"You're such a strong girl, Bailey Jones. Strong and smart," he said. "You knew to drop the locket and come here. Knew that eventually I'd find you." He kept talking to distract her as he carried her to the entrance. Luke was there waiting for him.

"I h-hoped you'd understand and find me."

"I'll always find you. We need to get you back now, love. Get that leg looked at."

"Angie?"

"Is in custody."

Between him and Luke they got her up the rest of the bank. This part wasn't as steep, but still an effort for a woman with a bullet in her leg. He felt every hiss of breath Bailey took, but she didn't complain. Once he'd reached the top, Luke pulled out his phone.

"I'm going to get clear of the trees and find some coverage and call Jack to bring transport. You hold on now, Bailey."

Joe watched his brother sprint off through the trees, and then looked at Bailey.

"I feel—"

Joe watched her eyes roll back in her head as she lost consciousness. Picking her up, he followed Luke. He was relieved when he heard the hum of the ATV a short while later.

They got her to the house, and into Luke's pickup. Luke drove, breaking every speed limit, and they reached the hospital in minutes. Joe carried her in, and soon she was on a gurney with nurses and doctors taking her away from him.

"Let's go." Jack took one arm, and Luke the other, and they dragged him to the waiting room. The same room he'd sat in to wait for news on his brother.

"Drink."

He took the coffee Piper handed him later, but refused the sandwich from Aunt Jess. The Robbins sisters brought him a scone, which Miss Marla broke into pieces and fed him one bite at a time. He didn't have the energy to refuse. Worry gnawed at him, and fear held his body tense.

"Angie is in custody, alongside your father," Fin said. "They're both going down for murder, although Angie could end up pleading insanity."

"I don't care where she ends up as long as she pays, but it won't bring Elijah back, or take back the hurt that was inflicted on Jack and Bailey." His words were a growl.

"This is not your fault, Joe."

"Angie did this because of me, Fin."

"So her insanity and your father's greed are your fault suddenly?"

He blew out a breath as guilt ate away at him. "No, I know they're not. But the fact is Elijah died because I broke things off with Angie."

"Which you would have done eventually anyway—or she would have ended up killing you."

"I guess... hell, I don't know." Joe lowered his head into his hands. "It's a fucking mess is what it is."

"The doctor's here, Joe."

He was on his feet in seconds.

"I need you to tell me she's okay, Doc."

"I can't tell you anything, Joe, as you're not her next of kin."

"I'm her fucking fiancé. So speak!"

"Joe," Luke clamped a hand on his shoulder. "Dial it back now."

The doctor didn't look intimidated.

"Come on, Doc, you can see he's distraught, and like he said they're engaged," Jack added coming to Joe's other side. "Besides she has no next of kin in town, her grandfather's left," Jack lied.

"All right, but if I get into trouble for this, I'm blaming the Trainer family."

"Fair enough," Jack said.

Joe kept his eyes on the doctor, willing him to say Bailey was okay.

"She'll recover, Joe. The bullet passed through the fleshy part of her thigh, so that's the good news. But it will take a while to recover from this, and she'll be in a lot of pain."

"I'll look after her," he made himself say. All he could think about was that Bailey would come through this. "Can I see her?"

A nurse came and got him when she was in a room, and Joe found Bailey lying on the bed, eyes closed, and tubes going everywhere. Monitors beeped, and lights flashed, and she looked so small and pale. His angel. Leaning over, he kissed her soft lips.

"I love you," Joe whispered, dragging a chair close to the bed with one foot. He lifted her hand, opening it and sliding his fingers through. Closing his, he held hers inside. He then just watched her.

BAILEY WOKE SLOWLY. It felt like she was swimming through a thick cloud of fog. Forcing her eyes open, she moved slightly, wincing as pain tore through her thigh. She remembered everything then. Her hand felt heavy, and looking down, she found Joe sleeping. He sat in a chair, with his head braced on an arm. His other hand held hers.

"Joe."

His eyes opened and looked straight at her.

"Bailey?" he croaked.

"I'm all right."

Joe got to his feet, pushing the chair away. Leaning over her, he cupped her cheeks and kissed her softly.

"Marry me?"

"Yes," Bailey whispered, running her eyes over his face.

She saw the tension in him, the sadness in his eyes. "This is not your fault, Joe. You couldn't have known Angie was unstable."

He managed a smile. "I know. My family and Fin have been telling me that, but it's going to take time to believe it."

"I'll help you." She touched his face.

"I know, you always help me." He kissed her again. "My beautiful Bailey. How the hell did I manage without you for fifteen years?"

"I've never loved anyone like I love you, Joe."

"I know, baby, me either. How's the pain?"

"Okay, just an ache now."

"You're not a very good liar, Bailey Jones."

She closed her eyes as he stroked her cheek.

"I thought it hurt last time you left." He breathed the words against her mouth. "But that was nothing to the pain I felt knowing you were out there somewhere with Angie."

Bailey slid her fingers into his hair and held him close.

"I'm sorry about what happened in my office."

"Joe, there's no need—"

"Let me talk." He brushed a kiss over her lips. "I should have asked you first to marry me, but the words just came out. And I can't promise that I won't spend money on you again, because spoiling you is going to be one of my life goals. Plus, there's that protective streak I have, that may be associated with me appearing pushy."

Bailey managed a smile.

"When I knew you and Angie were out there some-where, I realized that nothing else mattered in my life but getting to you, and having you back with me safe. I couldn't contemplate a future without you in it, Bailey."

"Oh, Joe, I love you so much."

"I love you too. My friend, soul mate, and lover. Never leave me again."

"I'll make that promise if you will?"

"Deal."

She felt her eyes start to close then, as tiredness once again dragged her under.

"Sleep now, baby. I'm here, and you're safe."

Epilogue

"BUT I'M sure it has cinnamon in it, Miss Sarah." Bailey heard Buzz bark his agreement from somewhere behind her.

"It doesn't, Bailey, try again." Miss Marla urged her on. "And you can be quiet, Buzz, or there's no more biscuits for you."

Bailey heard the door open, and knew it was Joe who entered, simply because the air felt different. Which was ridiculous, but it was always the same. "You can't see me, Joe. It's our wedding day, so get out of here now!" It really didn't bother her, but she knew the women who were trying to keep her busy would mind. At present they were tasting tea, and she'd gotten every one wrong.

"You can't see me, so technically we're good. How's my girl doing, Miss Marla?"

"No good, I'm afraid. Do you want to try, Joe?"

"Sure."

Bailey heard him pull up a seat beside her, but didn't remove her blindfold. Instead she took another sip of tea.

"Give up, sweetheart, you know I'm gonna kick your

ass." The deep words were whispered in Bailey's ear, and made her shiver.

"I don't think so." Bailey turned and let her lips brush his cheek. She was rewarded with an indrawn breath. She then heard him swallow a mouthful of tea.

"Lemongrass, ginger, and licorice root."

"All those things and cinnamon, was what I meant to say."

Joe huffed out a breath beside her. "No, you didn't mean that, and there is no cinnamon in there, Bailey, so give it up."

"I know that right about now you have that really smug look on your face that you get when you beat me at this."

"I know, baby, but now's not the time to pout, even though it looks cute on you. Those things that are twisted in your hair really do something for you."

"What the hell are you doing in this house, nephew!"

"I'm leaving, but first I wanted to give Bailey her present."

"Another one? I had that beautiful necklace yesterday, Joe."

She felt his lips on hers; it was brief, but so sweet it left her breathless.

"I'm sending it in, but I just wanted to tell you I love you, and can't wait until you're my Mrs. Trainer."

Someone made a gagging sound, and Bailey suspected it was Piper.

"Now go." Aunt Jess made several shooing noises, and Bailey heard the door shut.

"He's gone. You can take off the blindfold, Bailey. Then turn around."

She did as she was told, and found her brother standing there.

"Beau!" She leapt from the chair and ran at him.

. . .

JOE WASN'T EXACTLY NERVOUS. He knew Bailey would come down that path strewn in rose petals at any minute, but still, there was something fluttering inside him.

"The place looks good," Fin said.

"It does." Joe looked around. They'd decided to marry out in the gardens of the main house, which had been transformed with flowers, ribbons, and lights. White seats were lined up in rows, and filled with guests, all smiling at him.

His life had changed so much since Bailey had stepped back into it. Changed for the better. He felt complete now, as if all those places inside him that had still held anger or darkness were gone. He went to bed holding her in his arms, and usually woke with her draped across his chest. He loved it. Loved everything about her. It had taken adjustment on both their parts, but they'd managed it because of the love they shared, and now he couldn't imagine his life without her in it.

"Game on," Luke said, looking down the aisle.

She appeared on her brother's arm. Joe had contacted Beau Jones after the date was set, and decided on surprising Bailey with his arrival today. The smile on her face told him she was happy.

Her dress was cream silk, and she took his breath away. The top was fitted to her lovely body, and the skirt seemed to float with each step she took. Joe couldn't take his eyes off her. Her hair fell in curls, and a circlet of flowers sat on her head. In her hands was a bouquet of yellow and cream flowers.

"I'm tempted to knock you out and step in," Fin whispered, but Joe said nothing, his eyes on Bailey as she drew near, just as hers were on him. Her smile was shaky, but she held it as she reached his side.

He shook Beau's hand, and then Bailey's brother took his seat, and Joe and Bailey faced the front together.

"You take my breath away."

Her fingers brushed his, and they hooked pinkies as the service began. It was short and sweet, and Joe was soon asked to kiss his bride, which he did without hesitation.

"Hello, Mrs. Trainer."

"Hello, Mr. Trainer."

Joe briefly rested his forehead on hers. They'd spent years apart, but had never forgotten each other, and now they would spend the rest of their lives together. He could honestly say he had never looked forward to anything more.

THE END

From This Moment

Book two in the Ryker Falls Series is available now!

To keep himself safe, he trusted no one

Sixteen years after leaving, FBI Profiler Dylan Howard is returning to Ryker Falls to see his sick father. He doesn't do emotion or friendship, this is about duty and nothing more. He didn't need to connect with the two sisters who were strangers to him or catch up with his old school buddy. The only problem with that is one sexy brunette called Piper Trainer. From the start, she's determined to make him feel, determined to make him see how empty his life is. He can feel himself changing, but then someone from his past surfaces, and suddenly those he cares for are in danger. He must keep them safe, but to do that he needs to push them away and Dylan fears he's not strong enough to do that for a second time.

Trust was the only thing that kept her safe

Piper didn't need or want a hot, sexy man in her life. Especially not when her best friend died and she takes custody of her one-year-old daughter Grace. But Dylan Howard is like a burr under her saddle, and everywhere she turns there he is. She watches him try and remain emotionless when faced with his family and friends but the cracks are starting to appear, and the good guy surfaces. Just when she thinks that maybe there could be a chance for them, he pushes her away. Piper takes refuge in her family, but too late, she realizes that she's given Dylan her heart. Now she must fight for her happiness with the only weapon she has: love.

Printed in Great Britain
by Amazon